YOU

Rachel could no longer hear the music. None of the night sounds penetrated the bubble that enclosed them. Sam dropped her hand and raised both of his until they threaded through her hair.

She felt as if she had lived her entire life in the space of time it took for Sam's mouth to fuse with hers. The anticipation only heightened her reception of him. His face blurred into gentle focus as it came closer. His lips were soft and wet and tantalizing when they touched hers. He knotted his fingers in her loose hair, but held her as if she were breakable. He cradled her to him, his mouth meeting and lifting from hers in a dance that sent erotic sensations through her being.

Passion exploded inside Rachel. In seconds she was clinging to him. Their mouths fused into one as the kiss took on a life of its own.

Rachel looked up at Sam and suddenly the bubble burst. The night sounds returned, loud and discordant, as if someone had turned on a stereo with the volume too loud. The music from down the beach accosted her.

"Rachel."

It was the strain in Sam's voice that drew her attention back to him. "Sam—" She wanted to say more, but could find no words. "I'm sorry," she finally said, and pushing herself free of his arms, ran into the night. She didn't stop until she was inside her cabin. It was dark and scaffolding covered a lot of the floor. She leaned against the door, waiting. For what, she didn't know. For her own heart to settle down? For her mind to return to her head? For reason and intelligence to slither back into her through her ears, if that's how it got out?

What was the matter with her? Sam Hairston was a cop and she distrusted him. And he was Bill's brother. How could she feel so . . . so *good* in his arms?

death and destruction while they learn to trust each other and fall in love. Ms. Hailstock is a master of suspense."

—*Bridges Magazine*

Legacy
Winner of the Waldenbooks Award
Chosen as one of the 100 Best Romance Novels
of the Twentieth Century

"[Legacy] ... will put the reader through an emotional roller coaster. From a deep and abiding love, to spine-chilling suspense, *Legacy* has it all."   —Dinah McCall, author of *Jackson Rule*

"Beautifully drawn characters and a riveting story combine for a marvelous read! Exciting, sensuous *and* suspenseful. What more could you want?"   —Suzanne Forster, author of *Angel Face*

"*Legacy* is a riveting drama that blends the best elements of romance and suspense to create a quality literary liqueur too smooth and too lush not to be addictive!"   —*Romantic Times*

White Diamonds
Glamour Magazine "Fall in Love Again" List

"*White Diamonds* is a fast-paced romantic suspense that entices readers to finish in one sitting. . . . The audience will shout, 'Hail, Hail,' to Shirley Hailstock for a great story."   —*Affaire de Couer* 4+

"Gripping. A powerful drama—a powerful love story."
     —Stella Cameron, author of *Glass Houses*

"Shirley Hailstock has once again raised the ordinary to extraordinary, the sublime to exquisite and bathed it in an exotic romantic fantasy."   —*Romantic Times* 4 1/2 (Excellent)

Opposites Attract
National Readers Choice Award Finalist

". . . Hailstock thoroughly explores the emotional conflicts of her characters. . . ."   —*Publishers Weekly*

"*Opposites Attract* is a complex, emotional love story with ribbons of poignancy pulling the romance together in a treat that is just too good to resist."   —*Romantic Times*

You Made Me Love You

SHIRLEY HAILSTOCK

DAFINA BOOKS
KENSINGTON PUBLISHING CORP.
http://www.kensingtonbooks.com

DAFINA BOOKS are published by

Kensington Publishing Corp.
850 Third Avenue
New York, NY 10022

All Kensington titles, imprints and distributed lines are available at special quantity discounts for bulk purchases for sales promotion, premiums, fund-raising, educational or institutional use.

Special book excerpts or customized printings can also be created to fit specific needs. For details, write or phone the office of the Kensington Special Sales Manager: Kensington Publishing Corp., 850 Third Avenue, New York, NY 10022. Attn. Special Sales Department. Phone: 1-800-221-2647.

Dafina Books and the Dafina logo Reg. U.S. Pat. & TM Off.

First Printing: April 2005
10 9 8 7 6 5 4 3 2 1

Printed in the United States of America

To Ayanna

Chapter One

If she was going to return from the dead, this was the place to do it. Rachel Wells had died at Lake Como. It was the perfect place for her rebirth. She'd returned every summer since her personal emancipation. For three years she'd visited The Lake. She hadn't stayed more than a weekend and had avoided anyone she might have known in her other life. She'd wanted to walk the paths of her last summer here and remember a time before her life became a bitter secret.

Rachel had come those three years with supplies, food, and clothing, every anticipated necessity down to candles and matches, packed in her Jeep Cherokee. She'd stayed in the family cabin. It had no running water or electricity. She'd swum in the lake, under the cover of darkness as she did now, and walked miles through the trails that surrounded the water. In the back of her mind she'd thought, hoped, she'd run into Bill. That he would know she was alive and find her, that their summer on the lake was as clear and safe in his memory as it was in hers. Yet nothing like that had happened. Her hiking expeditions began and ended in solitude. Her midnight swims brought no visitors. In her short two-night stays not once had she seen Bill or even his brother, Sam. No one crossed her path except the owner of the diner where she ate. The woman had bought the facility three years ago and had no recollection of the Wells family who'd once occupied the small cabin near the water.

Rachel was back now, swimming in the lake. Her trip two days ago had required nothing less in the way of supplies than her previous visits. But this time she was here to stay. This time she was here for good. She planned to let people see her, contact old friends, make new ones. She was starting over. But so far she hadn't had the nerve, hadn't run into anyone she knew. Not even Bill's brother, Sam, who used to prowl the lake and the trails as if he were an explorer looking for a new country.

Rachel swam toward the center of the water. It wasn't the safe thing to do. No swimming instructor would ever teach students to swim away from the land, toward the opposite shore, not on a lake this size. The safe thing to do would be to swim parallel to the shoreline, keep the lights of the cabins in view, and not swim alone. But Rachel was finished playing it safe. She'd played it safe for nine years. She was done.

Or she would be.

Tomorrow, she thought. Tomorrow she would go to church, walk down the center aisle while Reverend Williams spoke, if he was still the minister. Wouldn't it surprise everyone? What would Woody Norris or

Hallie Jomatti have to say? Hallie had been away the summer of the explosion, that bright summer afternoon when the engine of their boat exploded and Rachel and her parents had supposedly died.

Rachel continued to swim, arm over arm, taking a breath in as she lifted her head and pushing it out under the water. Her legs kicked, her feet barely breaking the surface, the way she had learned at Lake Como High School in a swimming program during the summer she was eight. She was on her way to a scholarship that seventeenth summer. Hidden away from everyone, except Bill, was her wish to be an Olympic swimmer. But that wish had been drowned when the boat exploded and she disappeared.

Lake Como was three miles across at its widest point. Three miles was nothing for her. She had done twice that and more. The water felt good, the perfect contrast of mountain coolness against her warm skin. She moved through it as she moved through time, back to her seventeenth summer, back to an innocent history before life changed, before the recorded deaths of her and her parents, the mistrusts and experiences that had taken residence in her mind, back to the freedom of knowing a world of opportunities stretched before her like a country road, long and straight, shimmering in a mirage of heat.

Stroke for stroke, she propelled herself through the formless liquid. She reached the midpoint. There had been a raft there that summer. She and Bill had built it, hammered every nail in place under the guidance of her father, and launched it onto the quiet waters of the lake with the pomp and circumstance of teenage laughter. They anchored it with marine chain and old tires to the lake floor and used it as their private meeting place.

Bill wasn't as good a swimmer as Rachel. She could make it to the distant shore, but he couldn't so they'd built the raft as a rest stop. On that raft they had talked about everything. Morning, afternoons, late in the evening, even at midnight or later. Time didn't matter. They had their whole lives ahead of them. They were permanent residents of Lake Como, two of the four thousand families who lived there year-round. During the summer the population swelled to twice that. Yet she and Bill could swim out alone at night and watch the moon and stars or allow the relentless sun to darken them even more than their heritage had done. Bill was an even shade of walnut, but that summer the sun had toasted him, brought out the mahogany in his skin. Rachel, a shade lighter than Bill, turned burnished gold. Her hair lightened until it was almost the same color as her body. Bill called her his golden girl. She smiled at that. Water filled her mouth as her concentration waned for a moment. Spitting it out she stopped at the point where the raft had been and treaded water for several minutes remembering herself at seventeen.

The shore looked miles away. Her cabin wasn't visible from the water. She stared at the place where Bill had lived, still lived for all she knew. It was dark. Was it abandoned? She wished he were here. That they could talk one more time. That they were seventeen and all the mystery and wonder of adulthood was ahead of them.

A moment later Rachel kicked off toward shore. She swam for the trees. They were closer to her own cabin and the place where she'd left her blanket and clothes. Bill's cabin was in the opposite direction. From one of the windows she could see a light shining that hadn't been there moments ago. Her heart kicked in time with the movement of her feet. She swam faster, her heart lighter, but as the weight of the water buoyed her up she wondered if it was his light. The pull to turn and swim toward Bill was strong, but tonight wasn't the time to meet him. She knew how it would look if she appeared out of the darkness, a long-dead ghost resurrected in the moonless night. Tomorrow would be soon enough to find out if he still lived on the Lake.

Rachel had often thought of finding him. While she lived on a small island in Washington state, attached to the mainland by a single bridge, it was easy to type his name into any of the search engines on the Internet and see if anything came back. She could call up the virtual yellow pages and look for his name. How many William Hairstons could there be in a place the size of Lake Como? Her fingers had skated over the keys more than once, caressing the letters as if she could actually feel the corded muscles of his arms. She hadn't done it. She was afraid. The computer could be bugged. People could be collecting data of any site that looked for anyone in Lake Como. U.S. Marshal Aaron McKnight had told her that and warned her to let her past go or it could get her and her family killed.

She didn't need the Internet now. All she had to do was crawl out of the water and take the short trip across the sand to the cabin that bordered Lake Como. That cabin and her last summer with Bill had kept her going. He was part of the fantasy world she'd created in order to survive in her new life. Her planned and controlled life needed a staple, a lynchpin to keep it from coming apart, and she'd clung to the memory of Bill and that one summer. But she was free now.

Free.

And alone.

There was no one left. Her parents, both of them, were gone. The only other person in the world who'd ever cared about her was Bill. And she couldn't bring herself to even type his name into the computer or walk fifty yards to a wooden door. The years had ground into her a belief that her past life was gone, dead and buried. She feared everything about it, knowing that it could get her killed. Yet she had been exhumed, no longer suspended between worlds.

She was alive.

Back from the dead.

But what did it mean? Did she just drop back into circulation like someone returning home from a long trip? Would her friends embrace her, welcome her into the fold, be glad to see she was alive and walking among them? She didn't think so. Some might be angry. And Bill—what would he feel? She'd left him just as they were beginning to find each other. He'd been interested in someone else and so had she. They had spent the summer together because they were in the same boat. The person they each really wanted to be with was away. What would he think when he discovered she had been alive all this time?

Her name had changed three times. She couldn't remember the first two. The last one, the one she had used the longest, was Jane Dunston. She'd never quite gotten the hang of being Jane, even though her mother thought it fit. She'd tease her, saying she was a lot like Calamity Jane. Rachel had smiled when she said it and wondered if she would ever meet her Wild Bill Hickok.

She didn't believe in astrology, but three years ago her stars must have been aligned in the right configuration, for death had released her from bondage. None of them were alive, her parents or the people they'd testified against. All of them were dead within months of each other, as if ordained by some conflicting god. There was no need for her to stay protected, no threat hung over her head. She'd only been seventeen when she went into the program. At twenty-six she had no reason to remain in it. She could go wherever she wanted to go.

Release had come while she was in the cemetery. The stillness of the place always made her silent and immobile. Even when there was a breeze and Rachel could feel it going through her, the place was draped in mournful quiet. Rachel looked down at the gravestones. Side by side, resting in peace, were the strangers. The names of Amanda and Charles Dunston had been etched deeply into the gray granite stone. Rachel stood between them, a hand on each stone, her head bowed in reverence. Beneath the stones, deep under the earth, were her parents. Not Amanda and Charles Dunston, Rachel knew no one with those names, even though Campbell and Tamara Wells had worn them until their deaths and into eternity.

A twig snapped behind Rachel. She didn't move. Her appearance showed nothing to indicate she wasn't focusing on the two gravestones. But her body had gone taut and her mind derived escape scenarios. She was alone in this part of the cemetery. Her parents had been laid to rest near the edge of the place. Trees shaded part of the area and the cemetery butted up against a natural woods. It was a peaceful place, but also one that provided hiding if she needed to make a run for it.

Rachel's ears perked up and she listened intently. She'd made a study of footsteps. She could tell a man's gait from a woman's, a playful teenager from a child, and a cop's footsteps from those of the man on the street. The footsteps behind her were a cop's. She gritted her teeth together and prepared to meet U.S. Marshal Aaron McKnight.

Rachel looked up at the sky. Her eyes were dry even though her throat was choked. She dropped her arms from her parents' graves and turned around.

She didn't care what McKnight wanted. She didn't want to see him, especially not here in the place where her parents were buried. This was holy ground and somehow he polluted it.

McKnight leaned against her car, his legs crossed at the ankles, his hands deep in the pockets of his tan raincoat. He straightened up when she came near him. Pushing away from the Jeep, he came toward her.

Rachel's stride didn't falter. She walked past him without a word, the anger in her body communicating itself in every step.

"Jane," he said.

"McKnight," she said. She refused to give him the respect of attaching a title to his name. McKnight fell into step with her as she headed toward the small lane and her Jeep.

"I've come with good news." He stopped her by

catching her elbow and holding it. She snatched her arm free.

"I have good news."

She eyed his smile. He had straight, even teeth and was a good-looking man, with dirty blond hair, piercing blue eyes, and a football player's body. Yet Rachel hated him. He'd manipulated her and her family and because of him they had to be relocated a third time. Once it had been her fault, and she took responsibility for doing something stupid, but she was a young girl and didn't really understand the consequences of her action. She'd learned fast. He'd put them in danger on purpose. She would never forgive him.

"You never come with good news." She took a step toward the car, but stopped at his words.

"You're free of me."

Rachel peered at him with the skeptical eyes of a hungry lion. She didn't like Aaron McKnight and she made no pretense of civility with him. "You're being reassigned?" Her voice was sarcastically hopeful.

He stepped back, taking a long and deep breath. "I am being reassigned," he admitted. "So are you, if you choose."

"What?" Anger rushed into her like a diabetic taking an insulin injection. "A new identity, why?"

"Not a new identity. Calm down and let me explain."

Rachel crossed her arms. She didn't know what was coming, but no message McKnight had ever delivered to her was good news.

"There is no longer a need for you to have witness protection."

"Why?" Suddenly she was afraid, but she frowned up at him to hide her confusion.

"Papa Graziano died two months ago."

"Who's Papa Graziano?"

McKnight rubbed his palms down his sides. "Papa Graziano was the head of a crime family. Your father worked for him."

"He did not!" she immediately contradicted.

"Hold on," he said, remaining in position. "You can get riled up faster than any woman I know." Rachel only wished it were true. Actually, he was the only person to whom she ever showed her anger. It was too dangerous to get out of control with anyone else. "He wasn't aware Graziano was his ultimate boss. He thought he was working for an investments firm. Only the money came from one and only one source—Papa Graziano."

Rachel's father had told her the whole story a few years ago, but without names. When he found out the company was a front for a money-laundering operation, he went to the authorities, who convinced him to nose around until they had enough to shut the place down.

He had. And their lives had no longer been their own. But now all the parties were dead. Rachel was unsure how to react. She'd lived looking over her shoulder so long that the thought of not having to do it was foreign to her.

"You said it was my choice?" she asked.

He nodded. "You can be relocated to wherever you wish. The department will make sure you have everything you need. If you wish to remain Jane Dunston you can. If you want us to restore your former life, that can be arranged too. From then on you're on your own."

Rachel stared at him for a long moment. She didn't know whether this was an elaborate joke or some test that she needed to pass.

"Arrange it," she finally said.

And now she was here.

At Lake Como.

Afraid.

Alone.

Hiding in the dark.

Trees curved about the small beach area. She could only see a few lights as she neared the shore. Bill's cabin called to her, but she pulled her mind away from it. Except for the one light, it was dark, uninhabited. Behind it she saw the sky painted upward with a soft pink hue from the lights on the highway in the distance. Rachel concentrated on her breathing, moving through the water with ease until she reached the shelf that allowed her to stand up and wade ashore.

Back to safety.

Back to life.

Sam Hairston stood in the darkness looking out on the lake. He often watched the water. It was calm and still and sometimes in the early morning with the mist rising in the gathering heat, it was like the dawn of time. He could easily imagine dinosaurs raising their long necks over the surface and calling each other in the low-pitched voices of prehistoric song. In the evening or dark of night the water was like a sheet of black glass. Under the moon it was silvery and reflective. Sam had always lived near a lake, this one or the Great Lake Superior in Detroit. He couldn't imagine being landlocked.

Tonight there was no moon. The water rippled as he cast a look over the dark, secretive surface. There was a woman out there. She drew his attention. He wondered who she was. She'd been there for the last three nights, swimming alone. He'd watched her, made her part of his ritual of listening to the night-quiet surface as the lake gave up its secrets of the day.

It was against regulations for her to be there. The beach was public property, but without permits and lifeguards it closed at dusk. Everyone around here knew the dangers of the lake. She must be one of the summer residents. Sam thought of going to tell her it was unsafe to swim alone at any time, but especially dangerous after dark when visibility was an added factor to safety. It was his job. As police chief of Lake Como he was responsible for its citizens.

But he only watched her.

He liked the way she moved, not so much in the water as when she got out of it. He'd seen her several nights in a row, always after midnight and always alone. He wondered about people like her, the loners, the ones who didn't make friends easily. They usually became known to him quickly. They were the troublemakers, the quiet ones, holding deeply rooted secrets. He hadn't seen that so much at the lake as when he was in Detroit and Seattle.

Here he dealt with wayward teenagers and an occasional disorderly or mild domestic violence. But the lake was swelling with people. Summer was on its way and the population increased as the warm weather drew in.

So far he didn't know where she came from or if

she would prove a problem. All he knew was she swam alone and he liked the way she walked. So he let her be. If she got into trouble he had time to reach her before anything disastrous happened. So he stood on his porch, watching, protecting.

She came out of the water, her hands raised, smoothing the water back over her hair. She was thin, though not unhealthy. Her legs were long and she stood tall with her shoulders back, her chest high. He wondered if she'd once been in the military, then he noticed the sensual way she carried herself, the way she used a towel to dry down her legs and across her arms. She squeezed the water from her hair with a long pull that lifted her breasts. Sam could only see her silhouette. He imagined the rest and found his body reacting to his mind's eye. Then he dismissed the thought.

She looked familiar, although he couldn't see her clearly from his porch. There was no moon, but even if there had been she never truly faced him squarely. Sam squinted, trying to focus on the familiarity he saw in the woman. Yet there was no one alive who came to mind.

Rachel hadn't known he was there at first. While she was in the water and wading toward the land she'd felt completely alone. But she'd felt his eyes on her almost the moment she stepped on the sand. Her senses had been heightened since her encounter years ago in the program. After they were forced to move a second time, she was instinctively aware of her surroundings, taking in all the angles, shadows, and people within range.

And she saw him coming.

Rachel had thought control would be in her hands. Her reentry would be done on her terms. She was going to appear in church on Sunday as her reintroduction. But the situation was about to be taken from her.

It was already Sunday if anyone wanted to argue the technicality of time. Rachel supposed this could be considered a church since no structure was actually needed as a place of worship, but instead of her walking down the center aisle it appeared this small stretch of sand would have to do.

She turned to face him. *Bill.* Her heartbeat accelerated. She swallowed the dryness in her throat. He walked differently than he had at seventeen, an easy gait, not rushed or determined, but with a strength that hadn't been there in the boy. He was twenty-six now, the same age she was. She wondered if her walk had changed. He was taller than she remembered too, but so was she. She thought she'd reached her full height by the time she was seventeen. Most girls did, but at five feet seven inches she was two inches taller than she had been the last summer she'd seen him.

It was dark and she couldn't see his face clearly. She wondered if he looked the same. He was wearing a short-sleeve shirt, open at the collar, and shorts that came to the knees. His feet were bare and kicked up small clusters of sand as he crossed the stretch of beach-land that brought him closer to her, closer to a past that could be frightening and unexplainable.

She'd kept him in her mind for nine years. Whenever things got tough she'd remember talking with Bill. The summer on the lake was the best in her recollection. It was a normal time in a life that would never be normal after the fatal boating accident. It was the time of a teenager, high school, dates, dances, summer fun, and self-discovery. Her greatest worry was what to wear to the dance and if Bill would try to kiss her good night. They'd never made it to a dance and he'd never kissed her at all.

She had wanted to be normal, but that wasn't what was happening to her. For eight months she'd existed in the program, hating every minute of it. Then she'd committed the worst mistake of her and her family's lives. She'd called Bill. Sam had answered the phone. Rachel said nothing, but she recognized Sam's voice and hung up. That tiny call was enough for her family to be found by the people looking for her father. She could still remember the gunfire that resulted seven days later. The running, hiding, her heart pounding in her head, and the guilt that this was her fault. She was sure her next step would result in her death or that of her parents.

They'd survived it, but had to be relocated a second time. A second set of names, another house, more jobs for her parents, and a different school for her. And the constant haranguing from the U.S. Marshals to never, ever call anyone she had known before. It was imperative that they maintain cover. Rachel was so riddled with guilt and scared that she could cause her parents' deaths that she never tried to reach anyone again. Her life became a cautious, controlled pattern of keeping to herself and never making waves.

Until now.

"Bill," she said, still watching the man coming toward her.

He stopped. He didn't move for so long Rachel

thought of a photograph freezing a moment of time.

She'd played this scene a thousand times in her head. She'd meet Bill after years. She'd say hello and run into his arms. He'd enclose her, kiss her, make her feel safe, and then lower her to the sand and make love to her. But that wasn't going to happen. He didn't believe it was her. To him she was dead.

"Bill, it's me. Rachel Wells. I'm alive."

He took another step toward her. She lifted her head so he could see her face. He stared at her, but she couldn't see him. He stood in shadow.

"Sam," he said. "I'm Sam."

His breath was gone, ripped from his lungs by some invisible hand. He tried to say her name, the one name that had come to his mind when he saw her from his porch. But he couldn't get his tongue around it. He couldn't make himself say the name of a woman who was dead. He'd seen the accident himself. That day remained as clear in his mind as if it were yesterday. The Lake had been busy with people swimming and sailboats floating on the smooth surface. It looked like a Norman Rockwell painting of a summer day.

Mr. Wells held his hand out to his wife and helped her step into the boat. Sam had watched her and then turned his eyes to her daughter. Rachel wore a purple swimsuit under a white T-shirt with the logo of the Lake Como Cheerleaders. She'd waved to Bill and him on the shore. Rachel's father had overhauled the six-passenger cruiser and his family was taking it out for the first time. Moments

YOU MADE ME LOVE YOU 25

later he'd witnessed that same boat explode in the middle of this very lake.

The force of the air pushing outward was like taking a full-body slam. With no choice he stepped backward, fighting to stay on his feet. It was the worst accident the small community of Lake Como had ever seen.

Bill screamed. He screamed. Both of them were in the water, frantically swimming toward the burning boat, without thinking that no one could have survived the force of the explosion. Neither had thought of what they would do when they got to the boat, what they would do if they came up with an arm or a leg or worse. Luckily he caught up with Bill at the raft. He was breathing hard and Sam got him to climb onto the square of bobbing wood he'd watched Bill and Rachel construct while her father supervised. Bill broke down then. He cried and the two brothers who hadn't touched each other in years knelt on the wood and held each other in their arms.

Later Sam would think how lucky they were that no other boat was near the cruiser when it exploded. The worst that happened was a few people falling down from the air-concussion.

"You're alive," Sam said, trying but unable to think straight.

His knees buckled. He dropped into the sand, unaware that he'd lost muscle control.

"I'm sorry." Rachel dropped down near him. "I know it's a surprise." She touched his arm. "I am real." The hand on his arm felt light, delicate, but solid. He expected an apparition, but something more solid had latched on to him. He looked at it

unaware of what to do. It was cool from the water.
He could smell the lake on her skin. He looked
into her eyes. They were bright and concerned.
His throat was full, clogged.

"I—"

"It's all right. I should have come over. I intended to, but I—" She stopped too. "It's hard for
me too."

Regaining some of his composure, Sam put his
hand over hers. He needed to make sure she was
there. The solidity of her hand made him sit down
on the sand. She went down with him.

"How have you been?" she asked.

He stared at her for a long moment. Then he
laughed. From a deep well inside him sound blasted
through his body and shouted toward the star-
spangled sky.

How was *he?*

That had to be the understatement of the decade.

Chapter Two

While the temperature around the lake dropped after dark and her wet bathing suit chilled her, the spot on her arm where Sam's hand had been was warm. She looked at it wondering why it was the only spot, why heat didn't radiate outward or fade to nothing. Instead it remained constant and contained. It had to be because he reminded her of Bill. He looked like Bill. She couldn't see him well in the gloom of darkness, but he was Bill's brother. Yet, she'd never felt anything like that when Bill touched her.

That had been years ago. They had been friends, the best of friends, but never lovers. She admitted she had thought about sex with Bill. Before the summer ended she was sure they would have experimented with it, but she hadn't lasted the summer.

"Where have you been? What happened? I mean I saw it. I stood right over there." Sam pointed to a spot in the clearing. "I watched you wave. Then the explosion. And no one has seen you since. All we found was part of your T-shirt. It was ripped and burned. What happened? How did you survive?" he stammered, trying to get the questions out all at once. He turned directly to her. His face was clearer. Rachel didn't think he looked anything like Bill. There was a family resemblance, but Bill's face didn't have as much character. Sam's eyes were widely spaced, dark brown, although she couldn't see their color. It resided in her memory. His nose was slightly crooked as if it had been broken. She wondered when that had happened. She knew it had been straighter before she left. The rest of him she could only see as the darkness outlined him. His legs were strong, his shoulders defined against the girth of his shirt. As he'd walked toward her, she'd seen his flat stomach and slight waist. She wondered if he was married.

"Rachel?" He called her name. She hadn't heard anyone say it in a long time. Even being out of the program for three years she'd maintained her alias until just a few months ago when the U.S. Marshals had told her that her former identity had been fully restored. She was alive again.

Sam was still looking at her. He'd asked about *that day*. Rachel had labeled it *that day* and that's how she thought of it when she allowed herself to indulge in self-pity.

She remembered it clearly. She could tell him the temperature, the airspeed, how fast the wind blew through the trees, the exact color of the summer sky, and what everyone was wearing, even Sam. That day was indelibly printed on the soft tissue of her brain, but she didn't want to talk about it. She didn't want to share. Not yet.

Rachel moved away, picked up her shorts, and

put them on over her suit. She stood fastening them with her back to Sam. Slipping a sweatshirt over her head, she warded off the chill of the air against her wet body.

"It's not easy to talk about," she finally said as she turned back. Sam was still sitting on the sand. Rachel sat down where she was. Several feet separated them. She hugged her knees to her, resting her chin on them.

Sam stared at her. He was waiting for an answer. She knew if she started it would only bring on more questions. She had nothing to say, nothing she was ready to talk about to a stranger. Sam *was* a stranger. She had known him most of her life, but she didn't really know him. He was Bill's brother.

"How's Bill?" she asked, changing the subject. "Does he still live here?" She glanced at the cabin at the end of the trees. She knew Bill. He'd kept her alive all these years.

"Bill?"

"Your brother, Bill."

His laugh was almost a snort. "Of course, my brother." He paused and looked out at the lake. "No, Bill doesn't live here anymore."

"Where is he?"

"He moved to Caulder right after he got out of college."

"Caulder is only twenty miles. You say it as if it were on the moon." Rachel regretted the words as soon as she'd said them. She could have been on the moon herself.

"Sometimes I feel as if it is that far away," Sam said.

"You two don't see much of each other?"

He shook his head. "We're both very busy."

"What do you do?"

"I'm the police chief here. And as such I have some questions."

Rachel let go of her legs and leaned forward. "You're the police chief?" She repeated his words very slowly. It was the last thing she expected to hear. Just as slowly she watched him nod. She hated cops in any form. For years they had lied to her, manipulated her, kept her in constant fear for her life. She never wanted anything to do with another cop as long as she lived.

"Is something wrong?" he asked.

"I thought . . . I thought you studied law, went to law school."

He smiled ruefully. Turning away from her, he looked out at the water. His face was shadowed even without switching his position, and now his expression was completely concealed. Rachel felt as if she'd touched a nerve. "I am a lawyer."

"I thought you said—"

"I did," he interrupted. She waited for him to continue. "I went to law school at night while I worked for the Seattle P.D."

Seattle, she thought. He'd only been across the bridge from where she was. She wondered if Bill had ever visited him and had the two of them gone out together? Could she have run into them on the street or passed them going into a restaurant?

"I thought you were going to school in Detroit."

"I was. Everything was set for that. Then at the last minute I decided to go to Seattle. In my second year my parents got sick and I came home. I finished law school in Detroit."

"So why aren't you working as a lawyer?" She

wanted to pull the question back as soon as she'd asked it. Maybe it was knowing he had been so close to her that made her ask the question. She knew better. Since she wasn't willing to share her story, how could she ask him to share his? She hadn't invited friendships in the past nine years. She knew the consequences of getting close to anyone, of sharing too much, and of having her family found. "Never mind," she added quickly, raising her hand. "It's none of my business."

"I almost killed my partner," he stated, staring directly at her. There was challenge in his gaze. "I knew it was time to come home then."

Rachel's hand flashed out to touch him, but the tenseness in him made her pull it back quickly. "I'm sorry," she said. "We all do things we're sorry for." She stood then. "I'd better go now. It was really good to see you, Sam. Please say hello to Bill when you see him."

Sam got up. "Where are you going?"

"The cabin." She couldn't bring herself to call it home. "It's late."

"You often stay here later than this."

An emotion akin to fear passed through her. "You've been watching me?" Her voice quavered slightly. The thought of someone watching her was unnerving. She'd been watched for years, felt it all the time. She never went anywhere without thinking someone was looking at her or looking for her. At any moment, she'd thought, it was her last. Yet she'd returned to The Lake for sanctuary. She needed to get away from prying eyes and dangerous men. She should have known nowhere was safe. For the rest of her life she would be hunted, uncertain of even the kindest-looking people, and of those who could warm her arm and take her breath away.

"It's just that I'm responsible," he said.

"You're not responsible for me." Anger was evident in her voice.

"I'm responsible for everyone who lives here." His voice hardened.

"Well, leave me off the list. I don't want you responsible for me and I don't want you looking out for me. I can take care of myself."

She turned away. Upset. Even a little afraid. She wanted to run, go back to her cabin, and bar the door. Sam grabbed her arm, stopping her flight.

"I watched you as a lifeguard, not a voyeur." The tightness of his hand on her arm spoke of his anger. "This area is closed and by right you were breaking the law. It was either make sure you didn't get in any trouble or haul you out of the water and arrest you."

She jerked her arm away as if his hand were poker-hot. "I'll make sure I adhere to all the laws of Lake Como from this moment on."

Twisting on her heel, she stalked away. He stared after her. She could feel his eyes boring into her back. Forcing herself to walk, she waited until she got through the trees and out of his sight before breaking into a run, not stopping until she was inside the cabin and the lock on the door had been driven home.

Damn. Sam picked up a rock and threw it as hard as he could toward the other side of the lake. He knew he couldn't reach the opposite shore, but he was so angry he needed to do something. It plopped in the water about fifty feet from where he stood. The quiet stillness of the water moved in circles toward him.

What was wrong with him? Meeting a ghost should account for his behavior, but he knew it was a little more than that. What was this going to mean to Bill? He was happily married with a new baby.

Sam was sure Rachel was still in love with his brother. His name was the first she'd called when she saw him. She expected to find him still living in the cabin. Sam had been there alone since his parents retired and moved to Florida. And what did Bill feel? Rachel had *died* so quickly, so unexpectedly. Did he ever get over *her*? Why was she here? Now?

He thought about Rachel and how she had been that summer. He'd been fresh out of college and planning to go to law school. The little high school kid who hung out with his brother the previous year had grown into a vixen. And she didn't even know it, which he thought was good. He'd been to school with women looking for husbands and some were blatant about it. Rachel hadn't displayed any of those tendencies as a teenager and for the past three days she'd kept to herself.

She'd never been comfortable around him and he had enjoyed taunting her. She was quiet and nervous whenever she had to wait for Bill and he was there. She'd try to make conversation, but he'd turn her words around until she was tongue-tied.

"You'll be leaving soon," she'd begun one day. "Going to law school, probably getting married—"

"I won't be marrying soon," he cut in. "I'm waiting for you." The comment scared her. She stared at him. For a charged moment neither of them spoke. Then he smiled, grinned, and laughed. "Scared you, didn't I?"

"Of course not," she said, raising her chin. She wouldn't admit it, but for a moment she'd thought he was serious.

He didn't know it until it happened, but he was serious. Then he saw the fear in her eyes. He remembered she was his brother's girlfriend. After the explosion he never had to explore his feelings. Never let himself.

Until tonight.

Rachel was the same way on the beach as she'd been that day he'd told her he'd marry her. Nervous, unsure what to say to him. She actively avoided questions and he still needed the answers. If not for himself, for the safety of the town. Sam didn't think she was a criminal. He wanted to know where she'd been for personal reasons. And only one of them involved his brother.

Swinging his glance toward Rachel's cabin, he looked at the darkness. The sky was getting lighter. It was nearly morning. What would Bill say when he found out? What did he still feel for the beauty that lived in the woods? Sam had to go and call his brother.

And he didn't give a damn what time it was.

Rachel kicked the covers off and rolled out of her bedding. She struck a match and squinted as the sulfurous odor filled her nostrils. She lit a candle stuck in the neck of a soft drink bottle. It offered minimal light and threw garish shadows onto the walls. Her body was outrageously huge as it followed her about the room. It was past the middle of the night and she hadn't been able to do anything except think about Sam Hairston since she returned from her swim.

Pushing the curtains aside, she stood fully in front of the window and looked at the trees. No one could see her. There were no other cabins close enough to hers. This had afforded her enough privacy to keep to herself since she arrived a few days ago. She couldn't help looking in the direction of Sam's cabin. Bill wasn't there. It was no longer Bill's cabin. Bill lived in Caulder. Only his brother was there. And maybe his parents. Rachel had heard nothing about them, but on her earlier visits the cabin had looked so deserted. It didn't appear uncared for, just as if no one lived there.

Rachel didn't know how to restart living. She thought she'd ease into it, but she hadn't made a great start with Sam. Why had she flown off the deep end when Sam told her he was watching her? He hadn't meant any harm. He was really looking out for her the way any good neighbor would. She hadn't taken the time to think about being neighborly. She hadn't taken the time to think about anything. Usually she analyzed every situation, yet when he said he'd watched her, her hackles stood at attention.

She wasn't in the program any longer. She had to remember that. There were no people looking for her. They were all dead. She repeated it silently as if it were a mantra she had to learn the way she'd learned a new name, new Social Security number, new address, and new memories.

Then she thought of Sam again. He made her nervous. She didn't know why. She'd never understood it, only that he seemed to enjoy her discomfort. He'd laughed at her question about how he was. His laugh was hearty. Rachel had frowned when he did it, but she really liked the sound of his voice. It somehow reminded her of safety. Usually she hated jokes. It had been a while since she'd heard one and even longer since she'd told one herself, however unintentionally it had come out. She saw the irony in her words, inquiring about his health as if they'd only seen each other a day ago when, in fact, she was returning from the grave. Yet his voice had acted as a balm. She didn't understand it.

Letting the curtain go, she looked back at the room. The cabin needed work. A lot of work. It had been empty for nine years. Some of the wood had rotted, the floors were warped, rust stains lined the sinks and tubs, and she wasn't sure the electricity would work. She had only a cellular phone and not a single person to call. She'd been here three days. It was time to begin to live. Tomorrow, no, today—the clock had long since changed one day into another—she'd apologize to Sam. And on Monday she'd call and have the services resumed. It would be good to have electric lights and a hot shower. On Monday everyone would know. The entire community of Lake Como would come to see if it was true. The moment she put her name on the rolls of the electric company the word would go out.

Sam, she thought about him again. Why didn't she think of Bill? He was the one whom she'd spent the summer with. He was the one whose memory she'd held on to when life got out of hand. She'd lie in bed and remember their talks on the raft. Sometimes those talks were the only thing she had that seemed normal. Sam wasn't normal. His hand on her arm hadn't been normal. She put hers on the place where Sam had touched her. She knew it was impossible, but she was sure it was still warm, as if his touch had seeped through her skin.

She could use a cup of coffee right now. But she had no means of making it and it was too early to drive to the diner out on the highway. She reached for the half bottle of warm cola she'd left on the window seat. Taking it and blowing out the candle, she slid a long sweatshirt over her head, then padded surefooted through the cabin and out the back door. She sat down on the weatherworn steps and drank the tepid liquid.

Over the treetops the horizon blushed as if someone had spilled wine and it was soaking upward. The day was about to be born. Nothing could stop it. She thought about the days when she wanted to stop the sun from rising. Today wasn't one of them, although she had her fears for what it would bring. She was no longer in hiding, her seclusion ended when Sam saw her on the beach. By noon the entire community would know she was back. Her heart quaked over meeting people she hadn't seen in years, explaining what had happened, looking into their inquiring eyes. She wished she'd run when Sam came toward her. At least for one more day she'd be free of the searching eyes. But she'd thought he was Bill. And Bill would honor her secret.

Leaving her seat, she moved almost before she'd decided to ask a favor. She didn't know if Sam had gone to sleep. There was only one way to tell. If he was awake, maybe she could convince him to keep her presence unknown until Monday. All she'd ask for was one day. She wanted to control her reentry. She walked briskly, brushing the low pine branches aside as she passed them, the way she had always walked when she went to find Bill.

Car lights swung around and caught her in their beams. She stopped, raising her hands to shield her eyes from the brightness. The car stopped in front of the cabin with the lights trained on her. The cabin door swung inward. Sam came out wearing the shorts and shirt he'd had on earlier. Rachel could see his outlined form in the doorway. The car door opened and a man got out. He slammed the door and looked in her direction.

"Oh my God!" she whispered and stood rooted to the spot. This time it was Bill.

Chapter Three

The brothers stood side by side. Both stared at her. She was too far away to hear what they were saying, but their gazes focused on her whenever they weren't looking at each other. Sam had to be telling Bill that what they had seen nine years ago was faked. That she was alive and standing only a few yards from him.

She was afraid. She'd come here to ask Sam to keep her secret one more day. It was too late. He'd already told Bill.

"Rachel!" She started as Bill called her name. Looking up, she saw him coming toward her. Sam hung back by the car. Bill walked fast, cutting through the car's light beams, before breaking into a run. "Rachel!" he called again before he reached her. His face was wide with the smile she could identify blindfolded. He grabbed her in a bear hug and swung her around, then stood her on the ground and stepped back, keeping their hands linked and looking her over from head to foot. Rachel felt self-conscious, but happy. She hadn't dressed and her eyes must be puffy from lack of sleep. "Rachel, why didn't you tell me you were alive?" He pulled her back into his arms and hugged her again, repeating the full circle swing. Then he did something he'd never done. He kissed her. Kissed her hard. On the mouth. Her eyes closed and she responded. His hands raced over her, up and down her back and hips, over her arms and shoulders, as if he were making sure she was really there. That she wasn't a ghost who would disappear into the morning mist. He lifted her again, a sound of pure joy coming from his throat as he screamed to the silent sky.

"Set me down, Bill. I'm getting dizzy." He set her on her feet but held on to her.

"You should have called me. Let me know."

She had tried to tell him once. The results had been disastrous, but Bill didn't know that. She'd held on to their friendship until she thought she would go crazy. Finally, she'd picked up a phone and dialed his number. The outcome of that had sent her family into a crisis. Rachel couldn't tell Bill about it. She even refused to think about it herself. "I wanted to tell you, Bill. I couldn't," she said.

"How have you been?"

"I'm all right." She shook her head without committing anything. She couldn't tell him how it had really been, how she felt like a target all the time, how meeting new people caused her extreme anxiety, how she distrusted anyone who was nice to her or overly hostile. She was too used to the minimalist method: say as little as possible. Only answer the question. Don't elaborate.

"You look great," Bill said.

She bowed her head, threading her fingers through her thick hair. She knew she looked like a freak. She hadn't combed her hair. She wore a knee-length sweatshirt over her nightgown and no make-up.

"Come inside. It's cold out here."

Rachel let him lead her. They passed Sam and went up the stairs. Sam followed and all three went into the lighted living room. Rachel squinted. The cabin had changed since she was last there. All the furniture was different. The soft rose-colored sofas had been replaced with beige ones. Brown-striped pillows accented the color scheme. The mantel over the fireplace, that had held a huge clock and scores of photos, had no clock and only two framed pictures. One of their parents and the other of Bill and a woman. Rachel picked that one up.

"My wife," Bill explained as she turned to him. He'd taken a seat on the arm of the sofa. Sam stood by the door watching her.

Rachel looked at him, the photo in her hand. "You're *married?*"

"Four years now. We have a daughter. She's three months old."

Rachel looked down at the photo again. The woman was shorter than she was. She had the same coloring, but there the resemblance ended. Her hair was short and shaped in one of those styles that even looks good wet. "She's beautiful," Rachel said over the lump in her throat.

Bill was married. He'd found someone else. She hadn't thought of that happening, especially after he'd just kissed her. Now she saw the gold band on his left hand. She'd kept him in her mind for years. The news made her feel numb. All these years she'd imagined him the same as he had been that summer, that life had somehow been suspended in Lake Como, that when she came back everything would be the same. The water would be just as cold and refreshing as she remembered it. The summer sun would cast the same amount of light over the area. The trees would not have grown an inch and everything would be as she remembered it. No one would age or die. No one would marry or have children. They would just wait for her arrival to reanimate them. Then the world could turn again.

But the world had turned and not only for Bill. She was different too. She'd had time to get used to her changes. She'd seen herself in the mirror every day for the last nine years. Her world had changed a little at a time, making it impossible for her to see the minute transformations. His world came as a complete surprise. She hadn't been prepared for it. Like Sam's, Bill's face had more character. He had grown from the angular boy into a man. His hair, so often bleached lighter by the sun, was winter-dark as if he worked mainly inside. He had a family, a wife of four years and a baby. And Sam hadn't said a word. Why had he told Bill she was alive, but not told her Bill was married?

"Congratulations," she said to Bill, surprised at how calm her voice sounded. "I didn't know." She threw a glance at Sam. Anger surged through her and she sent a silent message to the police chief that his actions were less than warranted. He'd deliberately kept information from her, something she had a need to know. Rachel shouldn't be surprised at that. He *was* a cop. He'd only told her that Bill lived in Caulder. Why? she wondered. In some way was he trying to protect his brother? Or like the other officers of the law, was he manipulating her?

Everyone at The Lake had known she and Bill had a special relationship? They were together all the time. It started out because they were alone, away from the people they really wanted to be with, and it was easy to talk to someone you had no romantic interest in. But the ease with which they slipped into each other's lives made it seem as if they were a couple. Some people might have thought she'd slept with Bill. She wondered if Sam was one of them.

She knew now life had gone on, people grew and changed. She was no longer the same person who had lived in Lake Como. There was nothing between herself and Bill really. Only the promise of what could have been. For a moment she regretted that promise. Yet it was in the past and she had vowed to live for the future. But she'd pictured Bill in that future. Something inside her died knowing that would never be.

Bill didn't know he had kept her alive, kept her sane in the night when she felt the oppressive weight of hiding from the world, when she wanted to scream or run away. He was her connection to the outside, the *real* world, not the illusion in which she had existed. However unfairly, she'd made Bill her anchor. She'd thrown her hopes on him being there when she returned, even knowing she might never return. Now reality stared her in the face. She looked at the photo still in her hand.

A wife and a child.

"You'll have to tell me what she's like." Rachel replaced the photo on the mantel.

"She's a lot like you," he said. His smile was wide and happy and there was an indefinable glow that said he loved the woman he talked about. "She loves midnight swims and talking in the moonlight." Bill's smile infected her. She returned it. "You'll have to meet her soon."

"I'd like that." She gave the expected response and tried valiantly to make it sound genuine, but she didn't feel it. She felt as if her heart were being pulled out of her chest. Rachel knew there was no fairness in her reaction. Bill hadn't been part of her fantasy. He hadn't even known about it. She hadn't really thought of it as such either. She'd begun by holding her memories to herself, replaying them when she felt unhappy. They helped to bring her out of the depressions she'd fallen into.

"What about you?" Bill interrupted her thoughts. "Where have you been all these years?" He leaned forward in his seat. "What happened when the boat exploded?"

"I'm really sorry about that, Bill. It happened so fast. There wasn't time to explain anything. I couldn't say good-bye. I wasn't given the choice."

Both brothers waited for her to go on. She looked at Sam, whose quiet nature intimidated her. His position was casual, his arms loosely hanging at his sides, but she could see the deeply interested cop-eyes boring into her.

"I can't explain it now."

"Why not?" Sam asked. She felt as if a drill had twisted into her.

"It's a very long story and I'm not ready to tell it."

"When are you going to be ready?" Sam asked.

She swung her glance between the two brothers.

The resemblance was there, subtle things like the same hairline and bone structure, but the differences were more apparent. Sam's eyes were piercing, while Bill's were clear and open. Bill smiled easily. Sam smirked or snorted, but rarely laughed. The one occasion on the beach when he'd laughed full and hard came with nine years of unanswered questions. Bill's body was strong and sure. Sam's was hard and unyielding.

"Tomorrow," she answered Sam. She accepted the challenge in his eyes, but he said nothing. She could tell he wanted to. She could see it in the line of his body, the underlying tiger that wanted to unleash its fury on the current target—her. "I came over to ask you if you'd hold off telling anyone about me until Monday. I'll have the electricity and water turned on and—"

"You don't have water and electricity?" Sam left his position and took a step into the room. "What have you been doing?"

He made her feel as if her father were chastising her. "I haven't been here that long. I eat at the diner out on the highway and I bathe in the lake."

She saw his hand ball into a fist and release. A gleam in his eyes told her he understood her midnight swims. Yet he was angry with her. Why?

"I promise I will explain everything. I just need some time before everyone finds out."

"I'll keep your secret," Bill said. She turned to him, more to get away from Sam's stare than to acknowledge his statement. "The Lake hasn't changed that much. People will still come by. Everyone still gets into everyone else's business. You won't have a moment's peace once they know."

Rachel shivered. She wasn't looking forward to

explaining what had happened. "That's why I want another day of solitude before I have to recount the past."

Sam dropped his head. He looked as if he understood.

"Did Sam tell you we held a memorial service for you and your parents?" Bill said.

"No." She looked at Sam inquiringly. His face remained unchanged, closed. "We only had a few minutes on the beach tonight. There wasn't time to catch up on all that's happened."

"It was a beautiful program. Everyone came. We threw flower wreaths in the lake. Some of your friends said a few words. Sam spoke for me. I was too—"

Rachel stopped him. "Don't. Let's not go into it." Tears sprang to her eyes. She hadn't thought of anyone mourning them, of the community of people they loved coming to grips with their deaths. She had been bereft at the new situation, but had never thought of the neighborhood grieving. She'd only wondered about Bill and what he thought. She wanted to know if he missed her. Then she'd begun to create fantasies in order to survive. In them she would imagine herself on the raft talking to him.

"Bill, maybe you should let Rachel rest," Sam said, breaking into her thoughts. "It's been a long night and I know you'll spend the rest of it asking her questions."

She was suddenly very tired. "I am tired." Tonight wasn't the first night she was back at The Lake, but it felt as if she'd been on the witness stand.

"I'm sorry," Bill said. "I wasn't thinking. It's so great to see you again." He rose and joined her in front of the fireplace. "Come on, I'll walk you home."

"Rachel." Sam stopped them before they'd taken a step. "There's no one in the guest room. You can stay in there tonight. I'll call and have your services turned on in the morning."

"That's not necessary." She took a step forward and realized he was blocking her exit. "I've been there a few days. I can stay one more night."

The challenge was in his eyes. She remembered his words when he found her on the sand. She couldn't swim there after dark.

"That's a great idea, Rachel. Too bad the raft is gone. I miss some of the times we had out there." She looked at Bill, seeing him with the eyes of a seventeen-year-old. In many ways he was still seventeen. But she wasn't. "Whenever I come back here I stay in my old room. You can sleep in Sam's."

Heat vented in her face. "Where's Sam going to sleep?"

"I sleep in the master bedroom now." His voice was low and rumbled as if it were being dragged across sheets. Rachel felt it stir her insides. She pushed the feeling aside, telling herself it was exhaustion.

"I think I should go back." She took a step toward the door. Sam's hands slid into the pockets of his shorts.

"You don't even have a working bathroom there." His voice was strong. "Sleep here. You look like hell. A good night's rest won't hurt you."

He turned and left the room before she could reply. Rachel knew she looked tired, but it hurt to have him say it. What was wrong with him? And what was wrong with her? Why did his words bother

her? And why was she thinking of sheets and bedrooms when he looked at her?

"Is he always like that?" she asked Bill.

"He's had a rough time of it the last few years."

"His partner?"

"He told you about that?" Bill's eyebrows rose in surprise.

"Only that he almost killed him."

"Her. His partner was a woman. Since then he's changed a lot, but when you nearly die it changes you."

Rachel understood the volumes in those few words. Bill probably had no idea what he'd said. She'd been dead for nine years. Not to the memory of The Lake, but to herself. She had gone through the motions of living, but to herself she'd been dead, just unburied.

"Sam nearly died?" A tremor ran through her. "What happened?"

"You'll have to let Sam tell you, but he doesn't like to talk about it. I'm surprised he told you about the shooting. You two haven't seen each other in nine years. He hasn't really told anyone other than me."

Bill reminded her of her own quest for time to explain her secrets. Yet she wondered what he meant or, more, implied about her and Sam. Rachel glanced at the place where Sam had stood before leaving the room. Why would he tell her, if he hadn't told anyone else? They hadn't been friends. They saw each other often, but rarely talked to each other. Yet tonight he'd told her something he kept from most people.

Rachel couldn't think why he did it.

Bill broke into her thoughts. "Come on, I'll show you to Sam's room."

Sunlight poured through the windows when Rachel woke up. She liked sleeping with the curtains open. Her mother had said she had stars in her eyes. She liked looking at them at night and waking to the sun in the morning. This morning she remembered where she was. Not in Seattle, not in her own bed. She was in Sam's house.

In Sam's bed.

Trophies of his accomplishments were everywhere. Plaques on the walls, statues on the bookshelf, ribbons with medals hanging from them on a bulletin board. He'd been on the swimming and diving teams and played football. The room was almost a memorial to his sports achievements.

She wondered about him. There was something deeply hidden inside him. Bill had said he'd changed after his partner was nearly killed and he almost died. She knew that was enough to change a man's life, but his attitude toward her seemed out of focus. She felt that he accused her of something each time he looked at her. But what?

Sitting up, she pushed the covers back. Her sweatshirt lay across the bottom of the bed. She didn't reach for it. The room was warm. The bed had been warm too. The mountains around the lake district accounted for the weather patterns. It was often cold in the morning and evening and hot during the middle of the day. Her cabin was cold in the morning. She couldn't build a fire in either of the two fireplaces until she had the chimneys cleaned.

Some mornings she thought how nice it would be to sit by the fire while she finished the second cup of diner coffee she often brought back with her from breakfast.

Sam's room was masculine; a deep maroon and dark green spread covered the bed. The curtains followed the major color scheme. And the room had the definite presence of the man who used to occupy it. She could feel Sam's aura as if he were present, and it was as contradicting as it had been when she lived in Lake Como. He'd taunted her then, always appearing to force her to say something or do something she had no intention of doing or saying. Last night's challenge was no different. He'd practically forced her to stay the night. If Bill hadn't stood between them like a buffer he probably would have barred her from getting to the front door.

She went to the bathroom. Fluffy towels sat on the sink counter waiting for her. On top of them was a new toothbrush and a tube of toothpaste. A comb and brush set sat next to them. Sam had been in this room. She grasped the sink counter and held on while a wave of distrust passed through her. Him being in her room while she slept, watching her when she was helpless, scared her. She saw the towels again. Putting her hand to her throat, she calmed herself. This was Lake Como, not Seattle, not Charleston, not anywhere she could be hurt. Sam hadn't meant anything more than being a good host, she reminded herself. He wasn't one of them. He didn't know about her. Trying to calm her beating heart, she drew in large gulps of air.

While she'd slept he'd come in and given her the things she would need. She picked up the brush and looked at it. He was being nice, nothing more. Samuel Hairston was trying to make her comfortable. There was nothing sinister about it, she told herself. Looking in the mirror, she saw the frightened woman she'd become, pale, eyes large and dark. She shook inwardly, unable to ward off the feeling that she was being watched. She stood there for a moment or a lifetime, she wasn't sure. Finally the color began to return to her face. The shakes stopped and she calmed down. It was ironic, Sam trying to make her feel welcome. A small smile lifted the corners of her mouth.

She brushed her teeth and looked at the bathtub. It was pristine white without any rust stains. She wanted to sink into it, with water up to her neck. She wanted to fill it with scented salts and allow the hot water to wrap around her body in soft fragrant bubbles. But she resisted. She didn't want to get too comfortable here.

Rachel stopped herself again. And again she looked at the huge bathtub. She could submerge herself if she wanted. There was nothing stopping her, nothing pressing, and no one waiting. Yet she decided against it.

After a quick refreshing shower Rachel was reluctant to leave the bedroom. Both Bill and Sam were somewhere in the house waiting for her. All she had to wear was last night's sweatshirt. She didn't even have clean underwear. Reluctant to face Sam again, with the accusations in his voice and eyes, she spent as much time in the bedroom as she could before she had to leave it. Opening the door, she slipped out and went down the stairs. Voices came from the kitchen. Her stomach growled. She smelled fresh coffee and cooked bacon.

She had to pass the front door to get to the kitchen. For a moment she wanted to leave, run while she still had time. She could go out the front door quietly and leave the two of them alone. Sam admitted they didn't see each other often. They could catch up on old times. She looked at the door, the pull to escape strong in her mind. But it would be rude to go without saying a word, especially after Sam had given her the use of his shower and his bed.

"Good morning," she said from the door. Bill sat at the table. Sam stood by the counter with the coffeepot in his hand. He had on a white shirt and dark trousers. His suit coat hung from the back of a chair.

"We've been waiting for you," Bill said, getting up. "Sam checked—"

Sam cut him off. "Would you like some coffee?"

Rachel wondered what he was about to say. Checked what? Checked her room? Sam picked up a cup and filled it. He offered it to her. Rachel accepted it and took a seat at the table opposite the one with his jacket hanging on it.

The kitchen was almost the same as it had been *that* summer. The white linoleum had been replaced with pale yellow no-wax tiles, but the table and chairs were the same. The copper pots that hung from a rack in the corner stood in the same place. The counter appliances were as she remembered them. There was a cluttered desk and computer in another corner that hadn't been there before.

"Thank you for the towels and brushes," she told Sam.

"Your hair looks nice," he said flatly, turning to replace the coffeepot. "Breakfast?"

Her heart fluttered at the compliment, then fell when he turned away. He had said she looked like hell the night before and he'd given her the comb and brush. He could only comment on the fact that she used it. "What time is it?" She looked for a kitchen clock. "The radio in the bedroom is broken. I thought it was at least lunchtime."

"It's after one. You missed church," Bill said. He had the same look on his face he'd had that last summer when they had skipped church to go swimming.

She looked down at her sweatshirt. Pulling the collar, she let it snap back. "I had nothing to wear." As expected Bill laughed. "You haven't changed a bit," she told him. He still had a boyish face and under his suit, which probably belonged to Sam, he had broad shoulders. He wasn't as wide across as his brother or as tall, yet he was taller than she remembered. His hair was shorter, but his movements were the same. That invisible magic that underlined the nature of a person was still there. Bill was happy, successful at life, which she thought was more important than being successful in the eyes of the world. She didn't know his financial situation, but whatever it was, he'd found happiness. Her throat clogged at viewing the man he had become. She was sorry she hadn't been there for the transformation.

Sam on the other hand was moody. He shaded his eyes from her, hiding his feelings and holding everything inside. Only on the beach last night had he shown any emotion. She attributed that to her surprise appearance. He opened the refrigerator and took out milk and eggs. Her stomach growled again.

Ten minutes later he set a platter of scrambled eggs with Canadian bacon and wheat toast in the middle of the table. Juice, coffee, and milk followed it. Two kinds of jam, butter, marmalade, and apple butter were added to the meal. Rachel watched him adding things as if he were expecting all the residents of The Lake to show up.

"Sam likes breakfast any time of the day or night," Bill said, filling his plate with food.

"You never complained," Sam said. He took his seat and began filling a plate for himself.

"I like breakfast too," Rachel said, drawing the tension that had somehow gathered in the room. "I can eat it anytime."

"You two would make a great couple," Bill said.

Rachel didn't look at either of the men. She took care to fill her plate and not comment on Bill's unbridled statement. As always he never thought about what he said before he said it. Words just bubbled out of his mouth. It was strange that Sam didn't say anything either.

They ate in silence for a moment. Rachel put a forkful of food in her mouth. It was the best food she'd tasted in months.

"What's Hallie Jomatti doing now?" she asked.

"She's Hallie Alaria now."

"You're kidding." She put her fork down and couldn't help the smile that played at her lips. "Hallie and Joe Alaria got together? They hated each other in high school."

"Got four kids."

"Four? Has there been time for that?"

"You've been gone nine years," Sam reminded her.

She cut him a look. What was his problem? Why was he treating her as if she were a criminal? She'd done nothing wrong. She hadn't decided to fake her own death and go into the witness protection program. She'd had no choice. If there had been another solution her parents would have found it. But there wasn't.

"She has two boys and a set of twin girls," Bill said, pulling her attention back to absent friends. "They live over in Caulder too. Joe works at the county engineer's office. Hallie finished college on the Internet and started her own home-based business building Web sites. She's got some big corporate clients. Last time I talked to Joe, she was doing so well he said *he* could retire."

"The Internet is a great tool."

"If it's not abused," Sam interjected.

"I know kids get hooked on it and some get in trouble." She looked directly at Sam. "I imagine you have to deal with that."

"Not yet, but I'm aware of it."

Rachel was stumped. What was Sam trying to do? Each time he spoke she felt as if she shouldn't have said anything. She was only trying to make conversation, but she couldn't understand his attitude. He'd been a totally different man on the beach. She could almost like the guy on the beach. But this one . . .

"What about Woody Norris? I always thought he and Hallie would hook up." She turned her attention to Bill.

"I thought the two of you would get together," Bill returned.

Rachel smiled. "I did have a heavy crush on him." When *that* summer began Rachel had been devastated that Woody would be spending the entire summer away from The Lake, but after she and Bill began spending time together, her teenage affections changed.

Bill shook his head. "Woody never really returned after he got out of college. He went to MIT, met a girl, married her, and they live in Texas. He works for a big software firm."

"That's great. I'm glad to hear it. He loved his computer. He even helped me learn to use mine."

"When was this?" Bill asked. "You were always out on the lake."

"Not always," she said. "I remember a certain time when you were pursuing Amelia Cooper. . . ."

"Don't remind me." His smiled gleamed.

Rachel laughed. It felt good. She hadn't laughed in a long time. Glancing at Sam, she expected to see him smiling too. He often teased Bill about Amelia when Bill was trying to get the cheerleader to notice him, but his face was set. He held a cup of coffee, and when he drank from it he closed his lids, preventing Rachel from reading the dark expression in his eyes.

Bill looked down at his empty plate. Shaking his head, he said, "I can't believe I was ever attracted to her. But those were the good ole days."

"They were," she agreed. She felt better thinking about the past with Bill than she did when she was alone. His comment didn't immediately bring back the years of separation, but she felt more comfortable than she had in a long time. If it hadn't been for the tension Sam created in her she would have been totally at ease.

Sam drank from his cup in silence, refilling it once.

Rachel stood up. She'd had all she could take. If he didn't want her around, why did he insist that she spend the night? "I better go now."

Bill stood up too. "I'll walk you home."

"I'm sure you have to get back to your family."

"I have a little time."

She looked at Sam, then wanted to kick herself for the thought that she needed his approval for Bill to leave with her. Did he think the two of them would run to her cabin and jump into bed? After nine years of life without each other, did he think they were dying to pick up where they'd left off that summer?

As she thought it Rachel knew that's exactly what she had wanted. She'd assumed the two of them would continue as they had before she left, but finding out Bill was married had shocked her into reality. It would take her some time to adjust, but she had adjusted to many things before. She could do it here too. Things weren't the same anymore and she couldn't walk back into Bill's or anyone else's life and expect everything to be as she'd left it.

"Thanks for the bed and the food," she said tightly as she left the kitchen.

"Anytime," he said, but waved her comment away with his cup as if it meant nothing.

Rachel and Bill went out the door. She took a breath, sucking in the air as if she hadn't been able to breathe in a long time.

"I apologize for Sam," Bill said as they walked through the wooded area. "He's usually more hospitable than this."

"He offered me a bed and breakfast."

"And he made you pay for it with his company."

"Believe me, I've been in worse company." She felt scathed, unwanted, as if her presence at The Lake would upset the delicate balance that Sam had single-handedly achieved here.

The walk was short. Just before they turned to go up the path where they couldn't see the water, Rachel stopped and looked at it. Life here had changed. The oak tree near the water's edge had a knot that completely grew over the basketball plate her dad had nailed to it when she was twelve. The lake looked smaller, the trees bigger, thicker, the cabin more forlorn. But she had been happy here.

"Do you think we can ever go back, Bill?"

"Back to that summer?"

She nodded.

He shook his head. "Life isn't set up that way." All the boyishness about him was gone. He was nine years older, a father, a husband, and wiser. Here he was a man. "Was it bad, Rach?" He called her by the name he'd used that summer.

"Not all of it. I missed the lake and you. . . ." She looked into his eyes. "I missed all the things about living here. I didn't even know some of them until I came back."

"You can only go forward. I know it's easy to say put the past behind you and go on, but it's the only way."

She looked at the water, then at him. She thought of all the times she was unsure, afraid, told one thing by the government only to discover lies and secrets. Everything was a conspiracy. It was hard to tell who were the good guys, whom she should believe. In the end it was no one. In the end it was clinging to The Lake memories that kept her from losing herself in the travesty that seemed to be designed to drive her mad.

"I'll handle it," she told him.

He hugged her, pulled her head onto his shoulder, and kissed her hair. "However bad it was, you lived through it. And now you have people who'll be here for you if you need help. You know how we stick together here."

She looked up at him. "I thought of The Lake often. Mainly of the times we spent on the water, looking up at the stars and talking about everything, life, our futures, me swimming in the Olympics." She laughed at their lost youth. "I'm sure we were no different from any other teenagers. But we found out life doesn't always play by the rule book we designed. It has its own book."

Bill nodded, but he seemed to understand. It was their relationship, their raft conversations that allowed him to empathize with what she wasn't saying.

"You're back now." He lifted her chin and smiled. She returned the smile. "Your friends will gather you back to their hearts and you'll forget all about the bad times."

She stepped back, but he kept her fingers linked to his. "Even Sam?"

"Especially Sam. He's the law around here and he's known for helping people."

"I'm not sure that includes me. I rub him the wrong way. I always have."

"You just don't know him." Bill took a step closer to her. Rachel wondered if he was going to kiss her again. She wanted him to. She wanted to feel all the emotion she was sure would flow between them, but Bill didn't. "Sam's been through a lot in the last few years. He wants people to think he has everything together, but there are places in him that hurt."

Rachel should understand that. She knew about places inside that hurt, places that screamed for help when no one could hear. She was hurting now too. The man in front of her had been the pinnacle of her dreams. She had spun lives for the two of them, lives together, yet it wasn't to be. She couldn't think of Sam and his hurt. Her own heart hurt too much. Instead of trying to understand, she said, "He's your brother. You have to say that."

"Just give him some time."

"He's had nine years."

Chapter Four

The U.S. Marshal's offices in Syracuse, New York, had none of the poshness of its D.C. counterpart. Aaron McKnight had been in the D.C. office many times in his fifteen-year career with the marshal's service. He remembered the red, white, and blue decor, the windows, and the airiness of the room. The conference room he was in today was little more than a storage room. The table in the center was circumvented with boxes, leaving little room for people to move around. Boxes sat on the floor, the corner chairs, and the heating and air-conditioning vents under the windowsills. Some had labels in handwritten marker designating office supplies, other government or department acronyms.

McKnight studied the boxes. Everyone had convened and he was the only one who didn't believe in this action. He'd given his attention to the boxes and not engaged in the easy banter that took place before the meeting came to order. The director took his seat and Aaron turned his attention to the man at the end of the conference table. Luke Bland, director of the Syracuse office, was anything except what his name implied. He was a peacock, wearing loud, bright colors and sporting the image of a darkly tanned playboy. In point of fact, he was a Rhodes scholar, holding degrees in both criminology and law from Columbia University and Harvard. His suit today was bright yellow and he'd coupled it with a black shirt and yellow-striped tie. Aaron couldn't imagine anyone even selling clothes in those colors and he would never wear them. His suit was gray and his shirt white with gray cuffs.

The room was crowded with the team, the team he referred to as the Rachel Wells Coffin Assembly, RWCA. He was sure the plan they had devised would fail. They were burying a twenty-six-year old and she didn't know it. They hadn't asked her to cooperate or to participate. Aaron was thirty-seven and he'd decided this was his final job. He'd see this project through to the end, because he admired Rachel Wells and how she'd handled what she had already been put through. The belief that her every move would result in death, several relocations with new identities, only one of them precipitated by her, her parents' deaths within months of each other; it was a miracle she wasn't confined to a mental hospital. She'd been a strong child and now she was a strong woman. He'd do his best to keep her alive, but when this was finished, he was finished too.

He hadn't made any decisions about what he'd do with his life after the marshal's service, but he was certain law enforcement was not on his list of things to pursue.

"Is everything in place?" Bland asked.

"She returned to Lake Como as expected," McKnight reported.

"We got a break there," Jerry Wheaton, a three-year rookie, said.

"How so?" Bland asked. "We expected her to return to her hometown."

"True, but the first person she reintroduced herself to is the police chief."

"Have we contacted him?"

"Not yet, but if we don't, he'll surely call us." Bland waited for Wheaton to continue. "Samuel Hairston, a former Detroit street cop. Spent a stint in Seattle doing Internet crime, but returned to Detroit after a year. Left the force several years ago. Has a law degree, but works as the local police chief." He recited the facts as if he were reading a dossier. "He's got an exemplary record and would have made detective if he'd stayed. He's the kind that doesn't like mysteries, and if I read Ms. Wells correctly she's not one to openly explain her past."

Aaron knew that was right. They had trained her. She'd seen the consequences of talking about her family and he knew she'd learned the lesson well. It was too soon for her to be completely comfortable talking about herself. And that would arouse suspicion, especially in a man with Hairston's record.

"She'll be a puzzle and the police chief doesn't like puzzles. He'll try the normal channels, then call in a marker." The rookie was speaking when Aaron brought his attention back to the room.

"Do we know with whom?"

"An ole buddy from the DPD. Works for the bureau now. Name's Gregory Vancamp."

"Get to him and feed him the intel."

The rookie nodded.

Bland continued his meeting update. "What about the Grazianos?" He looked at Zack Price.

"We've leaked a little information. We expect he'll pick it up soon." Zack was the inside man at Security Investments, Inc. It was purported to be a stock brokerage firm, but more mob money went through there than legitimate investments. Zack was good at picking stocks and he was making a lot of legitimate money, but he knew who the real players were and a statement dropped here and there would make its way to the single pair of ears he wanted it to find.

Graziano was dead and usually all debts died with the godfather, but in the case of Tamara and Campbell Wells, Rachel's mother and father, Carmine Edgecomb, Graziano's grandson, was out for revenge. It was reported that he was on his own. The family didn't condone his actions and he'd been ordered to forget it, but Bland knew he wasn't doing that. So they'd set up this operation. And it would bring down more than Carmine Edgecomb. But in McKnight's opinion, it would also bring down Rachel Wells.

"We're ready for Carmey when he makes his move." Zack's voice grated on McKnight. The room was suddenly quiet. Everyone looked from Bland to McKnight.

"McKnight?" Bland called. "Are we ready?"

Aaron took a moment to survey each of the faces around the table. Most of them were veterans of the service. They had seen a lot of action and few took any job as a sure thing.

"This isn't the same type of operation we're used

to taking on," he began. "First, Ms. Wells is unpredictable. We don't know how she will react when someone from Graziano's family shows up. She won't even know they are from the family or that she's in any danger. There's a huge unpredictability factor here that concerns me. Without her cooperation she can unintentionally get some of us killed." He took a silent moment to let his gaze move from face to face. "And we can do the same for her."

A-wop-bop-a-loo-lop-a-lop-bam-boo, tutti-frutti. The radio blared on as the current time coincided with the set alarm. Rachel shot up in bed. She rolled over, crouching into a kneeling position, her feet instinctively going into her shoes as she reached for the neatly folded stack of clothes under the nightstand next to the bed. Except there was no nightstand and no bed. She was in a sleeping bag.

Panic skated through her like lightning. Her eyes darted around the unfamiliar space as she sought an escape route. Where were her parents? She got to her feet and started for the door. She knew better than to open it. She would listen first. Then she'd move and move fast. As she pressed her ear to the cold wood, memory forced its way past the panic that hammered in her head. She wasn't in Seattle. She was back in New York, back at Lake Como. The electricity was on. Her hand went to her wildly beating heart and she breathed a sigh of relief.

She moved to the radio. She'd brought it with her because it had a battery-backup system, but the battery had run down and she'd unthinkingly plugged the device into the dead wall socket. Music from an oldies station blazed through her bedroom. Listening to a station that played music from decades ago reminded her of her parents and was remarkably soothing, at least when it was played at a decent decibel level. The volume was as high as it could go. The control knob probably got changed during her trip to The Lake or when she unpacked the Jeep. She turned it down to a livable volume and hit the Off button. Silence stunned the room. Her head was buzzing from the scare of being so abruptly awakened.

It had happened to her before and there was always the threat of it happening again. They'd come in the night, the U.S. Marshals, awakening her from a restful sleep and plunging her into a nightmare. She'd heard the voices in the other room, angry voices that made her heart beat in fear. In seconds her father would burst through her door.

They had to move.

Had to go.

Now!

They left through the back window with nothing, no clothes other than the ones they were wearing. No shoes, or money, not even a tube of lipstick. They'd been discovered and relocation started anew. After that her father insisted they keep a set of clothes ready in case they had to leave the house in the dead of night.

It was a practice she'd continued. Her clothes were stacked in the corner of the room. They were her security blanket, one that she thought she might have to use this morning. She looked at the pile, a pullover blouse, jeans, socks, running shoes, and a hooded sweatshirt. She had no mementos, no jewelry, books, or maps to identify her. Everything she needed to survive had been committed to memory. In the woods she'd stashed some money in a watertight pouch and she never let the Jeep's gas tank fall below half-full.

Caution was ingrained in her. Thinking before she acted, analyzing what she'd say before she said it were as much a part of her makeup as her fingerprints.

The clock read 10:27 in bright green numbers, but it was really only three minutes past eight in the morning. The time was wrong, but both clock and radio worked. She was a night person, used to prowling the house alone or spending time on the Internet. She rarely rose before eleven.

Suddenly Rachel whirled around. She stared at the clock. The thought came back to her that it was plugged in. The electricity was on.

"Damn," she cursed. "Sam!" Rachel got dressed. Usually she'd head for the diner and breakfast, but not this morning. Sam had done this. He'd called the electric company. She probably had running water too. She went into the bathroom and twisted the knob on the cold water faucet. For a second nothing happened. Then it spurted and coughed. Involuntarily Rachel took a step back. A whoosh of water came out of the pipe as if someone had sneezed it through, before the steady stream ran like Niagara Falls.

Anger replaced the fear in Rachel. Did he think she couldn't take care of herself? Did he think she wouldn't know whom to call for services? What if she didn't want electricity and running water? Of course, she did, but what right did he have to remove her options? He was acting like McKnight, making decisions without her approval and taking action without so much as a word to her. If she wanted the electricity on, it was her duty to arrange for it. Not his. She wasn't a child anymore and she didn't need people doing things for her without her permission, not even cops. Especially not cops.

Rachel didn't know why she was so angry and she didn't stop to analyze the reasons. She drove quickly in to the center of the small town and parked in front of the police department.

The building was small and unimposing. It looked like a storefront restaurant, except the words LAKE COMO POLICE were painted in white letters across the windows. It could just as easily have read TONY'S BAR AND GRILL or MAISEY'S SEWING AND NOTIONS.

Rachel expected a bell to ring as she pushed through the front door, but nothing like that happened. Inside she found herself on a small carpetless pedestal two steps up from the floor leading to the counter. A third of the space had been delegated to a makeshift ramp for the handicapped. A uniformed policeman stood behind the counter, which was free of bulletproof glass to protect the constabulary from the citizens of Lake Como. Rachel counted herself lucky that she didn't know the man.

"May I help you?" he asked. A shiver went through her. No matter what level of the law she encountered, be it the FBI or the cop on the block, they each had the same rough edge to their voices, the straight pinned-back shoulders and booted feet of larger-than-life cartoons, and the same authoritarianism that caused her to lock her jaws and grind her back teeth.

"I'd like to see the chief."

"Is he expecting you?"

"Yes." A voice came from an open door to the left. Both Rachel and the officer looked in that direction. Sam Hairston stood there in his full uniform. Rachel hadn't been prepared for that. He was devastatingly attractive. No, she corrected, the man was gorgeous. For a moment Rachel could only stare. Her mouth was dry, her tongue glued to the roof of her mouth preventing her from opening it.

She'd seen men in police uniforms before. The mere sight of the starched shirts, embossed with epaulets and badges, was enough to have her turning away, almost running in the other direction, but the sight of Sam had her rooted to the floor.

"Won't you come in?" He stepped aside to give her access to his office. Rachel found strength in her legs and headed for the open doorway. Passing him, she could feel the heat of his body and smell the scent of his aftershave. The office was spacious, without clutter, unlike the one in his kitchen. Light filled the room from two oversized windows. Before the desk, which held a laptop computer docked in a workstation and the normal accouterments of an office desk, in-box, out-box, pencil cup, etc., were two sturdy wooden chairs. Rachel plopped down in one of them.

"You knew I would come?" she asked after he'd seated himself behind the desk.

"Part of my job is to read people, assess their criminal tendencies."

The hair on the back of her neck went up. She didn't like being lumped in with criminals and she didn't like being assessed and put in a box.

"Which part of those tendencies has to do with having my electricity and water turned on?"

"Oh," he said as if the gesture held little significance. "You couldn't keep living there without services. And you know people at The Lake are neighborly."

"Sam." She stood up and leaned toward him, although she didn't touch his desk. "Let's get something straight. I am an adult. I am responsible for myself and I take care of my own affairs. If I wish to have any services turned on or off I will make the call, not you."

"You don't like me very much, do you?"

"What?" The question threw her. She hadn't expected him to make things this personal.

"Liking you or not liking you has nothing to do with this."

"I think it does."

"Then why was it you were one person on the beach and a total stranger in your kitchen? If I hadn't seen you before I'd swear there was a good twin and an evil twin both wearing the same face and clothes."

He rolled his chair in close to the desk, folded his arms along the blotter-covered surface, and stared down at them for a moment. When he looked up his eyes were as clear as The Lake on a sunny day, and as unreadable as its depths at night.

"I was a little startled," he said. "You had just risen from the grave."

"Why don't we just agree to keep our relationship the way it was before I . . . went away?" She stammered over how to describe her absence. "At that time I was Bill's friend and you were his brother."

Rachel waited a moment, her eyes locked with Sam's. Then she straightened up and headed for the door. When she had her hand on the knob, Sam spoke. "Bill's girl. Weren't you Bill's girl?"

Rachel didn't turn. She took a deep breath first. She had never been Bill's girl. They were only friends. Then she left and for the intervening years she'd told herself she was Bill's girl.

But she wasn't.

She turned back and looked at him. "Whether I was or not doesn't matter at this point in time."

"That's good to know, because the way I remember it, Rachel, back when you were Bill's *friend* I told you I was going to marry you."

The breath caught in Rachel's throat. She remembered that day in their cabin when Sam had teased her. The way her stomach knotted now, she didn't feel like teasing. She stepped through the door and closed it quietly, suppressing the urge to slam it hard enough to shake the building.

What the hell was wrong with him? Why did he say that? He'd *wanted* to get Rachel's goat. He'd wanted to anger her, make her react to him, especially after she'd brought up Bill, but he had no right to taunt her with that stupid marriage conversation they'd had a hundred years ago.

Yet she remembered it. That short conversation had flashed through his memory and she recalled it immediately. He could tell by the way the color painted her skin tones with an undershade of red. What did that mean?

Sam had no idea.

He hadn't thought much of marriage. The summer he'd teased Rachel he'd been playing with her. She was nervous around him and he did things to throw her off balance. He was younger then and prone to pranks. The hard days of his life were yet to come. Was he still doing that? Had Rachel's reappearance taken him back to a more innocent time? There was something about her, even back then when she was only a girl, that aroused him. She was no longer a girl. She'd developed into a sexy, alluring woman, made more so by the arm's length she invariably put out to keep him away. And the further she extended her arms, the more he wanted to walk inside them.

Sam got up and went to the window. Resting an arm along the jamb, he checked the street in front of the office. Rachel wasn't there. The street was normal, cars parked at an angle on both sides of it, others driving slowly through the main avenue, and people moving in an out of the businesses along the picturesque town. But Sam was changing.

He really didn't feel that bad about teasing Rachel. He might just want to marry her. He turned back to his office and reached for the phone.

"Vancamp," the voice answered on the other end.

"Greg, how's it going?"

"Well, Sam, I was just thinking about you." Sam heard his friend's laughter. "It's about time we got together again. Are you heading for the District anytime soon?"

"Not this time. I've got something here I'm pursuing and I need your help."

"Go on." Sam could almost see his friend pulling paper and pencil in front of him. Even though they hadn't seen each other in a couple of years Greg wasted no time on catching up. If Sam said he had an enigma, Greg was ready. They had been that way as partners in Detroit.

"Her name is Rachel Wells." He spelled it. "She's from Lake Como, New York."

"Trouble in your little town?" Sam heard his short laugh.

"I don't know."

"What else do you know?"

Sam told him everything he'd learned about Rachel, up to the day she returned from the dead. He'd come in early this morning and spent hours working through every law enforcement data bank he could think of, trying to find something on Rachel and her family. At every turn he would find a reference to the boating accident and that would be the end of it. Sam knew that wasn't the end of it. He had living, breathing proof that Rachel Wells had survived that accident. So why was there no record of her for the last nine years?

"Any idea where she's been?" Vancamp asked.

"No, and she's not talking. I'm hoping there's a logical explanation, but . . ."

"But in our business there rarely is," Greg finished for him. "Give me a couple of days and I'll see what I can find."

"Thanks, Greg."

"Not a problem."

Sam replaced the receiver, but continued staring at the phone. He'd tried every place he knew to find information on Rachel and come up empty. And as he'd told Greg, she wasn't filling in the gaps. Yet she was intriguing.

Damn intriguing. More so now than when she was sixteen.

Sam frowned. Why didn't she just tell him where

she'd been? He'd checked the prisons and mental hospitals. No one with her name had been admitted or released in the last nine years. Sam wanted everything to fall neatly in place. The Wellses had been nice people. Finding out things weren't as he thought they should be could rip the community apart. And he preferred law and order.

There was also that teasing statement that nagged at him. Marry her. Yeah, he could marry her, just as soon as he found out who the hell she was and where she'd been for nine years.

Rachel slammed the door of the Jeep and ran up the four steps to the porch. She went through the front door, wanting to slam it too, but she didn't. Sam Hairston was a jerk, she told herself. No man had ever made her so angry. Why did he have to bring up that conversation? It was ancient history. She'd been a nervous schoolgirl then and he was practically an old man in her eyes.

She took a breath and looked around. Silently she began counting. It was a mechanism she used to calm herself down before she said something she shouldn't. She hadn't done it this morning in Sam's office. He'd been standing in front of her, wearing his uniform and looking good enough to eat. And all her practical thoughts were lost to her.

Why did she go to see him anyway? Why didn't she just stay here and forget the lights? They weren't that important. Swinging around, she looked at the switch. She refused to touch it. Somehow she felt it was like touching Sam. And for some reason she couldn't explain, that frightened her.

Turning away, Rachel surveyed the room as if

she'd never seen it before. Despite the way she felt, it *was* good to have the lights on. It made the cabin less dreary, but it also highlighted the damage that time and neglect had left on the structure. Why the place hadn't been sold Rachel didn't know. She discovered it was hers the day Marshal McKnight found her at her parents' graves and told her she was free. She had a home. It had been waiting for her all these years. Rachel wondered if somehow, someone knew she would return.

She didn't think there was termite damage, but she'd need an inspector to evaluate the true state. There was, however, extensive water damage in some of the rooms, rotted wood and the smell of mold. Upstairs in the loft that overlooked the common room, one window needed replacing. It wasn't cracked clear across, although a small triangle in the right corner was completely missing. The glass couldn't survive another winter without breaking. Luckily she had time to get the work done. There were two large bedrooms on the first floor. Both of them seemed to have weathered the time with grace. Little work other than updating the paint and adding furniture needed to be done in them.

There wasn't much in the cabin in the way of furniture. Rachel had brought none with her. Most of what she had brought was still stacked in boxes in the middle of the living room floor. Her toolbox stood askew next to the neatly arranged cases. She opened it and removed a hammer. Staring at it, she felt its weight in her hand and the pull up her arm. Her eyes darted back and forth from the hammer to the wall. A smile nagged at the corners of her lips. Rachel lifted the hammer, twirling it around in her palm as if she were a practicing ma-

jorette. Then she raised it and buried it in the wall
with a force that created a significant hole in the
Sheetrock. A small cloud of silt puffed out around
her. She pulled the hammer free. It tore a triangu-
lar gap in the wall and the piece fell to the floor.

Rachel slammed the hammer again, holding it
with both hands like a baseball bat. It felt good.
She thought of Sam and plunged the hammer
with all her force into the wall a third time. Over
and over again she drove the metal head into the
defenseless layer, pulverizing it and feeling relief
with every strike. She should find something to
put over her nose, but she didn't move from her
task. She continued to pound the water-damaged
wall, ripping the face off the structure. Her hair
and eyebrows were covered in dust, giving her an
aged look, but she kept at it, as if the wall were her
enemy and she had to vanquish it.

Twenty minutes later Rachel was sweating. Her
arms hurt from the perpetual swinging of the
hammer and the cloud of dust in the air had her
coughing, but despite that she felt better—good,
in fact. She'd cleared the wall to the wood struts
that supported the cabin. The gap ran from the
door five feet across and as high as her arms could
reach. She could see the insulation and electrical
wires that were now exposed to view.

Busy with her own form of pounding-analysis,
she didn't hear someone knock on the door. With
the hammer in full arc she saw movement out of
the corner of her eye and tried to stop the motion,
but the hammer finished its forward tilt and em-
bedded itself into the Sheetrock.

Rachel yanked the wooden handle out of the
wall ready to use it as a weapon. She turned and

stared at a complete stranger holding a casserole dish with a cornflower-blue logo on the side in an oven-mitted hand.

"Rachel?" the woman said, not looking at all surprised to see her.

"Leanne?" Rachel whispered, letting out her breath. She took a step closer to her. "Leanne Higgins?"

"The one and only. Not that I could say that about you." Leanne's eyes swept Rachel from gray hair to dusty sneakers. "What are you doing?"

Rachel knew what she looked like without checking a mirror. She'd been surprised the first time she and her father had done a renovation. When they'd taken a break she saw herself completely gray-haired and covered in silt. She'd laughed, teasing herself that this was what she'd look like when she was fifty. Her father was forty-two then and had only a few gray hairs. She dropped the hammer. It thudded against the bare floor. Emotion rushed into her as quickly as if someone had injected her with a powerful drug. She wanted to laugh and cry and fall on her knees all at the same time. Leanne had been her closest friend nine years ago. The two had been almost as inseparable as Rachel and Bill that last summer. Running across the tiny space, she hugged the woman who was five feet three inches tall, but a mountain in stature.

"Where the hell have you been?" Leanne asked, stepping back to keep the casserole dish in her hand from teetering to the floor.

Rachel's defenses immediately went up and she looked for an evasive answer. Telling the truth didn't come first to her mind. Rachel reached inside for one of the many scenarios she'd learned to the point that she could repeat them with the conviction of truth. Yet to this question she had no ready answer, no practiced, drummed-in, learned response or syllabus to use for the proper reply.

"How did you know I was here?" She plastered a smile on her face, a disguise designed to seem natural and make Leanne feel as if the conversation were rushing over a waterfall. It also precluded Rachel's having to answer her question.

"Bill told me."

"Bill?"

"Oh, he swore me to secrecy, but I had to come. I work for CG&E." Rachel's frown was misinterpreted by Leanne and she continued. "Canadaigua Electric and Gas, the electric company. You do remember the name of the electric company?"

"Of course," Rachel said.

"I'm the director of customer service. Bill saw me on Sunday on his way home and asked me to have the electricity turned on in your parents' cabin. Of course I had to ask why and he told me you were back. It was a good thing he warned me too, because if you'd walked into that office I'd have keeled over myself."

Rachel heard what Leanne said, but she was having a hard time believing it. "Bill told you?"

"I ran into him yesterday afternoon at Skeeters. You remember, the ice cream parlor."

"Is that still there?"

"It's in the same place. You wouldn't recognize it though. That little hole in the wall is now a modern establishment with mirrors on the walls and party rooms."

"Bill?" Rachel said again, not meaning to speak

aloud. Bill had told her. Not Sam. Why didn't Sam say something when she was accusing him?

"You know how Bill loved ice cream. Well, he still does and when he saw me he asked me to get the services turned on here as soon as possible. I couldn't believe my ears when he said you were alive."

"I know it's hard to believe."

"Why don't I put this down and you wash your face so I can really see what you look like?" Leanne indicated both the casserole and Rachel's features.

"In the kitchen," Rachel directed her. As Leanne headed for a room she'd spent nearly as much time in as Rachel when they were girls, Rachel went into the bathroom. Her face, eyelashes, hair, and clothes were covered in a fine silt. She washed herself quickly, using the bottled water she'd bought, and without applying any makeup, joined Leanne in the kitchen.

Leanne was spooning the food into small bowls when Rachel saw her, macaroni and cheese with breaded topping. She turned and looked at her friend. A smile spread across her face and she set the bowls on the counter. By some mutual agreement they moved toward each other and the two hugged as if they hadn't played out the same scene moments ago. The emotion of being lost and rescued, found after a long scary night alone, rushed into Rachel and she closed her eyes to enjoy the sense of homecoming.

"Have you been camping out here?" Leanne asked when the two separated. She picked up the dishes and handed one to Rachel. There were only a couple of bowls in the cabinet. Rachel had bought them for cereal when she didn't go to the diner for breakfast, although until this morning she could only keep milk from spoiling in the cooler.

"I haven't been here long. Just a few days." She evaded a direct answer. The place looked uninhabitable, especially after she'd torn down a wall in the other room. There was little furniture and until this morning no lights or water. Everything in the place needed replacing or discarding. Rachel took her food and led Leanne back through the living room and out onto the porch where there were a couple of empty crates they could sit on.

"Are you back for good?" Leanne asked.

"Honestly," Rachel said, "I don't know." She looked across the lush landscape. Pine trees gave their incredible fragrance to the air. The soft hills rose in the near distance and the lake behind them provided an insular calm, a place where she was once happy. Could she be happy here again? Or had her time come and gone? Life wasn't the same as she remembered it. Would she always be trying to make it so? Would moving to a place where she had no history, no memories, be better for her? Rachel had to find out here first. If it didn't work she could always move.

Suddenly thoughts of Sam came into her mind. He would be a reason to leave.

"What are you planning to do here?" Leanne's voice broke into her thoughts. Leanne was looking at the door, inside to the pile of Sheetrock rubble as high as she was tall.

"Until I decide, I need to make the place livable." Rachel looked at the open door. She could smell the Sheetrock dust, which covered everything inside. "I thought I'd replace the water damage and maybe buy a bed."

"You don't have a bed?"

Rachel smiled. "I have a sleeping bag. And before you start," she said, stopping Leanne, who'd opened her mouth to speak, "I've slept on worse."

"Rachel, we have a guest room. You're perfectly welcome to stay with us until you can get the work done here."

"Thanks, but I'll be fine." She smiled. "And who is we?"

"Oh my God, I forgot you didn't know. I traded Higgins for Jeffers two years ago. My husband's name is Russell Jeffers."

"I don't remember him."

"You wouldn't. He's from Albany. He came to The Lake about three years ago on a civil engineering project. I fell for him hook, line, and sinker."

"Any children?"

"Not yet." She looked at Rachel over her bowl. "But we're working on it."

Rachel smiled. She envied her friend. Her life was normal and Rachel no longer knew what normal was. Maybe that was why she was here. In all her years of absence, Lake Como had represented, at least in her mind, normalcy.

"What about you? Anyone in particular these last nine years?"

Rachel shook her head. She hadn't been allowed any relationships. At least she hadn't allowed herself to become serious about anyone. She was too afraid of forgetting herself if she got close to anyone, of saying something that might force them to move again. She'd had dates, even been involved several times, but nothing that lasted. At least nothing she allowed to last. She'd resigned herself to a protected life. Inside the program she would do what was required. She'd follow the rules and keep in step. That meant no outside involvements.

"I hate to eat and run," Leanne said with a sigh. "I have a million questions, but I have to get back to work."

Rachel instinctively checked her watch. "Oh, I forgot." She didn't work outside the house. She made her money trading stocks on the Internet. Often she wouldn't remember what day it was.

Leanne set her bowl on the floor and stood up. Together they walked down the steps to her car.

Rachel spoke when her friend was inside her car and had rolled the window down. "It was really good to see you."

"It was great seeing you, too. We'll have to get together soon and maybe you'll feel better about answering questions on where you've been."

Rachel was stunned. She thought she'd side-stepped the questions she didn't want to answer, while the truth was Leanne had allowed her to do it.

"Leanne, I didn't mean to be mysterious. It's a long story and one I'm not inclined to visit right now."

Leanne patted the hand Rachel had lying on the window ledge. "I understand. When you're ready and if you need someone to talk to, remember I'm still here."

"I will," Rachel said. "Would you do me a favor?"

"Sure." Leanne frowned.

"Don't tell anyone I'm here?"

"Why?"

"I'm not ready to have visitors."

"Or explain."

Rachel smiled in return to her friend's statement. "I'm not ready to explain."

"I'll keep your secret, but you'll have to come out of the closet soon."

"I just need a little time."

"In that case if you see Lori Stiles coming, run the other way."

"Who's Lori Stiles?"

"Loretta Stiles. She came to The Lake about five years ago. She thinks she's a modern-day Walter Winchell. She's the biggest gossip in town and a reporter for the *Lake News*. Nothing is off-limits to her."

Rachel waved good-bye as Leanne pulled away from the cabin. When the car was out of sight, Rachel retrieved the empty bowls and rinsed them in the kitchen sink. The water was rusty. Taking up her hammer from its place on the floor, she looked at the gaping wall. Her heart wasn't in tearing the wall down any longer. Sam hadn't told Leanne to turn the electricity on. Bill had done that. Yet, Sam had taken her anger and taunted her over it. He hadn't denied her accusations. He only returned her barbs with humorous sarcasm.

Rachel wondered why that was.

With a measuring tape, pencil, and paper, Rachel put Sam Hairston out of her mind and went to work assessing each room, writing down what needed to be done. She measured windows, floors, walls, archways, molding, and wrote the figures down. She thought about floors, carpeting, hardwood, tile. In the kitchen she assessed appliances, cabinets, and lighting. Then a trip to the local home-improvement store had her ordering a battery of materials. Fixing up the house would keep her busy for months. It would give her the opportunity of making the place her own and to come to terms with her future.

She loved solitude and working with her hands. In the past she'd worked with her father. They were a do-it-yourself duo. He taught her everything she knew about fixing things, building additions, and small engine repair. What he didn't teach her was how to do it alone. That she had had to determine for herself after he died.

Several days later a truck arrived and two strong men paraded in and out for half an hour unloading the materials she'd ordered. Rachel directed them where to stack the stuff. She was glad the living room was empty of furniture, since the drywall alone took up most of the floor space. She'd had to move the boxes she'd stored there to the kitchen. There were metal pipes, buckets of joint compound, paint, boxes of ceramic tiles, a sink and toilet, a new bathtub, and a myriad of miscellaneous supplies taking up the rest of the room. Her windows and kitchen appliances would be delivered later. Rachel had to skirt around the maze they created to reach the inner rooms.

She'd decided to begin with the bathroom and the bedroom in that order. She didn't need the kitchen for much. She wasn't a good cook and had never enjoyed food preparation. So far eating at the diner provided her with adequate nutrition. Hard work and her morning swims in the lake— she'd given up on nights—would keep her weight at an acceptable level and her body trim and toned.

The good thing about the cabin was that the ceiling in most rooms was only eight feet high. The common room, however, stretched to the skylights and she would need the scaffolding she had to put together to reach the places that needed work. Rachel planned to begin with the bathroom. While she wouldn't need the scaffolding for a month or more, she had to put it together to get some maneuvering space. Grabbing a wrench she began the highwire work.

It was exhausting, but proved cathartic. By the end of the day, the scaffolding was up and she defied Sam by taking a quick swim after dark then falling into a deep and restful sleep.

The next morning she was ready to start again. Equipped with a full breakfast and an extra cup of coffee, she returned to the cabin and continued her plans. Placing the surgeon's cup over her nose and mouth and covering her hair with a shower cap, Rachel took a hammer and started gutting the walls of the bathroom.

She worked steadily for the whole day. The physical work was therapeutic. She thought of nothing, not even putting Samuel Hairston's head in front of the hammer as she cleaved it into the powdery wall. One wheelbarrow at a time she carried the debris outside and using a rigged-up electronic pulley elevator system, lifted the entire barrow and upended it into the Dumpster that now sat on the small square of blacktop that was her driveway. A spray of fine powder clouded the air each time she made the trip.

Then she'd go back to work. The bathroom was finally clear. She'd swept up the last bit of debris and shoveled it into the waiting wheelbarrow before carrying it outside. Moving the old cabinet sink and rust-stained toilet proved her worth for the day. As soon as she disposed of them she'd go for a swim and then to dinner. Rachel craved a long soak in a bathtub, but she had no bathtub now. She'd discarded it, as she was about to do with the sink and toilet.

Grunting and heaving, she levered them out of the room and onto wheeled pallets. Tackling the sink first, she pushed the pallet. As she reached the front door, and the makeshift ramp she'd set up to avoid the step down to porch level, Sam Hairston met her. His hands came out and braced themselves on the sink as she pushed from the back. The unit stopped.

"Hey," he said. "What are you doing?" His brow wrinkled in a frown.

Rachel stood up straight. She pulled her hands free of the work gloves and wiped the sweat off her forehead. What was he doing here? She knew she had to see him sooner or later. She owed him an apology. Since Leanne had told her Bill really had her services restored she knew she had to apologize to Sam, but she wanted to do it in her own time. Sam's presence was forcing her hand.

"You got a warrant, Chief?"

"Sam," he corrected. She refused to call him anything else since their altercation in his office. Rachel reminded herself at every turn that he was a lawman and despite the feelings that sometimes came over her when she thought of him, feelings she couldn't understand and refused to explore, he wasn't someone she wanted in her life.

"I only came to see if you were doing all right."

"There are four thousand permanent residential families of The Lake. At least fifteen thousand during the summer months. Check them all out, do you?"

"No." He shook his head. "Only those with intriguing lives."

"You think I'm intriguing?"

"You're an enigma."

And he didn't like enigmas. Rachel could almost hear him say it. Sam smiled and she felt a sensation snake through her like a hot squiggly arrow twisting and turning at her core.

He stepped around the sink and looked over the room. "It appears you have heavy construction going on. I hope you have a permit. You don't want to break any laws."

Rachel linked her fingers behind her back and rocked on her heels. "I'm planning to stay awhile and the walls needed work."

"You're doing it yourself?" He turned to face her, an eyebrow raised in surprise.

"No, I hired an army to help me. Don't you see them?" She turned around in a full circle and came to face him.

"Do you want some help?"

"Aren't you on duty?" Sam was wearing his uniform and she'd noticed the police car when she was at the door, before he invited himself inside. The former police chief, Rachel remembered, had driven his car home. She assumed Sam continued the practice.

"Just going off," he answered.

"Well, I'm finished for the day." It was actually

the truth, but it sounded as if she were making it up to avoid him. Rachel did want to avoid Sam, but she didn't want it to appear so obvious. She'd found obviousness generated interest and she'd learned that interest was something she didn't want to attract.

"What about tomorrow?"

He looked at the ceiling as if he was assessing how much work it needed.

"I can do it."

Sam considered the scaffolding she'd built and the pulley system she used to raise the Sheetrock and fit it into place.

"This is amazing. Did you do this yourself?"

She nodded.

"Alone?"

"Yes," she said, pushing her shoulders back for the negative comment she expected was coming. "Alone."

"You like being alone, don't you?"

"You like asking personal questions. You've seen me for all of three times and you're doing a character assassination already?"

"It's my job. And I'm not assassinating you."

"I thought you were off duty."

"Going off duty."

"You mean never off duty. I find that cops are always cops."

"Had a lot of experience with the police?" There was that raised eyebrow again. And she'd said something she didn't intend to say, revealed a part of her past that she wanted to keep secret. At least from him.

Rachel took a deep breath. She no longer had to keep her life hidden. She could say what she wanted, tell anyone what she wanted, but a cop was a cop. And there she drew the line.

"I am not your job."

"Who are you?" Sam asked, apparently throwing her a left hook. But Rachel caught it with the dexterity of a whale harpooner.

"What's that supposed to mean?" she hedged.

"It means I've looked in every database I can find and technically you don't exist."

"Then you're seeing a ghost."

Sam said nothing. His eyes swept her body from head to toe. She forced herself to remain in place. Even with the grime of the walls and the sweat of hard work clinging to her skin, she felt a pull toward him.

"Would you like my fingerprints to determine if I'm alive?" she offered, angry more with herself than him.

Sam quickly accepted. "Yes."

She could feel heat pouring into her face. "Accuse me of a crime then, and arrest me. Because you're not getting them any other way."

The two of them stared at each other across the space of the room. The air was as charged as the electricity lighting the work lamps she'd set up to see the walls.

"What gives you the right to investigate me? I've done nothing wrong."

"I'm the law here."

"I know the law and without probable cause you have no right to question me and I won't stand for being harassed."

"You think this is harassment?"

Rachel was getting angry. She took a moment to count to ten. "Chief, what do you want?"

Sam approached her. He came within a foot of where she stood. Rachel wanted to move away from him. His presence was huge and she suddenly felt closed in by him and the room.

"I want to know where you've been for nine years and why I witnessed an obviously faked accident on the lake."

Rachel found herself counting again. "Am I being accused of a crime?" she asked.

"No," Sam said, shaking his head.

"Then I want you to leave."

Sam dropped his shoulders. "Rachel, I apologize. I didn't mean to strong-arm you. I guess it's the big-city cop in me that suspects everyone he can't categorize. I've known you since you were a child. I should be more trusting."

Rachel didn't buy that speech for a moment. Sam had just changed tactics. "Apology accepted," she said. "But you can still go. I'm going for a swim and then—"

"Good, I'll go with you." He didn't give her time to refuse, but took her arm and started pushing her toward the door. Rachel yanked her arm free when they got to the pallet still standing where she'd left it.

"I'm not going to swim in these clothes. I need to change."

"Of course," he said as if he'd only just remembered she needed a suit. "I'll take this outside and wait for you there."

He turned and pushed the pallet through the door as if it weighed nothing. Rachel stood in the middle of the room. When had she agreed to go swimming with him? It was the last thing she wanted to do, but he was waiting and she had no shower or bathtub now that she'd gutted the place. She couldn't go to dinner in her present state and she couldn't avoid the cop in her front yard.

Chapter Five

The water was delicious. Rachel had missed this lake during her enforced absence. There were other bodies of water, lakes, pools, the ocean, places she had swum, but none of them compared to the mountain water. It refreshed her skin and took her worries away. She felt at home here unlike any other place she'd lived. It was calm and silent and peaceful.

The sun warmed Rachel's face as she floated. She lay that way for an eon, then arching her back she held her breath and dipped her head backward. She felt the spongy water pull her hair, making it both heavy and weightless at the same time. She went under headfirst and using her arms completed a full circle in the soundless, though welcoming, world where speaking was impossible. Like a mermaid, she was at one with the water.

Surfacing, she stretched out and headed for open water. She'd only taken three strokes when suddenly her foot was caught and she was pulled back.

Coming upright, she faced Sam, who she'd forgotten was there.

"Where are you going?" he asked, treading water.

"I was going to swim out to the raft."

"There is no raft. It's been gone for years."

"I know that. It's the halfway point. I do it all the time."

"Not today. You've been working in that cabin all day. You're too tired to go to the middle. Swim parallel to the shoreline." He moved around behind her as if he was blocking her direction.

Rachel knew it was an order, but she didn't feel like arguing with him. She started out toward her cabin, parallel to the shoreline as he orchestrated, but quickly reversed direction and swam the other way. Summer vacationers had crowded the portion of the water toward her cabin. Rachel didn't want to take the chance of running into someone she knew whose cousin or friend was up for the season.

She swam behind Sam's house. The beach there was small, intimate, and secluded. Few people went there since it was so close to his residence. She and Bill used to use it as their private beach. When she was in view of the blanket she'd spread on the small patch of sand, she headed for it.

As if leaving the weightless world of the water added poundage to her, she was suddenly exhausted. She fell to her knees, then facedown onto the blanket, her eyes closing as she did so. She hadn't intended to fall asleep. She only closed her eyes a moment, but when she opened them Sam was staring at her and she had the feeling he'd been doing it for some time.

"Oh." She sat up wiping her face and running

her hands through her hair. A towel that had been covering her fell away. "I apologize," she said. "I haven't done anything like that in years." Rachel removed the towel and pulled on her T-shirt.

"You were tired," Sam said.

"I suppose. It's a good thing you stopped me from swimming to the ra—" She stopped. She was going to say raft, but changed her mind at the last minute. "To the middle of the lake."

Sam grinned. She smiled back, but Rachel had the feeling he was gloating on knowing she was too tired to swim out and back.

"You don't smile very often, do you?" Sam asked.

"I don't know. Smiles are the things one doesn't record about oneself."

"You also don't talk much about yourself."

"Neither do you."

He dropped his eyelids and smiled in a way that had Rachel's stomach turning a flip. Her hand went to it, unsure why she should have a reaction to him.

"I'd better get home."

"Why? It's peaceful here. When the sun sets, it's beautiful across the water."

Rachel remembered the sunsets. She'd watched several since her return. The sun would set in an hour or so. She didn't want to watch it with Sam. It would be dark after that and she didn't want the intimacy of darkness around them.

"I'm rather tired and I need to get dinner."

"I have just the thing." He turned and pulled a picnic basket from behind him. "While you slept I went to the house and made some sandwiches."

Rachel couldn't refuse. He'd gone to the trouble of preparing her something to eat. It would be rude to leave without being neighborly. And other than Leanne and Bill, he was the only friend she had since she'd returned.

Looking into the basket, Rachel found it full of food. "You said sandwiches."

"Well, I added a few other things."

She looked in the basket again, then back at him. Some of the food inside required preparation time. "How long was I asleep?"

"Have something to eat." Sam avoided her question. He pulled a plastic container of fried chicken out of the basket and followed it with a salad, dressing, rolls, and corn on the cob, still warm. Rachel bit into the chicken. It was delicious. Everything was finger food. Sam hadn't brought any silverware, so they picked at the salad one piece of lettuce at a time, dipping it in the dressing.

Rachel could hear the muted sound of people having a good time at the other end of the beach. The area of sand wasn't that large, so the space got crowded early and usually remained that way. On this side, behind Sam's cabin, they couldn't see the main area.

"How much work do you plan to do in the cabin?"

"As much as is needed. And that's a lot." Rachel bit into the chicken. "I'm doing the bathrooms and bedrooms first, then I'll move on to the kitchen."

"Do you cook?"

"Not as well as you." She smiled as she dipped a corner of lettuce into her dressing. They laughed and talked easily as they ate. Rachel was surprised at how easy it was to talk to Sam. She didn't know if he stayed away from subjects she would find sensitive just to keep her talking or if he was really interested in her. She knew she couldn't keep her eyes from straying to him more than she expected. He hadn't put on a shirt since they'd come out of the water, but had exchanged his trunks for a pair of shorts. She had a clear view of his strong shoulders and long legs.

His skin was remarkably even in color, as if walnut-colored paint had been poured over him as a child and someone had used hand strokes to smooth it out. There were no brushstrokes, no marks or blemishes except for a small spot near his waist. It disappeared down his waistband and she refused to think about where it ended.

He obviously kept himself in shape, for as Rachel's eyes traveled over muscle and bone she could find very little fat. Standing six feet tall, he had a military look about him. His hair was short, a little fuller than a policemen's buzz and definitely not military. His chin had the hint of a cleft, enough that she took notice, but not enough that it would pull the eye away from the other features of his face. His eyes were dark brown and widely spaced, fringed with long eyelashes and hooded under brows that were the same color as his hair. His nose was slightly crooked as if it had once been broken.

Music started on the other side of the trees that separated this secluded area from the main beach. Both she and Sam turned toward it.

"This happens every night," he explained.

"I remember," she said. "Young people haven't changed."

Sam shook his head. "They still like to play music and dance in the sand."

Rachel dropped her head and turned away. Her crowd of friends had done that too. "Were you one of them?"

"Sure," he said, glancing toward the music. "Before leaving for college I was on the beach every night."

Rachel lay back and looked at the stars. "Bill and I used to swim out to the raft and talk under the stars."

"Totally against park rules."

"Do you always follow the rules?" Rachel regretted the question as soon as she asked it. "We knew it was against the rules, but it didn't keep us from doing it."

"Do you want to do it now?"

The question threw her. She turned and stared at Sam, wondering if he was serious. The thought of swimming out to the middle of the lake with Sam had her body going hot.

"The raft is gone," she said, repeating his earlier comment.

"Then let's dance."

"What?"

Sam stood up and grabbed her arm. She got to her feet, protesting. "I don't want to dance."

"You and Bill used to dance out here too. I could see you."

Rachel stepped back and stared at him. Had he been spying on them?

"I was one of the lifeguards, remember? I was making sure you two were safe."

"You mean you knew we were on the raft?"

He pulled her into his arms and started moving. "Yes, I knew."

Rachel forgot to be angry. Luther Vandross was singing a love song in the background, the moon had risen, and she could smell the lake on Sam's skin. The water with its unique blend of minerals and the sand in a kind of hot glassy mixture adhered to him. The combination had a unique affect on her. It made her warm and slightly dizzy. The sun had gone, but remained a part of him, along with the unmistakable smell that was all his own. Rachel closed her eyes and inhaled. Her head fell forward and she let herself be carried away by the slowness of the music and the feel of Sam's arms around her.

She'd hadn't been held in a long time. She liked the feel of him, the strength of his arms, and the solid way he supported her. His chest was bare and her hands skimmed over the heated skin of his back.

"Rachel." He whispered her name. She heard the depth of sound, as if he had to dig deep into his gut to say it. Rachel shifted against him, fitting herself into his body as if it were made for her. Sam groaned. Motion between them stopped. She looked into his eyes. Something magical happened to her. They stood in the sand, its heat rising up her legs while some force of nature encircled them in a web of passion. Rachel could no longer hear the music. None of the night sounds penetrated the bubble that enclosed them. Sam dropped her hand and raised both of his until they threaded through her hair. His eyes searched her face. His features were set. Hands caressed her hair, his thumbs massaging the skin of her ears. Rachel's knees weakened. With intended slowness he lowered his mouth to hers. She couldn't move, couldn't turn away. She didn't even know if she could breathe.

Rachel felt as if she lived her entire life in the space of time it took for Sam's mouth to fuse with hers. The anticipation only heightened her reception of him. His face blurred into gentle focus as it came closer. His lips were soft and wet and tantalizing when they touched hers. He knotted his fingers in her loose hair, but held her as if she were breakable. He cradled her to him, his mouth meeting and lifting from hers in a dance that sent erotic sensation through her being.

Passion exploded inside Rachel. She couldn't remember the last time someone had held her like this. She went up on her toes, arching toward him. In seconds she was clinging to him. Their mouths fused into one as the kiss took on a life of its own. His arms were so tight around her she could barely breathe. But Rachel didn't need breath. She needed the sensations rioting through her, the flash of color, storms, rainbows, raging rivers, and explosive fireworks. She needed the feeling of pleasure-pain to send her to that apex where she was breathless and weightless and needy. She needed, wanted this to go on forever. Somewhere in the back of her mind was a voice telling her Sam was the law, and she had no use for lawmen. Sam was Bill's brother and it was Bill she had thought about for years. But none of the messages got through to her body, which was ignoring them and clinging to the erotic song that Sam was playing.

He deepened the kiss as if he were suddenly hungry. Bending her back enough to throw her off balance and force her to hold on to him or fall, he devoured her mouth with his. His tongue dipped into her mouth and made her a part of him. Rachel circled his leg with one of hers to remain upright. It also aligned her body with his, bringing her legs into alliance with his arousal. She didn't know how long she remained in that position or how long the sensation of his mouth on hers went on. The night had disappeared. The beach was gone. There were no cabins, no trees around them. The only remaining part of the universe was the two of them and the overhead stars, only now the stars were all around them, as if they'd somehow been teleported to a realm high into the heavens, to a place that had no roof and no floor. They floated above the world in a place where sensation and passion ruled.

After a lifetime, Sam slid his mouth from hers and buried his face in her neck, continuing the kiss along the sensitive zone between her ear and shoulder. Streams of electricity funneled through her like bright-colored lights streaking through a Fourth of July sky. Rachel's breath was ragged and came in short gasps. She tried to regain composure, but she was too weak, clinging more now than she had when they were locked in an embrace. Her heart hammered in her chest, loud enough that she could feel it throughout her body. She was sure Sam could hear it.

Rachel looked up at Sam and suddenly the bubble burst. The night sounds returned, loud and discordant, as if someone had turned on a stereo with the volume too loud. The music from down the beach accosted her. Luther Vandross was no longer singing. He'd been replaced by the raw rhythms of a rock band. She could hear the sound of young voices singing along with the lyrics.

"Rachel."

It was the strain in Sam's voice that drew her attention back to him. "Sam—" She wanted to say more, but could find no words. "I'm sorry," she finally said, and pushing herself free of his arms, ran into the night. She didn't stop until she was inside her cabin. It was dark and the scaffolding covered a lot of the floor. She leaned against the door, waiting. For what, she didn't know. For her own heart to settle down? For her mind to return to her head? For reason and intelligence to slither back into her through her ears, if that's how it got out?

What was the matter with her? Sam Hairston was a cop and she distrusted him. And he was Bill's brother. How could she feel so . . . so *good* in his arms?

Sam Hairston yawned for the fifth time since his second cup of coffee. He hadn't slept well after Rachel ran off. Well, he hadn't slept at all. Any time he closed his eyes, what he saw was her face in his hands, her mouth opening to receive his kiss. He shouldn't have kissed her. He knew he was rushing things, but she was in his arms and her hands were roaming over his back. Her eyes were wide and he could see the desire in them. The idea of not kissing her didn't occur to him. If he'd been in his right mind he could have thought clearly, but where she was concerned he didn't seem to have a right mind.

The phone on his desk rang and Sam picked it up. He was grateful for a diversion, something to keep his mind off Rachel.

"Chief Hairston." He cradled the phone between his ear and shoulder.

"Sam, it's Greg."

Sam sat up straight and pressed the phone closer.

"Did you find anything?" he asked without preamble.

"Nothing," Vancamp said. "No tax returns, parking tickets, or credit cards. Not even a library card."

"There's got to be something on her."

"You say she's living in your jurisdiction."

"She showed up about a month ago, although she'd lived here as a child, attended grammar school and high school, was a cheerleader. Then when she was seventeen there was a boating accident and she and her parents were reported dead." Sam repeated the sketch he'd told Vancamp before.

"This tells me one thing only," Vancamp said.

"What's that?"

"Witsec."

The word hit Sam like a bomb exploding in his head, but it made perfect sense. An accident that didn't kill anyone, yet they were all reported lost. What else could it be other than induction into the Federal Witness Security Program?

"Then what is she doing here?" Sam spoke out loud, but he was really thinking to himself.

"I don't know," Vancamp replied, unaware that Sam's words weren't meant for him. "It's extremely unusual, in fact, I'd say impossible for someone in the program to be placed in their hometown."

Sam had to agree. The only other solution was also impossible, yet he voiced it anyway. "Do you think she's been removed from the program?"

"We both know the program is voluntary. You can take yourself out of it any time you want. But generally, once you're in, you're in."

Rachel was acting strange in Sam's eyes, keeping herself aloof and not doing much talking. For all he knew, that could be normal for her. She could be hiding out here, but with all the building materials she was planning to make it a long stay.

"What about a sting?" Sam asked. Could she be up here for a reason? But then why wouldn't he be told? He was the law in Lake Como.

"Again, rare to impossible."

Sam sighed. Every time he thought of Rachel the intrigue got darker and darker. And she was forthcoming with nothing.

"Can you access Witsec?"

"Sam, you know better than that. I'd have to go to the man himself. Or at least the man who reports to the man himself."

"Well, keep looking."

"If I uncover anything I'll let you know."

"Thanks, buddy." Sam hung up and leaned back in his chair. Initially, he'd teased Rachel about him being the law but now his cop instinct was rearing its head. She was here for something. He didn't know what it was, but if she was part of Witsec, that could only mean trouble of the major kind.

For once in his life Aaron McKnight had done what Rachel asked of him without a production number of reasons why it couldn't be done. Although Rachel couldn't be present for the reburial, her parents' bodies had been moved to the Como Lake Cemetery and the headstones above the fresh graves bore their correct names.

Rachel stood in the quiet morning air looking at the stones. The sun hadn't yet reached its highest point, but the day promised to be hot and humid. The mist was still present and swirled about the ground, giving the scene a surreal tone. A tear escaped her eye and coursed down her face.

She didn't talk to her parents out loud. She felt

they could hear her thoughts and know how much she missed them. She sensed they would rest better knowing they were home, back among friends.

Rachel closed her eyes and let the feeling of her parents' voices wash over her. She assured them she would be all right. Then she turned to leave. Sam stood waiting for her on the walkway leading down to the road that made a complete circle inside the cemetery. He wore his uniform and played with his hat in his hand. Rachel thought it was a nervous gesture. At least they were on an even playing field. She knew she had to see him again after her exit last night, but she hadn't expected it to be this soon.

"Hi," he said as she approached him.

"Morning," she said. It was awkward seeing him after last night. She hadn't slept much and she hadn't come to terms with what had happened. Why it happened and how she could feel so right in his arms. "How did you know I was here?"

"I saw your Jeep as I was patrolling the area. I wanted to talk to you about last night."

She stopped and faced him. "About last night," she repeated. "I suppose those words have been said a thousand times after something someone regrets doing the night before."

"I don't regret it," Sam said.

Rachel held the surprise and a little elation inside her.

"You might," he went on. "You ran away, so I can only surmise that you would rather I hadn't kissed you, but I don't regret it at all."

Rachel should regret it. She should feel shame or guilt or something more than the remembrance of the pleasure his mouth gave hers. She should feel that she'd somehow betrayed Bill, but she felt nothing like that. What she felt was a racing in her blood and a breathlessness she couldn't account for. Her body trembled and she could think of nothing else except reliving his arms around her again and again.

"I know how you feel about Bill," Sam said.

Rachel was pulled out of her musings. Bill? Her feelings for Bill? She hadn't thought of Bill when she'd looked into Sam's eyes after the sun set. She hadn't thought of Bill when his mouth was united with hers. She should have. She didn't know why she didn't. Bill had been part of her childhood and Sam was definitely not in the same class.

"I know it takes time to get over someone," he continued. "The fact that Bill is my brother probably means it was bad form on my part, but I can't promise you I won't kiss you again if the situation presents itself."

Rachel was supposed to say she would make sure the situation never presented itself.

But she didn't.

"Why don't we just forget it happened? You're the police chief here and I'm just one of the residents."

"Rachel, you can't believe that."

"Sam, I didn't come back to The Lake to begin a relationship. I admit Bill was on my mind, but he wasn't the only reason for me to return. He and I were on our way to starting something that summer." She paused. "But we didn't. And providence has sent us down separate roads. I respect that he's married and I have no designs on him."

"But—"

"Can we leave it at that?" She stopped him from

whatever he planned to say. "We're both adults. It was only a kiss. The world didn't stop revolving."

After a moment Sam sighed and nodded. "No, the world didn't stop revolving."

Rachel stared at Sam. His words didn't mean what he said. She could see it in his eyes, hear it in the underlying message of his words. Had he felt what she did? Had the world not stopped revolving, but spun out of control? Was he making an effort to control it as she was? Was he trying to keep things in perspective? And did he really want to kiss her again?

"Well, have a good morning." Rachel watched him walking toward the squad car. He got inside and started the engine.

"Sam," she called. He faced her.

"I don't regret it either."

The click of a camera shutter made Rachel look up. In front of her was a woman she didn't recognize, but Rachel had been warned. This was surely Loretta Stiles.

"The place is buzzing with your name," she said as if the two of them had known each other all their lives. "I'm Lori Stiles of the *Lake News*. Could I speak with you for a few moments?"

Rachel said nothing. She'd been trained to ignore the press. If they ever stuck a microphone in her face, she was to say nothing, keep walking, and get away from them. She shouldn't have a photo taken or cooperate in any way. And then she should call McKnight.

"Come on," Lori said as she hurried to catch up

with her. "You're news. You can't expect to remain hidden, especially in a town this small."

The Jeep was parked about fifty feet way and Rachel concentrated on reaching it without running. She thought it was rather vulgar of Lori Stiles to seek her out as she left the cemetery. Her parents' graves were fresh and their headstones had only been set that morning. There would be a ceremony the next day, but Rachel expected to be the only person present for it. She had invited no one else. But Lori Stiles was waiting as she emerged from the grave site.

"What's your story?" Lori asked. "Where have you been for nine years? How did you fake that accident on the lake?"

Rachel reached the Jeep and pulled the door open. Her anger was so acute, she wanted to ram Stiles's pen through the camera she kept using to take pictures. She slipped into the driver's seat and jammed the key into the ignition.

"Whether you talk to me or not, there will be a story." Lori clamped one hand on the edge of the open window. The other one held her camera and notebook. "Don't you want it to be the absolute truth?"

Rachel turned and looked at her then, her stare so glaring the woman should have burned to a crisp in the heat of it. Rachel started the engine, then in a lightning move reached out and plucked the camera from Lori Stiles's hand before gunning the engine and leaving her in the wake of spitting gravel.

* * *

Rain drizzled down the windows of the squad car. Last night's downpour had changed into a misty wet fog that seemed to swirl around everything. It was common weather in this area. In a couple of hours the sky could clear and the afternoon would be sunny and hot.

On the seat next to him was the latest copy of the *Lake News*. Loretta Stiles's byline appeared below the headline RACHEL WELLS, DEAD OR ALIVE? There wasn't much news in this community. At least not crime news. Sam took credit for the lack of it. He worked in a program to help teenagers and had spearheaded several projects to give them a place to blow off the bursts of energy that came with the hormonal changes in their young bodies. Because the newspaper covered several small towns in the small resort community, what Loretta Stiles had published this morning was bound to cause talk and curiosity seekers.

Rachel's high school yearbook picture appeared on the front page along with that of her parents' graves and a drawing of what the smiling cheerleader would look like today. Sam was on his way to Rachel's. He wanted to get to her before she saw the paper, if that was possible.

The radio crackled in the squad car and he picked up the receiver and pressed the button. "Hairston," he said. They didn't go in for protocol here. Codes didn't mean much since most of the calls were just to check in.

"This is Molly. Are you on your way in?"

"I thought I'd check on Rachel first."

"You'd better get in here. We've got company. And they're wearing suits."

It was a signal. A joke. In a small office where little more than teenage vandalism and occasional domestic violence were the only crimes, having suits show up was unlikely. Molly's voice held no humor.

"Feds?" he questioned.

"U.S. Marshal's office."

"I'll be right there."

Sam whipped the car around and sped through town. He didn't turn on the siren, not wanting to arouse attention. Instinctively he knew the reason the marshals had come.

Rachel Wells's return.

Greg was checking into Witsec and it was an arm of the U.S. Marshal's Service.

Had she left the program as they'd discussed? Was she a fugitive? He didn't think so. He hadn't been able to find anything on her, at least not under the name of Rachel Wells. He'd checked both U.S. and international databases. There was nothing on her that *he* could find. But obviously the marshals knew more than he did. And they were waiting for him.

Sam wasn't sure he wanted to know. He remembered the feel of Rachel in his arms, the softness of her body, and the taste of her mouth on his. He wasn't prepared to find out she was wanted by the feds.

Learning to cook hadn't been something that Rachel aspired to do. She liked working with her hands and had spent most of her time with her father learning how to build things. Her mother made delicious meals and after she died Rachel understood that there was a part of her education she would never get.

Gus's food at the Castle Diner wasn't as good as her mother's, but it was so close Rachel had no complaints. She went there every morning and was usually served by Gus's wife, Doris. Doris worked the counter and the tables and Gus cooked in the kitchen. Rachel had become friends with them the third morning she came in for breakfast. Now it had become routine. Only this morning Rachel got the news of her return from the dead and her breakfast in the same helping.

"I didn't know you were a celebrity," Doris said as she poured coffee in Rachel's cup.

"What are you talking about?"

Doris grabbed a discarded newspaper from farther down the counter and dropped it open in front of Rachel. Rachel had too-hot coffee in her mouth. Her hands waved from the heat and surprise of what she read. She swallowed the coffee rather than spewing it over the table when she saw her picture and read the headline.

"Are you all right?" Doris asked.

She nodded, but held her throat and took a drink of cold water.

"I can tell it's an old picture, but that is you."

"Yes, it's me," Rachel said, although her voice was so low she doubted Doris heard her.

"Says here you died on the lake?" Doris replaced the coffeepot on the burner and sat down on a stool behind the counter ready for Rachel to tell her the unvarnished truth of what had really happened that day. Rachel read the story Lori Stiles had written. It said nothing other than her death was obviously faked nine years ago since the prodigal daughter had returned to the roost. The rest of it was a rehash of what had happened on that fateful day. There was nothing she had current except the photos of Rachel's parents' headstones.

Rachel's appetite was lost. She wanted to get out of the diner. She knew that Doris believed they were becoming friends. And they were. But Rachel felt as if the walls were closing in on her. She wanted to run. Grab her prepared pack of clothes and rush into the woods. She wanted to take another identity and start over in another town.

Reaching for her purse, she took enough money out to pay for her meal and placed it on the counter. "Doris, I'm sorry. I'm not very hungry this morning. I'll be back later." She got up.

"Don't rush off with nothing," Doris said. "Let me put it in a bag for you." Rachel waited and took the food. Doris added a couple of muffins and a fresh coffee. Moments later Rachel drove out of the parking lot and headed toward the cabin, but her hands were shaking so badly she had to pull over. She got out and stood against the side of the Jeep, facing the woods.

She understood this would happen. She should have done it herself. She had hidden in the cabin. She hadn't gone out and let people know she was back, and now she was front page news. Rachel couldn't keep it a secret for the rest of her life. She knew that. She'd come back here to reenter the world, yet she hadn't done it. She'd hibernated, making herself as much a prisoner here as she had been in the program.

Taking a deep breath, she got back inside the Jeep and drove the distance back to the cabin. She expected a crowd would be waiting for her, but there was only one car next to the huge Dumpster taking up most of her driveway.

"I came the moment I saw the paper." Leanne got out of her car when Rachel got out of the Jeep. "Three people have already been by and several others have driven by without stopping."

The two of them went inside. The kitchen was the only place where they could sit. Rachel shared her muffins and coffee with her friend.

"It's all right, Leanne. I should have done it myself, but it's a moot point now."

At that moment someone knocked on the door and called her name. "I'll get it," Leanne said.

"No," Rachel said. "They're coming to see me."

She went to the door and opened it. Hallie Jomatti stood there. "I don't believe it," she said. "I read it, but I don't believe it." She pulled the screened door open and hugged her. "You look great. And you haven't gained a pound. I think that's just against the law."

Hallie was only slightly heavier than she had been when Rachel had last seen her. Her hair was shorter. It used to flow down her back and she loved to swing it over her shoulders. It now only brushed her shoulders and framed her face, which had filled out. Her smile showed the deep dimples that had had every boy in school lusting after her.

"Where the hell have you been?"

"Why don't you come out to the kitchen—" She was cut off by another knock. Both women turned as Perry Reardon pulled the door open and let himself in.

"What's going on in here?" he asked, looking at the various stages of construction in progress.

"Perry!" Hallie exclaimed. "I haven't seen you in years." She hugged him as old friends do. Perry looked at Rachel when the two separated.

"You look remarkably well for someone we buried a lifetime ago." The two of them laughed and Leanne came from the kitchen, joining in. Rachel didn't laugh, but she managed a small smile.

"We didn't bury her. We had a memorial service," Leanne corrected.

"She was just about to tell us what happened," Hallie said.

"Oh, hi, Leanne," Perry said, seeing her over the heads of the two women.

"Leanne, I didn't know you were here," Hallie said. Again hugs all around were the order of the day.

Rachel took a long breath and squared her shoulders. This was why she came back, she told herself. She wanted to reconnect with old friends. She wanted to return to the world in which she was comfortable and in which she had friends. This was the first step. It was a big step for her and as time passed the steps would get easier. She knew this to be true. She'd learned it. She only had to get through today. Tomorrow would be easier and the day after that even easier. But she had to get through today first. She had to tell the story. And already she felt closed in.

When they were all in the kitchen standing between boxes they looked at Rachel as if she were about to give them the cure for cancer.

"The accident on the lake was faked. My father worked for an investment firm that was a front for the mob. He became an informant and testified against them. Afterward we went into a protection program. I was not allowed to tell anyone."

The silence in the tiny kitchen took on a life of its own. Rachel couldn't believe she had summed up nine years of her life in a few sentences. She waited for the news to sink in. A moment later the questions started.

"Who did he testify against?" Leanne asked.

"The Graziano family."

"I remember that." Perry closed his eyes as if he were trying to bring the past into focus. "I spent a week in New York that summer. Talk of the trial was all over the news." He paused to look at Rachel. "I didn't pay a lot of attention to it. I was more interested in the tennis match that was going on."

Rachel nodded. Perry had once wanted to be a professional tennis player. He played all year and went to tennis camps during the summer and he never missed the U.S. Open.

"How did they fake the explosion?" Hallie asked.

"I don't know," she said. "We weren't there."

"But—"

She interrupted Leanne. "The people who got on the boat weren't us. They were made up to look like us, but we were already gone when it happened. We left a little after midnight the day before. I only heard of the explosion later when the marshal protecting us told my father we'd apparently been killed in an explosion."

"Wow!" Hallie said. "And you remained quiet all this time?"

Hallie's cell phone rang and she fumbled in her purse to find it. "It's Joe," she said. "He must have heard." She put the phone to her ear. "Joe, I can't talk—" She stopped at something he said. "I know. I'm here right now. I'll call you back." She didn't wait for him to reply. She closed the phone and returned her attention to Rachel. "I'm amazed your phone isn't jumping off the hook."

"I haven't had it turned on and no one knows the cell number."

"What are you doing in here anyway?" Perry asked, looking around and thumping on one of the boxes. "It looks like you're rebuilding the place."

"Only part of it," she said. "After lying unoccupied for years, some places need work."

"Skip the construction," Hallie said. "Tell me more about this program. Didn't you miss us?"

"More than I thought possible." Another knock came at that moment, signaling the order of the day. A steady stream of people came. It seemed the entire population of The Lake was crowding into her kitchen. Rachel felt claustrophobic. Didn't anyone have to work today? she wondered.

By noon she had a headache and was exhausted from all the people. Her throat was dry and she'd licked all her lipstick off. Relief flooded through her when she saw Sam walk into the room. They exchanged a look and she hoped he understood her predicament.

"Hey, everybody." The group looked at him and the greetings started again. He made his way to her. "How are you holding up?" he asked in a voice only she could hear.

"Would you mind if I left and hid out at your place? I'm thrilled to see them, but right now I want them all gone," she answered honestly.

Sam turned to the group and raised his hands for quiet. When he had the group's attention, he said, "I know all of you have some place to be and

I need to speak to Rachel in an official capacity."
There was silence. "Don't worry, I'm not planning
to arrest her."

They all laughed, but got up and started to file
out. Rachel shook hands and hugged people and
agreed to see them later as they left. When the last
car pulled away from the curb, she closed the door
and collapsed against the wall. She slid down it
and sat on the floor.

"Thank you," she told Sam. "I didn't know how
to get them to leave."

"You look tired," Sam said. He sat on the floor
next to her and put his arm around her shoulders.
She resisted a moment, but he pulled her against
him.

"They were all my friends and they were scaring
me to death," she said. "They kept looking at me,
asking the same questions over and over." She rested
her head on his shoulder. Sam's hand threaded
through her hair and he slipped his arm around
her waist.

Rachel thought she was stronger than this. She
was sure she could accept returning to the lake
and reentering the world. She hadn't known what
she expected. She knew people would be curious,
that she would have to explain what had happened but the press of people in her kitchen had
rattled her. She wanted to go out a back door and
find some open air. Sam arrived just as she thought
the last pint of oxygen had been sucked out of the
room. She was so glad to see him and have him understand her need for space.

She touched his hand as if in thanks and sat up
straight. Looking at the room, filled with construction materials, Rachel started talking. "When we

left here it was like becoming pioneers," she began. "We were in the government's witness protection program. The first time they settled us in Charleston, South Carolina. We did everything for ourselves. My mother planted a garden and raised some of the foods we ate. If something needed fixing in our house my father figured out how to fix it and we'd do it ourselves. I helped him a lot. We were closed in, unable to make new friends or talk about our past. It became normal to depend on only ourselves. Having so many people around me at one time was frightening."

"How many times did they move you?"

"What?"

"You said the first time they settled you. How many times did you have to relocate?"

"Three. The first time was leaving here. The second time was my fault."

"Yours? What did you do?"

Rachel shifted position and looked at him. He really did look like Bill. She wondered if that was the reason she found him so easy to talk to . . . or kiss. Suddenly heat started in her stomach and she pushed thoughts of him holding her in his arms away.

Going back to the story she was telling, she focused on Sam. "I called Bill."

Sam, who'd had his back against the wall, leaned forward. "You spoke to Bill? He had no idea you were alive. His reaction when I told him you were alive and back here had to be genuine."

Rachel shook her head. "I never talked to him. You answered the phone." Sam started to say something, but Rachel headed him off. "I never said anything. I only listened to your voice. I was so miserable. I wanted to talk to someone who knew me, someone with whom I didn't have to pretend I was someone else." Rachel had covered the receiver with her hand when she heard his voice. She had hoped that Bill would answer, and she was going to tell him who she was, that she was alive, but it was Sam. His voice was strong and deep, deeper than she remembered it being. It was late at night and he should have been asleep, yet his voice sounded wide awake. Rachel thought he must have just been getting in.

He'd said hello four or five times, then, "Who is this? I know someone is there." Rachel said nothing. She didn't even breathe. After a few more hellos she had hung up.

"I don't remember."

"It was very late at night and I knew Bill stayed up late. I thought he would answer the phone. I was sure you were away at school. You must have been home for a visit."

Sam looked at the ceiling. "I think I remember that now. Was it in February?"

Rachel nodded. It was clear in her mind. The phone call was another of the memories she collected and kept in her safe place. Lake Como was safe and she used it and her memories to keep herself from going into a situation that was out of her control. Sam had answered the phone and she'd listened to his voice, but in her memories, when she thought of it in the night as fear stole into her room and took up residence, she'd pretended it was Bill's voice. And she would be safe. But now she knew it was Sam she had been listening to and remembering all those years. It was Sam's voice she heard in the quiet of the night. Sam's voice that anchored her.

"It was February," she said. She was certain of it because after she made the phone call the month hadn't ended before they left everything behind and were resettled in North Dakota.

"I *was* home then. I'd just come in when the phone rang. It was the night of the Winter Cotillion and I thought . . ."

Sam trailed off, not elaborating on who he thought might have called. But Rachel knew he'd come home from law school to escort someone to the cotillion. He and Kim Kirby had dated a lot, but she'd left The Lake to take a job in California right after college, before Sam went to law school. She could have come back for the annual winter dance that had been a tradition since she could remember, but Rachel didn't think so. She didn't know who he'd taken, but Sam was a law student then with looks that could make your insides melt. Many girls at The Lake lusted after him. And at least one of them had angled a date to the Winter Cotillion.

"Apparently, the people after my father were relentless. We were moved immediately and went to live in North Dakota. I never stepped out of line again."

Sam reached for her hand. He held it in his lightly, allowing her to pull free if she wanted to. Rachel didn't.

"Our last relocation, before I came here, was to Seattle, Washington. We stayed on one of the islands off the coast." Her parents had died there.

"Why did you have to move there?"

"This time it was the government that tried to set up a sting operation to get a crime family. They leaked information on us and the operation went terribly wrong. We narrowly escaped." It had been in broad daylight. They were shopping in a local mall for a birthday present when shots rang out. Her mother was hit in the back. McKnight had appeared out of nowhere and run them through the back halls of the mall and out a side entrance. He'd saved their lives that day and her mother had only lost one of her kidneys. As soon as she was well they were hustled off to a new location.

"It's over now," Sam told her. "You're back and you're safe."

Chapter Six

She was back, but she wasn't safe. The meeting with the feds had given him more information than he thought would ever follow him to Lake Como. Their story was the stuff of places like Detroit and New York, not this sleepy community nestled in the Finger Lakes region of upstate New York. But he knew that communities had no boundaries any longer. MTV, *World News Tonight*, HBO, and the Internet had diminished the size of the world. Everything from frontline war to how to hire a hit man was presented in living color for the asking. Yet who would have thought the mob was looking for someone living in Lake Como?

Sam had told Rachel it was his job to protect her. He used those words often, so often in fact they were a cliché. Yet this morning the truth had come home. Although his uniform's arm patch said Lake Como Police, he was back in Detroit, back fighting criminals who killed with little provocation. And this woman, who'd been little more than a child when she was forced to leave her only home, was now a target. She didn't know it. And he couldn't tell her. All he could do was spend as much time with her as possible. And when he wasn't there he'd make sure someone else was.

"Well, I guess I'll get back to work." Rachel stood up and moved away from him. Lifting the netted cap she used to cover her hair, she pulled it over the thick mane that was slowly lightening from the sun. Sam knew if she spent more time on the beach her hair and body would become the same golden color. With her natural light brown eyes, the lack of contrast made for a strikingly beautiful woman.

Getting up, he said, "I could help out for a while." He was reluctant to leave her alone. Suddenly The Lake had become a forest where an assassin could lurk behind every tree.

"You have to go back to work. I'm sure there are other people in town who need your protection."

"I can be spared for a while."

"Sam, I'm fine. I can do this."

"The point is you don't have to. I can get you some help."

"I'd like to do it myself."

He walked toward her, stopping a few feet away. "You don't like people, do you?"

"Why do you say that?"

"You refuse help when it's offered. The people here"—he spread his arms to include the entire house—"they scared you. You've been here awhile and not interacted with anyone you used to know."

"It's not that I don't like people. I need time." She dropped her head, then quickly looked up as if she remembered that gesture meant she wasn't being truthful. "And I want to do this myself."

"Why?"

Rachel put her hands on top of the pile of Sheetrock that sat in front of her. She didn't answer immediately and Sam recognized that she was deciding if she should tell him her reasons. He wanted her to tell him. He wanted her to know she could trust him. But he also understood that police, people who should protect her, had let her down. Aaron McKnight from the U.S. Marshal's Service had filled him in on the details of Rachel's life. At least he'd given him some details. He hadn't told him Rachel's family had been moved three times.

He'd said Rachel didn't trust cops and Sam was wearing his uniform. She couldn't help but include him with the group of other law enforcement men who'd not lived up to their code.

"You don't have to answer that," Sam said, giving her an easy way out of confiding in him.

"It's for my mother and father," she said. "And for me too. This was the last place we lived when we were who we were. I want to restore that."

"There are things you can't do," he countered. "The porch. The roof."

"I'll hire a contractor to do those. It's the inside I want to do."

If she worked inside, Sam thought, he would know where she was and she wouldn't be a target working on the roof. The opposite side of that was whoever was after her would also have an easy time finding her if she stayed in the expected location.

"I'm not planning to make it a monument or a shrine to my parents," she said quickly, misreading his hesitation. "My plans are to restore it with changes. I'll show you."

She ran up the stairs to the loft and quickly came back with a laptop computer. Opening a computer-aided design or CAD program, she showed him the three-dimensional representation of what she had in mind. Sam moved around behind her to see the various rooms she had created. The cabin would look nothing like it had when she'd lived her before. The loft would remain as it was, but the placement and size of rooms on the first level were completely different from the past.

"I've said it before. You *are* amazing." Sam smiled, unconsciously placing his hands on her shoulders. The movement had seemed natural to him until he felt Rachel's response. She stiffened and went perfectly still as if a cold wind had suddenly frozen her solid. Sam released her and stepped back. If he was to be her protector he needed to keep his mind on the job and not let his emotions get involved.

Still her reaction irritated him. The way she had responded in his arms on the beach told him one story, but this coldness replaced it with another one.

Rachel reached for her work gloves and pulled them on. Sam took the action as his clue to leave.

"I'll be back to check on you," he said.

"Why?" Rachel turned and looked at him in surprise.

"To make sure you haven't fallen off all this scaffolding and broken your neck."

He was genuinely concerned about her. It was more than wanting to keep his record clean of any major crime in Lake Como. He had feelings for Rachel, feelings stronger than he had known. That kiss on the beach changed him. He was no longer

Bill's older brother, teasing Rachel because she was nervous around him. She'd gotten under his skin and he wanted the opportunity to explore all the feelings that her nearness brought to the surface.

She'd been dealt a raw hand for the last nine years. She'd left the world behind, refused to let it touch her, afraid of its hands, lest they be hard, angry, and hurtful. He wanted to make it better for her here. But he wasn't in a position to control what would happen, and before the feds finished their sting he knew much more would happen. He was going to make sure Rachel survived it.

Hot water. Bubbles. A clean and well-lighted room. Rachel eased down into the hot, soapy water. She closed her eyes and breathed in the lilac scent. The water came up to her neck as she slid down, allowing the contours of the bathtub and the water to buoyantly lift her. The bathroom was finished. The walls had been sealed and painted, the tub installed and caulked. The floor had been replaced, towel racks installed, and water pipes connected. She had hardly been able to wait for the caulking to dry before getting into the tub.

It was worth it, she thought, viewing her handiwork. All the lifting and setting, the washing and cleaning, the new sink and new tub, and the muscle aches and pains. She felt them easing, elongating as the therapeutic water replaced the taut strains with a relaxed balance. Her father would be proud of her. Rachel proved she could do it. And do it alone.

Today had been stressful, worse than she expected, but she'd survived it. Tomorrow would be better.

The ice was broken now. Her friends had come by, some of them at least, others would come later. She was sure of it. While their appearance had been overwhelming, it wouldn't continue that way. She would be able to handle the visitors. Suddenly she thought of Sam coming to her rescue.

She smiled to herself and settled farther down into the water. Things were falling into place. Tomorrow she would begin on the living room, altering her design of tackling the bedrooms next. According to her plan she'd make it into a huge great room. There wasn't much work that needed to be done in there. Everything felt good, she thought, not just the water, but she knew things would be all right. She was back. This was where she was supposed to be.

The files on Rachel Wells and her family arrived by special messenger two days after Sam had been briefed on where she had really been since the accident. Photographs of people he remembered lay on his kitchen table. He thought of the sweet cakes Mrs. Wells used to make and supply to the local kids as a summer treat. Even when Rachel grew to a teenager, her mom still baked those cakes. And she'd slip Sam one or two as she passed him on his way to the lifeguard's chair.

The thought that Rachel's whole life had been laid out for him embarrassed him. He knew things about her and about her father that she didn't know. The file was thorough, starting with her parents' births, their education, people they had known and had affairs with, thankfully before they met and married each other.

Sam's job wasn't to make sure Rachel didn't get in the cross fire of the FBI operation. He'd assigned that to himself. The FBI wanted him to keep a lookout for anything strange that might happen at The Lake. They didn't expect that Edgecomb would come himself. More than likely a hit man would try to kill Rachel. Sam had to figure out a way to stay close to her, but each time he got near her, she backed away.

On the beach he'd been sure she was with him and she told him she didn't regret kissing him, but he wondered if it was Bill she still thought about. Was that why she went stiff when he touched her? Sorting through the papers, Sam picked up Rachel's photo. It was an eight-by-ten color shot. The note on the back gave her name and the date. It was two months old. It had to have been taken just before she returned to The Lake.

Moving from the table to the door leading to the beach behind his house, the place where he had kissed Rachel, he took the photo with him. She was not smiling. Her eyes were wide open and clear, but undistinguishable as to what she was thinking. She was looking up and her hair flowed unrestrained to her shoulders. The photo was a closeup so Sam could not see what was behind her, but it was an outside shot. She must have been coming out of a building and looked up at the sky or a traffic light.

Moving his gaze from the photo to the backyard, he looked outside. It was dark now and she could be out in the water, taking her midnight swim. He'd checked the water when he came in and it was clear, as undisturbed as it looked now. There were no ripples from a solitary swimmer. He breathed out, thankful that she wasn't there alone and in the line of someone's sight.

According to the feds they didn't expect anyone to show up in Lake Como for at least another week, but it was Sam's experience that the expected was never the rule. Whoever they were expecting could already be here. He'd taken precautions. His small force was taking turns watching for anything and anyone who might pose a threat. But they couldn't be everywhere and they couldn't stop her from going through her daily routine, whatever that was. She had no job that Sam had found. The feds had mentioned no work experience. She had a bachelor's degree in finance and an MBA with a concentration in marketing. He'd checked her school records after discovering the alias she'd used, and she'd graduated with honors. Rachel also had taken a lot of psychology courses. That was something they had in common. He'd been keenly interested in how and why people behaved as they did. In his desire to be a lawyer, he wanted to understand motivations. He wondered if her experience inside Witsec had led her to try and understand the forces that placed her there.

Sam checked the water again. It remained as smooth as glass. Then he looked at the photo and walked back to the table. He'd check in with the watch before going to bed.

Lifting his radio, he called in. "How's it going?"

"No incidents. No visitors. It's quiet."

"She still awake?"

"Yeah. I gather she finished the bathroom today. The light in that room was on for more than an hour. I didn't hear any movement like nailing or that pulley system lifting. I believe she took a nice long bath. The light went out about fifteen minutes ago."

"Keep a keen eye out," Sam said.

"Will do."

Sam signed off. Images of Rachel's body, naked and slick with warm water as she was getting out of the tub, drove a stake into his groin. He needed an update on her, but the visual that accompanied it would keep him up most of the night.

The groan couldn't be suppressed. When Rachel opened her eyes, every muscle in her body screamed in pain. Where was that pounding coming from? Her head was spinning. Turning over in her sleeping bag hurt. She needed a bed, she told herself. She was too old to sleep on the floor any longer. Even with the pallet of blankets under her, the stiffness in her muscles grew worse every day. She was sorry she hadn't brought an air mattress. But even if she had, it wouldn't make a difference. Her pain didn't totally come from sleeping on the floor. She was cold and she'd piled everything on top of her, yet she shivered. She had a fever. Shivering and cold at this time of year was a sure sign.

She needed some aspirin. Rachel rolled over, holding her head, but the pain was too much. She leaned back, pulling the covers over her, trying to warm herself.

Her aspirin was downstairs. In the new bathroom. She'd been so proud of it. Unpacking the cardboard box that held her personal products had been a real pleasure yesterday, but she was paying for it today. Pushing the left-sided zipper down with her foot, she lay back as the effort took all her energy. Breathing hard, she felt the cold air rush into the open space and chill her body even more. Moving away from the cold, she pulled the fleece-lined bag closer to her shoulders and moved her legs to the opposite zipper.

What had she done to make her feel this bad? Rachel tried to remember yesterday. Had she gotten a chill somewhere and not remembered it? She had spent most of the day working on the bathroom. After it was finished and she took a bath, she spent time on the Internet, checking her stocks, which she'd neglected in light of the construction she'd been doing.

But now she had to get downstairs. She had to at least get a pain reliever to stop the pounding in her head. Pulling a long sweatshirt on despite the heat the day should already have, Rachel went to the stairs. She grasped the banister as the stationary steps seemed to accordion up and down. She looked away, closing her eyes. Her equilibrium was off. She recognized it. The first time it happened she'd been frightened, but a doctor had explained what happened and now she recognized the symptom. Unfortunately, she had no medicine to drain the water in her ears.

Rachel sat down on the top step and keeping her eyes closed went down the steps one at a time like a child. The pounding got worse with every step and she finally realized it wasn't inside her head, but outside on the porch. Someone was out there. When she finally put her feet on the floor, Rachel went to the bathroom first. She took no pride in her accomplishment this morning, only the fact that the distance from the loft to the downstairs bathroom felt like ten miles. She got the aspirin and using her cupped hand to hold water, she downed two pills.

Hanging her head over the sink, she braced her hands on the new console, waiting, hoping the pounding would subside. It seemed like it wouldn't with whatever was going on outside. She left the only completed room in the house and felt her way to the front door. She pulled it open and squinted at the light that hurt her eyes.

Sam was outside. He had his back to her and he was using a hammer to pound new wood onto the porch frame, which she'd planned to replace. There were other people out there too. Rachel didn't try to figure out who they were. She just wanted them to stop.

"Sam," she called, too low for him to hear. "Sam." Her voice was a croaked whisper, but he must have felt her presence. He turned to look at her and immediately dropped the hammer. "Please stop," she said.

He came to the door, which was open only a crack. "Are you all right?"

"I'm fine," she lied. The words came naturally. Unless she was talking to her mother or father, she never complained of anything. "What are you doing?"

Rachel was holding herself erect by the support of the door. Sam pushed it open and threw her off balance.

"Whoa," he said. "Maybe you should sit down." He grabbed her arm and leveled her as she started to move precariously across the floor. "Rachel, you have got to get some furniture."

Sam led her to the short stack of Sheetrock and

sat her on it. He put his hand on her forehead. "Do you have a thermometer?"

She shook her head. "I took some aspirin." Wanting to lie down, she leaned forward and placed her elbows on her knees. She could still hear sounds outside as if someone was working on the house. "What are you doing outside? Who are those people?" She remembered the others she'd seen.

"They're a few kids from my community service group. You said you'd get someone else to do the porch and roof. I assigned it to them."

"Without asking me?" Her words held no censure. She was in too much pain to summon any indignation.

"They're part of the community and so are you. Not only are they curious, but it helps to build character."

"You should have asked me."

"Do you mind?" He didn't wait for her to answer. He walked over to the uncovered windows and lifted an afghan lying next to a beach chair. Bringing it back, he slipped it around her shoulders and pushed her to a prone position on top of the Sheetrock. It wasn't as comfortable as her pallet in the loft, but the thought of going up the stairs was too much to consider.

"What is a community service group?" she asked, trying to remember something he had said earlier.

"Have you eaten anything?" Sam countered.

"I usually go to the diner out on the highway for breakfast." Its real name was the Castle Diner. It had a castle motif on the outside, but no one referred to it by name except tourists and the summer arrivals. "Doris will probably wonder what's happened to me."

"I'll drop by later and let her know you're ill. Now what's wrong with you?" Sam went into the kitchen and looked around. Her supplies were extensive, but unopened. If she were going camping she had everything she needed, but there was little in the way of breakfast foods. "I'm waiting for an answer."

Rachel groaned. She could hear him rummaging around in the cabinets, but was beyond caring what he was looking for. He came back and pulled a crate over to sit near her.

"I'm making you some soup. It should be ready soon."

"I'm not hungry."

"You're ill. You have to eat."

"Yes, Doctor," she said with as much sarcasm as she could muster. The aspirin was beginning to work. Some of the pain in her head was subsiding. She could distinguish between the pounding of her blood and the pounding on the roof.

"I'm fine, Sam. I just caught a bug of some type. It will go away."

"It's not good to be sick and live alone."

"Let's not make a federal case out of this." Rachel wanted to laugh at the cliché. She'd never have said anything like that to Aaron McKnight. It was proof she was getting better. Still she knew she had to get a prescription filled for the water in her ears.

The bell on the microwave rang and Sam got quickly to his feet. He looked like a giant from where she lay. He disappeared in the kitchen and came back moments later with a bowl that Rachel usually ate cold cereal from and a stack of crackers.

"It's not one of Gus's breakfast specials," he said, "but it will fill you up."

He helped her to a sitting position and handed her the bowl. The crackers he opened and laid beside her. Rachel ate unconscious of him watching. She was hungry and she was beginning to feel better.

"Thank you for coming by and checking on me, but could you tell me what is going on up there?" The pounding on the roof continued.

"These are troublesome kids. They're bored mostly, plenty smart, but get in trouble for lack of things to do. Judge gave 'em community service. They're working it off outside."

"I guess I'll have to thank you again. The porch, roof, short-order cook, and doctor, all rolled together in a policeman's uniform."

Sam went still. Rachel could tell she'd angered him. "I'm not one of them, Rachel."

She looked at him with a steady gaze. "Aren't you?"

"I wasn't there. I didn't set you up and I didn't put you here. Don't paint me with the same brush as the cops who betrayed you."

He was right. It was unfair of her, but she couldn't separate them, especially when he wore the outward symbol. He wasn't wearing it today. He had on well-worn jeans and an open-neck shirt.

"I apologize," she said, but the words seemed flat and insincere.

"I'll go out and make sure everything is going all right." He walked to the door and turned back. "Be sure you eat all that food."

Rachel lay back down when he went out. Her hand went up over her eyes. She'd been rude.

He'd come to help her, even had people outside working to get her cabin in living shape, and all she saw was his uniform. Pulling herself up, Rachel slid off her makeshift bed. As soon as she stood she lost her balance and fell back against the Sheetrock.

Being more cautious, she got up a second time and reached for the wall. Using it as a guide, she went to the door and opened it. She could see no one. The rotted porch planks had been removed and in some places only the support frame was visible. As luck would have it, the section directly outside the door was that way. Rachel gauged the distance between the door and the post. She would never make it. She looked to one side, then the other. A ten-foot section was missing in each direction.

"Sam," she called. He didn't answer, although all the pounding noises had ceased. There were cars and a van parked along the street, but they were all empty.

Rachel looked at the support rail. She stepped out on it, still holding on to the door. She put her other foot on the beam and pulled the door closed, but held on to the knob. Dizziness caught her. A fear of falling made her shiver. She couldn't move. The beam was like a tightrope and she was high above the porch, not just a couple of feet off the ground. She was paralyzed, afraid to go forward or backward, frozen in that place.

"Rachel!"

The sound of her name being called startled her. She looked toward the sound. Sam was coming toward her, but the rest of the world turned too. She lost hold of the knob. Her footing went and she screamed as she fell. Her leg slipped through the spacing and scraped along the rough wood. Her body fell onto the open planks. She felt her elbow bang and her side hit the wood. Pain radiated up her arm.

"Rachel." Sam's voice was immediately above her. He jumped into the well of space created by the missing porch slats. "Are you all right?"

She groaned. A crowd gathered. Many strange and young voices asked questions. Sam ignored most of them. He lifted her hair and pushed it away from her face. Rachel knew her expression was contorted in pain.

Sam wasn't on duty, but he pulled a walkie-talkie from his pocket and pressed a button. "I need an ambulance at—"

"No!" Rachel shouted. "I don't need an ambulance." Despite her headache and hurt leg, she was fine.

"Rachel, you could have a concussion. You could have fractured a bone. At least let me take you to the emergency room."

"Sam, I'm all right."

He canceled the call and replaced the unit on his belt. Looking over his shoulder, he ordered a tall dark-skinned youth to get some boards and put them across the hole in the floor. The boy ran to the end of the house and returned carrying several long boards. He and Sam slatted them across the beams and Sam set her on them near the front door before hopping up on it too.

"Are you hurt anywhere?"

"My leg, arm, and this side." She pointed to her left side. He helped her to her feet and took her inside. "You guys get back to work," he said over his shoulder. Rachel looked at the small crowd. They were mostly teenage boys, but there was a girl here and there. One of them stared directly at her with a pained expression on her face.

"What were you doing out there?" Sam asked as he looked at her leg. "I'll need a first-aid kit."

"There's one in the kitchen. In the far cabinet." He went looking for it. "I came out to apologize," she said in answer to his question.

"You'd already apologized." He returned with the white metal case.

"I didn't think you believed me."

"I got the impression you didn't care what I thought."

"I don't . . . I mean it was rude."

He tore open a cleansing packet and pulled out the white paper cloth. "There are worse things than being rude." He applied the alcohol rub. Rachel winced when he touched her. "I'm sorry," he said.

"It's all right." Still she clenched her teeth as he cleaned her leg wound. "You're also Bill's brother."

His hand stopped in the air. "Being Bill's brother gives me some sort of special consideration?"

Rachel swallowed. He was making her nervous. His hands had become tender on her skin and while the scrape burned, his touch seared.

"Sort of," she answered.

"Why?"

"Bill saved my life."

Sam waited for her to continue. Rachel didn't feel like she wanted to go on. Yet she'd opened a door and she knew Sam wouldn't leave until she closed it.

"Sit up," he said. "How's your shoulder?"

"Bruised." She wasn't about to pull her sweatshirt over her head and allow him to look at her body.

"Can you manage it yourself?" He saved her from having to refuse his touch.

She nodded.

Sam took the seat on the crate in front of her again. "I'm waiting," he said.

"For what?"

"For the explanation of how Bill saved your life."

Rachel climbed down off the construction materials. She walked gingerly to the window, holding on to the Sheetrock to keep her balance. Her side hurt and he ear crackled as if a knocker were inside it. She put her finger in it to stop the ricocheting in her head. Her back was to Sam. "From this window I can see the tops of pine trees and a small patch of sky. When Bill and I lay on the raft, I could see the whole sky and all the stars in the universe." She glanced at Sam. He sat in the same place, no doubt wondering where she was going with this.

"The public thinks witness security is all cushy and good. It isn't. It's a life of looking over your shoulder, growing eyes in the back of your head, developing instincts that no ordinary citizen even thinks about, and never knowing if today is the day your life ends. Each time you put your key in the ignition, you wonder. Opening the door to your house can be fatal. You question whether someone is inside waiting for you, waiting to shoot you on sight or torture you until you beg to die. Every step in the open air could be your last. Doing normal things like shopping makes you mindful of lifting bags of food and putting them in a car. You're vulnerable, a target. You could be picked off with a silencer or kidnapped in broad daylight. Your body winds up until you feel you'll explode if something doesn't happen. Some days you wish it would. You want it to end, to be put out of your misery, you're ready to end the torment."

Sam came up behind her. Rachel felt his presence and turned to face him. Anger had welled up inside her and she knew if he got too close he'd get the brunt of it. She backed away, coming up against the wall. The solidity of it helped her dizziness and allowed her to go on. "It was nine years, Sam. The anguish of it made me call Bill that night in February. After we were relocated I followed all the rules, but the strain was even greater than I thought it would be. I knew I was headed for a breakdown. My mother knew it too. She tried to help me, but what could she do? She couldn't take me on a trip, we couldn't spend the day at the beach, in the open. We couldn't even go to the mall and spend the day doing girl things. So I turned to Bill."

Rachel stopped to take in a breath. She'd never talked to anyone about this, not even the psychologist that had been approved by the service.

"What do you mean?" Sam's voice was soft, low, as if he didn't want to disturb even the air in the room. He wanted her to go on and Rachel obliged him.

"I know what it is now. I took a lot of psychology in college. I made a safe place for myself. It was with Bill. I would imagine myself back here, back in a time before our lives became harassed by people who were supposed to protect us." Her tone was venomous. She counted to ten and transferred her attention back to the window.

1/2

"I replayed stories in my head of things we'd done that summer, reviewed conversations under the stars. I kept it up until I could relax, until I could cope with the knowledge that there were things I couldn't foresee. That there were people protecting me and I was totally in their hands. If they slipped, it could mean my life, but I wouldn't allow myself to dwell on it. Whenever I'd begin getting depressed, I'd think of The Lake and that summer."

Rachel felt drained. She hadn't meant to unload on Sam, but he seemed to always be around. Once she'd begun her story, it poured out of her like rainwater over a gutterless roof.

"Are you still in love with Bill?"

She faced Sam. The pain in her ear and her body felt secondary to the emotions that passed through her body.

"The truth is I don't know." Sam didn't look as if he wanted that answer. "I wasn't in love with him when I left. Both of us had interest in other people. We only spent time together because we were in the same boat, so to speak."

"But while you were away," Sam offered, "while you were remembering your days and nights out on the raft . . ." He left the answer hanging.

"I fell in love with him?" Rachel finished for him, but shook her head. "I don't think so. I think I fell in love with the idea of having someone love me." She hesitated a moment. "It was a fantasy."

"Did it get out of control?"

"What?"

"The problem with fantasies and the continuous 'dreaming'"—he used both hands to suggest quote marks—"is that you lose track of reality."

Rachel smiled. Her ear hurt and she put her finger up to stop the pain. "You believe I'm fantasizing? That I no longer understand what is real and what is not?"

"I believe you're hiding in an imaginary world."

Keeping her back against the wall, Rachel looked over the room; scaffolding, Sheetrock, caulking guns, joint compound were everywhere. "You think this is imaginary?"

"Not the room. You. You're hiding here. You've moved your fantasy world into this house. This is your raft and you're on it alone. You can use all this"—his arms encompassed the room—"to rebuild the perfect world. But it's not perfect. It can be burst with a pin. Nobody lives in a perfect world. You shelter yourself here, doing everything yourself, proving you are an island unto yourself."

Rachel was angry, but not as angry as Sam seemed to be. She didn't know why.

"This is impressive," he went on. "Who would have thought to set up a rig like this to lift heavy objects inside a house? It looks as if you're constructing the Sistine Chapel in here. Why not hire someone to do this? You could fall off that thing and lie here for days before someone came by to help you."

"I doubt that," she countered. "You're always here, wanted or not."

Sam didn't reply. He glared at her for the space of a lifetime, then dropped his shoulders in defeat. Without another word, he turned and walked out of the house. Rachel didn't understand him. For someone who didn't like puzzles, he was one himself. She couldn't put a personality in place. Each time she thought she was seeing the real Sam, he changed.

What had she said that angered him so much? He came this morning and made her soup and crackers. The crackers were still on top of the Sheetrock where she'd left them. He was tender and caring as he carried her into the house and saw to her wounds. Then he went into this other person, someone she didn't know.

He took all her breath away. She hated fighting, and each time she came in contact with him they seemed to end the day with a fight. Bill was utterly different. He and Bill couldn't be further apart on the spectrum. Where Bill's temperament was even and predicable, his brother's was moody and volatile. Rachel had dreamed of a life with Bill, playing out scenes in her head that were composed and serene. It was a relationship like the lake on a quiet summer morning, windless and stationary. Yet Sam was a whirlwind. He was a surprise at every turn and even though he could drive her nuts with his mood swings, there was something overwhelmingly attractive about him.

Chapter Seven

By the time the pounding outside stopped and Rachel heard car doors slamming and engines starting, the pain in her ear was back and her leg and sides had suddenly awakened to the nerves in them. Every one of them screamed for relief, magnifying the pain in her ear. None of it showed any sign of abating without further medication.

She couldn't help but wonder how much of her physical pain had to do with the scene between her and Sam. She wanted to say he was wrong, that he didn't know her, that he had no right to make the assumptions he had, but he *was* right. She'd walled up her world. As surely as if she had built the sturdy frame of the cabin herself, she couldn't have constructed a more solid fortress.

Rachel bit her lower lip as the thought of what she needed came to her. She'd open up the space. She'd put in windows, big windows, huge windows, to let in the light and the outside world. It was a small way of going out, but she could only take baby steps at this point. While she wanted to miraculously morph back into the person she was at seventeen, slip invisibly back into that life with the ease of an ethereal ghost or a pliable teenager, it was not happening. She found it as difficult to release the years of living cautiously as it would be to move through an alternate universe. She'd have to do it a small step at a time.

But first she had to get something for this pain. Putting her hand to her head, she held it there, hoping to stop the pounding pressure. A moment later she decided to get more aspirin. As she turned, she jumped and screamed, then caught her ear. A woman stood on the other side of the room.

"Who are you?" Rachel asked, her back teeth clenched as she controlled her voice.

"Oh, excuse me," she said. "I'm Alex. Alex Lytelle." Her voice was hesitant and young. "I didn't mean to scare you."

Rachel hadn't expected her. She hadn't even heard her come into the room. That disturbed her more than finding her there. There was a time when she could hear everything, when she was attuned to every sound, every movement, every change in the normality of her surroundings. She had created her universe. She'd carefully constructed it with beams of memory and the wallboard of a past life. She'd electrified the rooms using the light of her parents' love and insulated the structure with only one candle of hope to light the entire world of darkness. She'd set every piece of furniture in place, plugged in each lamp, and memorized the two floorboards that squeaked. Being back was different. The Lake was a different, if not a new, place. She hadn't learned to be aware of her surroundings here. She felt vulnerable, exposed, as if someone could steal into her protected environment and bring chaos to the order she was trying to establish.

"Were you with the others?" Rachel asked.

The girl nodded. Rachel could see she wasn't as old as she'd first thought. She was a teenager, maybe fifteen or sixteen. She was gangly with a bit of awkwardness. Her hair was a dark brown and richly thick. It was her best feature. Her face was pretty and in time she would come to be a beauty. Rachel could also tell that at this time Alex Lytelle felt ugly.

"They're all gone," Rachel told her. Alex said nothing. "Did you want to see what I looked like?"

The young girl raised her eyes and looked directly at her. Rachel could tell she'd hit on the reason the girl had walked in on her.

"Well, what do you think?" she tried to joke. They both smiled. It seemed to break the ice—for them both.

"You look more alive than dead."

Rachel grabbed her ear as she tried to laugh and the pain arrested her attempt.

"Are you all right?" Alex took two steps forward, then stopped. Rachel knew she was concerned, but cautious.

"I have an ear infection, probably swimmer's ear. It's painful and affecting my balance."

"You should go to the doctor. I used to have those chronically when I was younger. My mother was always taking me to the doctor."

"I agree, but I don't think I can stand up long enough to get to my car."

"I'll drive you," she quickly volunteered.

Rachel was going to ask Alex to help her to the car, but instead she asked, "You can drive?"

Alex smiled. "My car is outside." She walked over to Rachel. "That pain isn't going to go away."

At that moment Rachel felt that clicking in her ear and a burst of pain went up her head and into her eye. She gasped, clamping her teeth down on her lower lip to keep from screaming and grabbing the side of her face.

Alex took Rachel's arm and within minutes the two were headed for a doctor's office. Rachel hadn't asked where they were going and Alex took over as if she'd done this many times before. She parked in a space next to the medical arts building and came around the tiny car to help Rachel out and hold onto her as they went inside.

Rachel expected to spend the rest of her day there, but after Alex spoke to the receptionist Rachel was called in ten minutes later. Alex stayed with her, shepherding her around and standing between her and the stares that naturally came when anyone heard her name.

Forty minutes after they stepped into the doctor's office they had picked up her prescribed antibiotics from the pharmacy and were headed back toward her cabin. Alex had even thought to buy her a cold bottle of water to wash down the pills.

"Are you feeling better yet?" she asked as she parked in the driveway as close to the house as she could get.

"It usually takes antibiotics a while to kick in. I

probably won't have any real relief until late to-morrow."

"Heat will help. Do you have a heating pad?"

"No," Rachel said. She'd had one, but she'd left it behind when she decided to move back to Lake Como. "I'll use a warm, moist towel. I'll heat it up in the microwave."

Back in the house, Alex asked, "Do you want to go up to the loft?"

"Not yet." Rachel lowered herself to the floor near the window where she and Sam had talked. "Why don't you sit down?"

"I'll get you a towel first."

"They're in the bathroom." Rachel had installed a tall cabinet with towels, soaps, tissues, and sup-plies. Alex dropped to the floor with all the agility of youth after she'd found a small towel, wet it, and heated it. Rachel sighed as Alex pressed it against her ear. It felt heavenly.

"You're very good at caring for other people. Are you planning to be a doctor or a nurse?"

"I don't know yet," she said. "I haven't decided what I want to do. The counselor at school says I have time before I need to make a decision."

"Anything you're leaning toward, something you like?"

"I liked working on the roof and the porch." She smiled fully for the first time. Rachel thought her face was very pretty when she did.

"Maybe you can start your own construction company."

Alex's look was one of surprise.

"What?" Rachel asked. "Don't you think you can do it?"

"I know I don't know a lot about doing things. Officer Sam teaches us a lot."

Rachel could see she liked Sam, but the mention of his name made her heart jump a beat before settling back into routine.

"What are you doing here?" Alex asked, looking up at the ceiling and then at the piles of building supplies on the floor.

"I'm remodeling. This is everything I need to fix that wall." Rachel pointed above Alex's head. "And to section off that area over there and make a separate room. I'd like a small office, a place to put my computer equipment."

"Are you good with computers too?"

"Not technically. I can go on the Internet and find things. I do a lot of trading there."

"You mean like eBay?"

"No, I mean trading stocks."

"The stock market? We learned a little about that in school. I thought of trying it myself, but my mother would . . ." She trailed off.

"It's expensive. If you can't afford to lose the money."

"Yeah." She looked at her hands and volunteered nothing more. Alex turned her attention back to the remodeling. For a few minutes she only talked about the house; what Rachel's plans were; where did she learn to do the things she could do? A sadness had come over her. Rachel didn't understand what caused it, but she could feel the change in her.

"You know how to do all that?" Alex asked in amazement.

"My father taught me."

Alex looked down, her hands drawing circles on the bare floor. "My father's dead," she said softly.

"So is mine," Rachel said in the same soft-as-cotton voice. She refused to allow emotion to clog her throat. Alex was on the verge of tears and one of them had to remain in control. The job fell to her.

Then the girl smiled tentatively. "It was three years ago. I still miss him terribly. We lived in Rochester. After my dad died my mother got a job here and we moved."

"It's been hard," Rachel stated.

Alex nodded, her eyes still cast toward the floor.

"Kids in school mean to you?"

"Some of them."

"What about the summer thunder?"

She looked up. Beautiful blue eyes, wide and clear, looked out at Rachel. They questioned her knowledge of how superior some of the summer residents had been known to act.

"I grew up here," Rachel explained. "Every summer they come, like a storm, pale, white bodies, roasting in the sun until they get as dark as possible. When the winds of autumn arrive they blow away all red and gold and brown."

Alex giggled. "I never heard anyone describe them that way. It's very poetic."

"Bill and I made it up."

"Bill?"

"He's a friend I grew up with. Officer Sam's brother."

"Officer Sam's nice." She paused, then rushed on. "He was stern in the beginning, but I think he really cares about us."

"Did he tell you about me?"

She nodded. "He told us that we were coming to work off some of our community service here and that you had been thought dead for a long time."

"Is that all?"

She shook her head. "It was in the newspaper. We all read it."

"And were curious." Rachel finished the sentence for her. The warm cloth had turned cool. Rachel moved it and felt the coolness rush into her ear, but it didn't cause her any additional pain.

"Do you want me to reheat that?" Alex was already rising.

Rachel stopped her. "It's all right. The pain is subsiding."

"Sometimes I wish I could go away."

"Why?"

"There's nothing to do here."

Rachel knew that wasn't the reason. Alex had started telling her something about herself, but she wasn't sure she wanted to confide in a stranger. Yet Rachel had the feeling she kept things to herself, bottled them up inside and didn't share them with anyone. Rachel should feel privileged that Alex might share with her, but she knew this was a classic move for people in trouble. They would tell complete strangers things they wouldn't talk to their family about.

"You don't have many friends, do you?" Rachel asked.

"They don't like me . . . they think I'm . . ."

"It's hard being the new kid." Rachel helped her out by not pressing her to answer. "How long have you lived here?"

"A little over a year. I had some friends." She

rolled her eyes. "At least I thought they were friends. It's because of them that I got caught."

"Doing what?"

"They got some beer on the beach one night and we were all drinking. We ran out and someone suggested we ride into town and get some more. We all piled into the cars, but when we got there they started throwing cans at the shop windows and making a lot of noise. The police pulled us over and . . ." She paused. "They called my mom. She was so mad. We had to go to court and the judge said I had to do twenty-four hours of community services."

"Did you know drinking as a minor was against the law?"

She nodded. "I only wanted to fit in. But not anymore. At least not with them."

"You want to hear some advice from me?"

Alex looked up at her. Her eyes were clear, but she didn't agree or disagree.

"You're a very nice person. Look how you helped me, taking me to the doctor and getting my medicine. If you'll just be yourself you'll find friends."

Alex smiled. Then she got to her feet. "It's almost time for my mother to get home. I better go."

Rachel got up. The floor had become hard and she thought she'd go to the loft and sleep awhile.

Alex stopped at the door. "Do you mind if I come back sometime?"

"I'd like that."

The young girl smiled and went out. Rachel liked her. They were both fish out of water. And they both had Sam Hairston in their lives. Only Alex worshiped him and Rachel wasn't sure of her feelings.

* * *

The prescription bottle on the kitchen counter was dated today. Sam picked it up and read the label as he set down the bag filled with the fixings for tonight's dinner, spaghetti with meat sauce, garlic bread, and salads. Rachel was dressed the same in her long sweatshirt, although her hair was tussled from sleep. The temperature had fallen a little and would continue to cool throughout the night.

Sam thought even ill she was the most beautiful woman he'd ever encountered. She'd been under his skin for years.

She'd opened the door when he returned in the evening. When Sam left earlier she looked as if she couldn't fix herself anything to eat, and other than the protection part of his job, he wanted to see her. Food and her being alone and ill were perfect reasons for him to return. He carried a bag and went toward the kitchen. Rachel followed him, sat down on a crate, and leaned against the wall.

"Where'd these come from?" He turned to her with the brown prescription bottle in his hand. He didn't know what they were. Her car was parked in the same place as it had been, but this was a world of drive-through convenience. She could have had a prescription called in from anywhere in the United States and then the small bottle delivered to her house.

"They're for my ear. Alex took me to the doctor." She brushed her hands over her hair, pulling it back and looping it behind her ears. Sam watched her movements as if they were in slow motion, the choreographed way her hands floated through the air, the pull of her sweatshirt over her breasts, the way her hair moved as her fingers combed it. He wanted to go to her and slip his own fingers through the thick hair that was streaked with the heat of the sun. She looked much better tonight than she had when he'd seen her this morning.

"She came in after everyone left. I needed medicine for my ear and she took me to a doctor." Rachel's soothing voice broke into Sam's thoughts.

"Alex?" he said, suddenly remembering whom they were talking about.

"She's a very nice girl."

"I agree. Why did she come in?"

"She wanted to see what a dead woman looked like."

Sam stared at Rachel, but saw no insincerity in her expression. He turned back to the food he was preparing. Knowing she might not have the pots and knives he needed, he'd brought his own. "Apparently, you'd told the kids who I was and she'd read the story in the newspaper. When she saw I couldn't walk, she took over like a little mother and got me to a doctor, then the pharmacy before going home."

"This was *Alex?*" He smiled widely.

Rachel nodded.

"She's so timid. I'm surprised she didn't run away when she found you looking at her."

"She's a very unhappy young lady."

"I know. She doesn't think anyone likes her. She really needs some friends." Sam turned around and began taking food out of the bag. "How long did she stay?"

"Including the time in the doctor's office, a couple of hours. She was very interested in what I was doing in the other rooms and how I'd learned to do it."

"She's very lonely. She wants to fit in," Sam said. "It's that need that got her in trouble. She fell in with the wrong crowd."

"She told me," Rachel said and again Sam turned to look at her.

"It took me three weeks to get her to tell me the slightest bit of personal information and she told you her life story within two hours of meeting you?"

"It wasn't her life story, but she needed someone to talk to. I gather her mother works a lot."

"Charlotte Lytelle. She's the plant manager at Long's. Everyone calls her Carly." J.T. Long's Container Corporation was the town plant. It manufactured all types of containers, everything from corrugated boxes to perfume bottles. "She's a wonderful woman and concerned mother, but she's a widow and works long hours. Alex took her father's death hard, and not having her mother around most of the time is not a good combination."

"She says the kids make fun of her too."

"She's smart, geekish, kind of like you were, except she doesn't think she's pretty."

"And I did?" She sat up straight.

"Don't get angry," he cautioned her as he browned ground beef on one burner of her hot plate and had spaghetti boiling in a pot on the other. "You had plenty of friends and you had parents who supported you in everything you wanted to do. You were popular at school. Alex transferred in. She wasn't born into the cliques around here. She's in a position where if she's smart, she loses, and if she's dumb, she loses. Her self-esteem is a little low. It will take time, but she'll find her way. All she needs is a little guidance. We're trying to give her that."

Sam cut up some bread and added butter and garlic. He slipped it into the toaster oven and turned it on.

"Who's we?" Rachel asked.

"Her mother and a community program for teens." Sam had a sudden idea. "Why don't you come down and help? If you got Alex to talk to you, maybe you can reach some of the other kids."

"I don't know," Rachel began.

"Don't refuse so quickly. You've already proven you can reach one teen. They're kids trying to find themselves. We need people who can guide them to the right path."

"You're not asking me so I can have counseling at this center, are you?"

"It could help you, too."

Rachel's eyebrows went up in question. "How?"

"It'll be a way to get back into the swing of things around here slowly, at your own pace, and without people asking a lot of questions. Anyway, we meet Tuesday night at seven o'clock in the Community Center."

Sam drained the spaghetti and heaped it on two plates. Using a couple of sawhorses and a piece of board, he constructed a table. Pulling a tablecloth from the bag, he covered it and set a wine bottle containing a candle at the center.

"Wow," Rachel said when he lit the candle. "Should I have dressed?"

Sam had to keep from voicing the first thought that entered his head or he'd have told her she could come undressed. "I can do much better than spaghetti, but your kitchen is lacking in the necessary conveniences for my gourmet talents."

He laughed and she joined him. "Do the people of The Lake know you're such a clown?"

He shook his head. "It's one of the best-kept secrets around."

Stacking two crates on top of each other, he fashioned chairs and helped Rachel sit on one.

"This is very good," she said, tasting the food. "I probably wouldn't have made myself more than a sandwich."

"Then it's a good thing you have a cook."

The sun shone through the loft windows and woke Rachel. She opened her eyes and quickly raised her hand to cover them. She turned away from the brightness. What a difference waking up this morning was from the day before. Although she couldn't remember going to sleep.

She was hot in the sleeping bag, sweating hot. Pushing it down, she saw she was wearing the long sweatshirt she'd had on yesterday. She wiggled it over her head and took it off. The T-shirt she'd slept in the previous night was under it. Cool air kissed her skin and felt delicious. Tilting her head from side to side and rolling it around on her neck told her she was pain-free this morning.

Why had she slept in that? The last thing she remembered was sitting on the floor with Sam. They'd finished dinner and he'd cleaned up. Then they went into the other room and watched the stars. Rachel had wanted to go outside, but Sam thought with her ear infection the night air wouldn't be good for it.

So they'd stayed inside. When did he leave? And how did she get into the bedroll?

Chapter Eight

It was back, Rachel thought. She'd felt it days ago when Alex took her to the doctor, but she shoved it off as part of the sickness. She stepped out onto the new porch that Sam and his team had finished and painted. It was then that she felt the eyes. She looked left, right, and straight ahead, but saw no one, heard no one. Yet she had the feeling. The same one she'd had many times while she was in the program. Eyes were on her. Someone was watching her, stalking her movements.

Rachel shrugged as if she were dropping an overcoat from her shoulders. It was silly, she told herself. She was safe. There was no one left to spy on her. No reason. It was over. She was free to come and go as she pleased, without the thought of a threat. Yet, she hadn't been able to abandon the feelings in the past and she couldn't shake this one now.

She hadn't been out of the cabin for three days.

Sam had come to see her regularly, and spent at least an hour talking to her. Alex and the other teens had finished the roof and painted the porch. Rachel had yet to complete the inside, but she'd spent most of the day working on the office she was constructing. Alex had come and the two talked while Rachel worked. Then Alex got up and started to help. She proved a quick study.

The drive into town was short. Rachel meant to slip into the back of the Community Center unobserved, but Sam saw her the moment she walked in. He smiled at her and her stomach did a funny little flop. Rachel's hand came up to quiet it, but Alex rushed over and grabbed her arm, pulling her to a seat next to hers.

Sam was speaking, giving introductions of new teens there for the first time. When he looked at her a sudden coldness went through Rachel. She was afraid he was going to single her out. She breathed a sigh of relief when the group apparently broke up and he didn't.

"What's happening?" Rachel asked. "Is it over already?"

"Oh no," Alex said. "We break up into smaller groups and talk about what got us here and how to prevent it from happening again. The older ones help the new arrivals. "Come to my group." Alex stood up. "Our leader isn't here tonight. Officer Sam was going to stand in, but you can do it. You can talk to us."

Rachel glanced at Sam, who nodded to her, as she followed Alex to an area in the back of the room. Three other teens had already gathered there and others were coming. Across the room young students were dragging chairs and forming circles. The noise of scraping wood and raised conversation made it hard to hear. Yet Sam's voice could be heard above the cacophony as he directed them to get to their groups as fast as possible. Rachel had a moment of déjà vu. She heard his voice over all the other noises. It came to her ears as if through a telephone line. And she grabbed at it for support.

All around her kids were looking at her, some openly staring, others trying to be coy about it. Whispers went through the room as a form of gossip played from person to person. If anyone there didn't know who she was, by her estimate within five minutes her fame would have increased fourfold as another generation learned of her return.

Alex held her hand and had a smile on her face. Rachel felt as if the young girl finally had someone to support her. "This is my friend," Alex said to the group when they were seated.

"We usually talk about the effects of alcohol since we're all here because of it," a girl wearing a name tag with Melissa written on it said. "But can we talk about you?"

Rachel had known this would happen. She could handle it. The initial crack in the wall had been opened and she'd survived. Alex had talked to her, a complete stranger. She could surely talk to teenagers. They were less threatening than adults.

"What would you like to know?"

"How did you disappear?" name tag Jim asked.

"Nobody can disappear, Jim," she told him. "It's all an illusion. You're just no longer in the same place."

"I wish I could disappear sometimes," Jim said,

more to himself than anyone else, but Rachel heard it.

"Why?"

"My parents just don't get it. They're living back in the eighteenth century."

Jim had several earrings climbing up the curve of his ear. He wore an oversized black T-shirt with a rock band's logo on it to match the black shorts that hung past his knees and were three sizes larger than his sixteen-year-old frame. His hair was dyed jet-black and spiked on his head like a porcupine.

"You give them a lot of trouble," Rachel stated. "You're punishing them for their attempt at control?"

Jim looked down at his hands. The group was quiet, all waiting for him to continue his story.

"Yeah," he finally said.

"You ever think they are having a hard time understanding you?"

"No," Liza with a Z said. The Z on her name tag had been drawn in Old English lettering and colored in with red, black, and yellow markers.

"Why not?"

"They been here." Her voice was almost accusing. "You should remember. You ain't that much older than we is."

Rachel smiled at her. Her belligerence reminded her of herself at their age. Without even knowing Liza with a Z, Rachel was sure her use of language was all show.

"Didn't you ever do anything when you were a teenager?" Liza asked. "Or were you Miss Goody Two-shoes?"

Rachel looked over the group. There were six people in front of her. Four girls and two boys. Liza,

Jim, and Melissa had already spoken. Alex had only introduced her to the group. Kramer and Shelby had yet to join in. Rachel leaned forward. She was sure the group made the same move.

"I wasn't Miss Goody Two-shoes. I'm sure my parents would have been glad if I were. I was just like you." She paused and looked at each one of them. "I was growing into my new body and I wanted my way. But I had another restraint. Anybody know what it was?"

"Witsec." The reply came from Kramer. Everyone looked at him as if he'd said something foul. "Stands for Witness Security. I looked it up on the Internet. Is that all right with you?" He crossed his arms in a defy-me gesture that dared anyone to oppose him.

"Kramer is right. I had Witsec. I was seventeen, same age as some of you. I wanted to go to parties and dances. I wanted to talk to my friends on the phone, hang out at the mall. I wanted to share my secrets with my best friend, go to the movies with people I knew, spend the night at a sleepover."

"You couldn't even go to the movies?" Melissa frowned as she asked the question.

"I knew no one. I had a different name, which I had to keep remembering was mine. I was so afraid I'd say the wrong thing and give us away that I stayed at home. I couldn't even go to programs like this one and talk to other people in the same situation as I was. There were no other people in my situation. I was totally alone."

"Man, what a life," Liza said. Her tone indicated that her own life wasn't as bad as what Rachel had gone through. And Rachel hadn't told them the really bad parts of her life inside the program. She was thankful for her father and mother. They had understood what she was going through since they were experiencing the same kind of withdrawal.

Rachel found the kids refreshing. She didn't mind talking to them. After their initial curiosity of her wore off, they opened up and told her their own stories. She didn't try to solve their problems or give them solutions they should try. She asked them questions and allowed them to think of their own solutions.

"What do you think of the world, Kramer?" she asked after he'd told her he'd broken into someone's house after he'd been drinking.

"It's a big place." His comeback was immediate and caused laughter in the group. Sam, who hadn't been near her group, but had sat in on all the others, looked over at the sound of laughter. Rachel felt that flutter in her stomach again.

"How much of it have you seen?"

He consulted the ceiling. "Let's see, I went to Mexico one summer."

"You didn't go to Mexico," Melissa contradicted. "Rio Nuevo is a border town, not the real Mexico. It doesn't count."

"Well, I've seen Niagara Falls. From the *Canadian* side," he stated, daring her to oppose his comment.

"Would you like to see more of it?" Rachel asked.

"I guess so." He shrugged as if the answer meant nothing to him.

"Ever wonder what girls are like in North Carolina or California or France?"

"I hear them French girls is hot." The girls groaned. The boys laughed, nodding their heads in agreement.

"There's only one way to find out," Rachel said, using her hand as if it were a plane taking off.

"Go to France?" he asked.

"Go to France."

"I can't go to France."

"Why not?"

"My parents will never let me go or give me the money."

"Earn your own money. If you earn it yourself and show your parents you're responsible and trustworthy, you might be surprised at which century they really live in. And just think of what you can learn spending time in another country."

"I can't speak no French." He added his own obstacle.

"Maybe it would be fun to learn." Rachel lowered her voice. "I'm sure you can find *someone* willing to help you with the language."

Rachel smiled slyly. The girls did too. It took the boys a second, but suddenly they were all smiling.

"Yeah," Kramer said, crossing one arm over the other in the typical bad boy fashion. "I can get a job after school. Make some money."

"Kramer, you have to keep your grades up. That's important to parents."

"I can do that," he said confidently. "Yeah, yeah, I'm going to France."

The room had cleared out except for Rachel and the group she was leading. Sam had observed them throughout the evening. All of the students in her group wanted her to give them advice on something they could do. It was positive. It was a start on them becoming productive citizens. Suddenly they all wanted to please their parents, even if they didn't understand that was what they were asking.

"Hey, man, you coming?" Jeff Taggart, a curly-headed blond boy with grown-up muscles stood in the door. He wore gym shorts and carried a basketball and directed his question to Jim.

"In a minute," Jim said.

The blond disappeared. Sam heard the smack of the ball bouncing against the floor. The boys usually played basketball after these sessions. The girls played cards, some of them used the indoor pool, and there was always a volleyball game or a table tennis match in play. Others gathered and talked until their parents came for them or they drove themselves home.

Sam thought it was good to give them an outlet for their energy. They looked at it most nights as a reward for sitting through the programs. Rachel's group had defied convention. For the first time, they actually wanted to stay and continue talking. He hadn't gone to her group, but he'd eavesdropped on what was going on. At first they were curious about her, but then they accepted that she had had experiences similar to their own. He wished he had more counselors like her.

"Time to break up," Sam said, walking over to the group. "Don't wear Ms. Wells out. We'd like her to come back."

The six of them stood up, and smiling, saying good-bye, and thanking her, started filing out.

"Thanks for coming," Liza with a Z said, smiling as she moved away. "I hope you come back." She glanced at Sam and whispered, "She was *really* good."

Sam nodded.

"Me too." Shelby reiterated Liza's comment. Shelby was a quiet girl and had said nothing the entire evening, but Sam knew she missed nothing.

"Officer Sam, can't she be our group leader?" Kramer asked.

"We've had requests for her by the other groups."

"Aw, no," several of them said in unison. "She's ours." Alex took Rachel's arm as if she were her personal property.

"She came as a guest tonight, guys. And your group has a leader."

"Not like her," Melissa said.

"Thank you all for the encouragement," Rachel said. "I enjoyed talking with you. And I hope you follow through on some of the things we discussed."

"We will," Kramer said, speaking for the entire group.

"Maybe I could come back sometime and be a guest again."

When they started to protest Sam stopped them. "Why don't you all go upstairs? I'm sure you'll see Ms. Wells again soon."

They said good night to her and left, each one pausing to tell him how much they wanted her back.

"See you tomorrow," Alex said and waved.

When the last one went through the door, Sam faced her. "What did you say to them? They left raving. And the other groups were jealous of all the fun your group was having."

"I only asked a couple of questions. They saw the possibilities in themselves."

Sam sat down. "You're a natural at this."

"I am not."

"I saw you tonight. I heard some of what you said. And if I hadn't, I know those kids and they aren't the best of the bunch, but they listened to you. I mean really listened."

"They were more interested in *me* than in anything else."

"Maybe at first, but not in **the** end. And I meant it when I said the other groups really wanted to know what was going on over here."

Rachel was quiet. She dropped her head.

"Have you ever done anything like this before?"

"Counseling young people?"

He nodded.

"No."

"You're good at it. Very good. It's obvious the kids want you to come back. And there is always a need for people the kids can relate to. Will you think about it?"

She nodded.

"Come on. I'll see you home."

"It's all right," she said. "I drove over. My car is outside."

"Then I'll follow you home. Make sure you're safe."

"Chief, don't tell me Lake Como isn't a safe community."

Sam hoped she didn't see his reaction. The Lake was a safe place to live and raise kids. At least it had been until he'd become privy to her story.

* * *

The stars provided a beautiful crown over the town. A huge moon hung over the water in the distance as if it were something out of a song. The air was fragrant with the smell of summer and a light breeze was riffling the air. Rachel was at peace, or at least she should be. The moment she stepped out of the center she felt it again.

The eyes.

Unconsciously she took Sam's hand and looked over her shoulder.

"Anything wrong?" he asked.

She smiled to hide her concern. "I was just thinking how perfect the town looks. It's a nice night for a swim. The big moon, the stars, it's very romantic."

"The air is too cold."

"Often the air is cool, but if we stay in the water . . ."

"What about getting out?"

"We could make a fire to keep warm."

"You've just gotten over being sick. Going in the water too soon could make you ill again. I am up for a cup of coffee at the Castle."

"All right."

Sam drove her in the police cruiser. He was off duty and despite Rachel's protest that they could take her Jeep, he insisted that if there was an emergency he needed to be prepared.

It wasn't late when they went through the door of the Castle. There were a few customers scattered about the tables and counter. Sam led her to a booth in the back, near the kitchen. They could be alone there, away from the other customers. And the way Sam sat, he could see anyone coming through the front door.

Rachel would have preferred that seat, but he'd helped her into the one facing the swinging kitchen door. She usually took the seat facing the entrance and she always looked for escape routes. Sitting in the back didn't bother her. When she came here alone she sat near the rear. Most people opted for the few tables near the front windows. They liked looking out on their cars in the lot or watching the slow scenery of vehicles that ventured this way en route to summer homes, sun, and fun. Rachel needed to know she could get out at a moment's notice.

Doris worked the morning shift and stayed until five. Sherry was on duty tonight and she came over, steaming coffeepot in one hand and two institutionally thick cups in the other.

"Coffee?"

"Please," Sam said. "Sherry, meet Rachel."

Sherry smiled and color went up her face. "I read about you in the paper."

Rachel wondered if there was a single soul in the entire county who hadn't read that story.

"How's that kid of yours?" Sam asked.

"Growing like a weed. He'll be five next week. All he can talk about is his birthday party." She glanced at Rachel. "Can I get you anything else?"

"A piece of chocolate cake and a large bowl of vanilla ice cream," Rachel answered.

"A sweet tooth," Sherry said. "I like her. What about you?"

"The same."

Sherry nodded and left them.

"So tell me, what did you think of tonight?" Sam asked.

She hesitated as was her nature. "It wasn't as bad as I expected. The kids were curious, not prying."

"And you've gotten it out of your system?"

"Well, let's just say I survived it with no visible scars." Concern marred Sam's features and Rachel smiled to take the sting out of her words. "So now that the ice is broken, so they say, can I ask you a question?"

"Shoot." He leaned against the back of the booth, apparently relaxed in who he was. Rachel wondered if she would ever get to that place. Would she ever be able to live in the moment and not constantly be aware of everything and everyone around her? Even though Sam looked relaxed, Rachel felt a tightness in him. It was the way he looked around the room, constantly taking in the scene. She gave his actions up to him being a cop. Just as they'd arrived here in his cruiser, he was always on duty. It didn't matter that he wore an open-neck shirt and khaki pants, or that his feet were in deck shoes without socks. Every line of his body said he was still a cop.

Sherry arrived with their cake and ice cream before she spoke. "Let me know if you need anything else," she said and sped off.

"Why are you working in the police department?"

"I'm the chief of police," he joked.

"You know what I mean. You were heading to law school nine years go."

Sam took a drink from his coffee cup, then set it back on the table. "I went. At the end of my second year my parents were in an accident. They required constant care for almost a year before they recovered. I had to drop out to handle things. I came home, lost my financial aid, and it took a while to make enough money to return. They wanted to help, but they only had their retirement money and I could wait awhile. "

"Where was Bill?"

"Bill was a mess."

"Bill?"

Scooping a spoonful of ice cream on his cake, Sam ate them together. Rachel was holding her spoon, but her concentration was on Sam. She'd forgotten she even had food. She'd never thought of Bill falling apart. He was such a well-adjusted young man. He'd wanted to go on to college after high school, study engineering, and travel to exotic places building things that would leave his mark on the world. What had happened to their dreams?

She supposed life and circumstance had touched him in a way similar to her own fate. How much they thought they could be the masters of their universe was so easily refuted by some outside and unknown force. Bill couldn't have known his parents were going to require so much care.

"Anyway." Sam's voice brought her out of her memory episode and back to the diner. "Constantly taking care of two people who could do almost nothing for themselves was hard work and it didn't appear there was an end in sight. He wanted to go back to school, but felt too guilty leaving me here alone when I should have also been in school. He held the contradiction inside himself until something had to give. He needed me and I stayed. But it all worked out. I got a job and worked to save money to go back and finally got the degree."

"Did you pass the bar?"

He nodded.

"But you took the job of police chief here. Why?"

"When I left the Detroit police and came home the old chief was retiring. They asked me to take the job on a temporary basis, just until they could find a permanent replacement. I already had experience and Lake Como is no Detroit. I agreed. That was five years ago."

Rachel's ice cream was melting when she began eating again.

"I haven't given up on the idea of going into practice. There were some programs I wanted to get started in the community. Some of them are done. Some still on the drawing board. But I'll get to it. I've got time."

"More coffee?" Sherry surprised Rachel by suddenly appearing at the table. She was holding the pot the same as she had when she first came to serve them. Rachel assumed it was part of her make-up. She pushed her cup toward the waitress and the woman filled it to the brim. Sam passed on more coffee. He asked for water instead. Sherry moved away like a firefly, flitting about the room serving in an orderly pattern that she'd perfected with years of practice.

Rachel folded her arms along the table edge. Sam was an interesting man. She enjoyed talking to him and he genuinely cared about the people of this town. The kids at his center respected and liked him. Rachel wondered about his moods. She couldn't tell much about him and she admitted she'd had little practice other than the psychology courses she'd taken. There had been men in her life, but not many and not for long.

"Bill told me you nearly killed your partner." She wasn't sure how to broach the subject or even if she should. But Sam had listened to her tale. He'd almost insisted she tell him. She wanted to know about him too.

"I was on the Detroit P.D.," he began after Sherry had placed his glass of water on the table. "The days were eighteen hours long in the summer and just as lengthy in winter. We'd been on a routine call. Domestic violence. We pulled the car up in front of a run-down house on the edge of the river. I could hear the screams long before we got out of the car."

Rachel swallowed. She could picture the scene in her mind.

"P.J. got to the door first."

"Is that your partner?"

He nodded. "Pearl Jamison. Everybody calls her P.J. more because she likes a rock group called Pearl Jam than because of her initials. She got out of the car and stopped. I knew something was up then. She was looking around. There's a way she would stand, a way her head would cock as if she were sniffing out the crime going on. She'd throw her head up, her face intense, and listen, it seemed, to the air. This was a ritual when she had 'the feeling.'" Sam raised his hands and waved two fingers on each one. "The feeling meant something was wrong. Things were not as they appeared. Thank God for it. She didn't have to tell me. I immediately called for backup.

"P.J. got to the door first and identified herself as Detroit P.D. The noise inside stopped as quickly as if someone had switched a CD player off. We waited for the door to open, but no one came. P.J. knocked again. And all hell broke loose."

Sam never wanted to relive that night, but he had no choice about it. It would go away for months, sometimes a year, then sneak up on him, fill his dreams with surreal images of the gunplay that lit up the waterfront. In the midst of it all was P.J. directly in the line of his gun. A split second and a glint of her shield came too late to keep him from pulling the trigger. The thought of killing P.J. had chills running up his spine, just before the sweat poured over him. He'd wake with his teeth chattering or fighting the covers trying to get away from the massive amounts of expended heat soaking his body. As many times as he tried, the experience shook him. He had quit the force and returned to The Lake.

Rachel hadn't said a word sitting across from him. She quietly ate her cake and ice cream, but he knew she was waiting for him to continue. "The door exploded inward. P.J. dove to one side of it. I went the other way. Gunfire erupted from everywhere. I couldn't see P.J., but I knew where she was by the returned gunfire. I also heard her hand radio crackle as she reported that we were under fire.

"The houses were close together and had alleyways between them. The alleys were long and narrow. I could run down them, making myself a target for a speeding bullet. Staying where I was, my back pressed up against the porch lattice, wasn't the best option either. Sooner or later whoever was firing bullets from inside the house would come out and find me or P.J.

"I could no longer hear P.J. I wondered where the backup was and why they were taking so long, but within the 139.6 square miles of the city of Detroit something was always happening that required the services of the forty-seven hundred officers and civilians on duty. I tried the radio and noticed it had a bullet lodged in it. I can't tell you the fear that went through me when I realized that bullet would have killed me if it hadn't gone into the radio.

"Behind me I heard glass breaking. A window halfway down the alley blew out and a booted foot and jean-clad leg came out of it. I had to make a decision. It's not protocol to separate from your partner, but I started down the alley. The man coming out of the window looked at me and fired. I ducked and returned fire. He went back in, but continued firing. I was pinned down, too far into the alley to go back and not close enough to do anything effectively. I heard the sirens of the backup vehicles coming, but they weren't going to make it in time. All I could do was fire and keep firing while I backed out of the alley."

"What about the people in the house?" Rachel asked.

Sam saw her shoulders tighten as if she were living the episode as he had done so many times.

"I thought about them, but I had to take my chances. Backup arrived as I got to the end. More than just a couple of cars converged. A full SWAT team pulled up. DEA agents jumped out of cars and vans. The whole place became a war zone. Firepower was exchanged from more than the one house. It seemed like the whole neighborhood was alive. I heard a sound in the alley and I turned. I didn't see who it was. I was sure it was the man who'd tried to come out of the window and I fired."

He couldn't say it. Rachel saved him from having to do so. "It was P.J." Her statement was soft and without emotion.

"She'd circled around the building. When she heard the sirens and saw me she started down the alley."

Rachel reached over and took his hand. "I'm sorry," she said. "But she's all right, isn't she? She's alive."

"She's alive." Sam sighed. "The bullet went through her, piercing her spine, as it exited her back. She's a quadriplegic and lives in a nursing home for disabled police officers."

"I'm sure you've been told it wasn't your fault."

Sam drank from his now cold coffee cup. He nodded. "I've told myself that too."

"But your dreams haunt you." She stated it simply, without the need for a question, said the words as if she understood them, and Sam immediately knew she did. Her fate had been different than his, but they each had their own demons. P.J. did not blame him for her fate. She'd known there was risk involved when she entered the police academy. She hadn't called out to identify herself and there was shooting going on as she approached a policeman from the rear. It was a series of errors, but the result was the same no matter how different his dreams might be. He couldn't change the outcome.

"You're still a cop here. You didn't leave the force when it seems you would have even in a place with as small a crime rate as The Lake."

"I told you why I did it."

"You did," she agreed. "I'm sure you've told yourself that too."

"What do you mean?"

"The people in the house. Back in that alley in Detroit. When everything was over, what was the outcome?"

"Several wounded, a couple dead. We rounded up thirty people. It was a major drug bust."

"How old were they?"

"What?"

"The ones that died. How old were they?"

Sam didn't know how she knew, but he was sure she already had the answer to her question. "Barely teenagers," he finally said.

"That's why you stayed on the force here. You're trying to fix it, save the teenagers here." When he didn't respond she went on, "It's a noble endeavor, but have you thought of what you'll do if something major happens here?"

She had his complete and full attention with that question. "Do you know something?"

"No, but you need to be prepared for whatever might come. You told me you were the law here. You have to *be* the law here."

"If the need comes, I'll handle it." When the words left his lips, he was confident they were true. He was the law and he would handle it. He'd been in the grips of P.J. and his part in her fate for five years. He couldn't change the past and he could no longer allow it to hold him prisoner.

Yet, while his prison walls were being skillfully deconstructed, the woman tearing them away brick by brick was using those same bricks to reinforce her own cage, only hers was a prison of fear.

Chapter Nine

The car doors slammed with the click and slap of the rocker and knob mechanism engaging. Sam had taken her back to the Community Center to pick up her car and followed her home in the squad car. Before she'd turned off the ignition, he was there to help her out of the Jeep. He'd been very attentive tonight and open with his story of his life in Detroit and what had brought him back to The Lake. She knew he was reluctant to share his story, but she had told him hers.

Rachel was also attracted to Sam, more than she thought she could ever be to someone who wore a uniform. She wondered if she'd always been attracted to him. Was that the reason he'd thrown her off balance when she was seventeen?

She slipped out of the cab and into his arms. They closed automatically around her. She felt warm and protected with him. A cocoon insulated them in the dim light of the open door. She looked up at him, seeing the desire in his eyes. Her breath caught and she stood, unmoving at the depth of what she saw. She didn't know how long Sam stood holding her, why his mouth, only a kiss away from her own, never moved the microinch it needed to touch hers.

"Come on, I'll see you safely inside."

Rachel didn't hear him initially. She was still inside the cocoon, the place where only lovers go. They weren't lovers, she thought, and the bubble around her burst.

"All right," she said. He moved back to give her room and slipped his arms protectively around her as he led her up the new steps to the front door.

"I'll have a quick look around." He didn't give her the option of refusing. As soon as the door swung inward, Sam went inside. Rachel smiled, reaffirming the belief that the cop in Sam was always present. He turned on lights and looked in every room. He unhooked the safety strap that kept his gun from falling out when he sat or ran. Rachel noticed he didn't take it out and assumed he didn't want to scare her. He didn't know she was amused by his acting.

"Everything looks fine," he said, coming down from the loft.

"Did you expect to find a hit man up there or something?"

He returned her smile, then looked around. He commented on the state of the construction. "You've done quite a bit since I was here last."

She looked at the walls and molding that had gone up in the small space of time. "Alex comes by and helps me."

"Alex? I thought you wanted to do it all your-self."

"She needs the therapy more than I do." Rachel checked the workmanship. "She's good. She wants to learn everything she can. And when she works, she talks. She needs someone to take an interest in her. She doesn't believe her mother has time."

"Does Carly know she's been coming here?"

"I asked her that and she said her mother doesn't care where she is." Rachel didn't like the look on Sam's face. "Sam, I'm sorry if I did something wrong, but I didn't want her to get into any more trouble. She goes to summer school and comes after classes. She does her homework here and then helps out. There can't be anything wrong in that."

"There isn't. It's just that those two need to talk to each other and I wouldn't want you getting in the middle of it."

"You want me to send her home when she comes?"

"Maybe you should talk to Carly about her com-ing."

"Okay. I will."

Sam's hand reached for her and she took the few steps separating them and took it. It was strong and warm and a slight form of electricity went through her fingers and up her arm at his touch. He started toward the door.

"Think about coming back to the center. You were a wonder there and I know the kids appreci-ated you coming."

"I'll think about it."

At the door he turned to her. "I enjoyed talking to you tonight," he said. "Other than Bill, I've told no one the whole story about P.J. and the night she was shot."

"Thank you for telling me," Rachel said.

"I suppose I needed to get it off my chest. Put things into perspective."

"I found putting things in perspective helped me when I was in the program. It was hard getting through the day as it was. I used to remind myself of the things I could control. Dwelling on those I couldn't drove me crazy."

Sam pulled her into his arms. Rachel hadn't expected it, but she went. His arms encircled her and she felt the pressure of his lips in her hair. "It must have been awful," he whispered. "But that's all over now. You're safe here and I won't let anything bad happen to you again." He kissed her hair again. "I promise."

Rachel pulled back and looked at Sam. The catch in his voice disturbed her. There was something desperate in his tone, something she hadn't ever heard before, and it made her tremble.

Sam's eyes turned dark, their depths as dark as the midnight lake. Even with a full moon the bottom couldn't be discerned. And Rachel was drowning in them. Then his head dipped and his mouth touched hers. His lips were soft and featherlight against her mouth. The tip of his tongue touched her lips, outlining them in a slow, drugging circle that made her sway against him or lose her balance. His arms tightened around her as he raised his head slightly and began the feathering kisses again. Time seemed to mean nothing as he drew his mouth across every section of hers, one small centimeter at a time.

The cabin had no air-conditioning. The windows weren't open and the air inside caught fire. A furnace fueled her from the inside out. Its burn was searing and Rachel wondered how she could remain solidly inside her skin. She raised her arms and held him, wanting more. Her body aligned with Sam's. They weren't on the beach this time. The clothes between them were armor keeping them apart. She wanted to tear them off as Sam's arms crushed her against him and his mouth took hers. Rachel went into the kiss with a necessity born of a need so strong it consumed her. She kissed him like a wild woman, with an abandon that had never taken her before.

Their tongues and teeth clashed in a dance so fierce it had to be forbidden. Rachel was past caring. She wanted Sam here and now. Her hands roved over him, pulling his shirt free of his pants and running them upward over his moisture-rich skin. It was silky and dark and heaven to touch. Her sensitized fingers felt every layer of his skin. Rachel smiled and kissed the skin where his shirt opened, tasting the salt and inhaling the uniqueness of him. She didn't understand what plane she was on or how she had come to be on it, but it was like glimpsing another world, one in which only lovers were allowed, a world where the two of them lived on ecstacy, sensation, and passion, in a time zone that went neither forward nor backward. Yet the moment her hand hit the butt of Sam's gun the fantasy world she'd entered burst like a pin in a bubble. Rachel snatched her hand back, her entire body moving as fast and as far away as she could get.

"It's not the first time," Sam said after a moment. Rachel had no idea what he meant. "The gun. Many women abhor them."

"You mean women who've been as close to you as I was?"

He nodded reluctantly.

"It *was* the gun," Rachel said. "But it's not what you're thinking. I'm not afraid of the gun. I'm actually a good shot."

"Then why did you slide across the room the moment your hand touched it?"

"It's what the gun represents."

"What's that?"

"Mistrust, deception, death."

Rachel used to be able to tell the day's weather by the night sky. She and Bill knew by the smell of the water. They could tell by the whisp of fragrance in the air or the peek of stars through an overcast sky, that rain was on its way, that fog would greet the morning, or that rain would spoil any planned picnics or outdoor activities.

Tonight she watched the sky from her window. Yet the weather wasn't on her mind. Her eyes strayed in the direction of the cabin she couldn't see, to Sam's house. He'd left her hours ago. She should be asleep, but sleep eluded her. It was Sam's gun that kept her awake. It didn't frighten her. She frightened herself. Touching it had only surprised her. It had brought back the memories. Her mind had yelled at her that he, that Sam, that the man who held her in his arms, whose lips turned her body to liquid fire, was a cop. The feelings she had for him were raw and open. How could she feel this way about him when she knew that cops would as quickly have her killed as forget their duty of protecting her?

She hated what they had done to her and Sam was one of them. Even without the uniform, it was undeniable, he was every inch a lawman. He'd explained his job in Detroit and she'd been able to picture it in her mind. She could see him in control, see him angling down that alley, walk or run with him as he planned the capture of the criminal. The problem was there was no difference between herself and the drug-deal-gone-bad criminal. A sting operation was done regardless of who the players were. Rachel had been set up before and her trust in those who were supposed to serve and protect was as low as the subzero temperatures at either of the poles.

Yet when she thought of Sam everything thawed. When he held her in his arms, she melted, and when his mouth settled over hers, she could almost hear the sizzle of ice metamorphosing directly into gas without the need to go through the liquefied stage. Frankly, he scared her. Her feelings scared her. Why couldn't she have come home to find Bill waiting for her with the same feelings she had imagined in the dark nights of her captivity? Why did she have to find Sam in his place? And why did her nerves go haywire at the thought of him?

Like her first night back at The Lake, Rachel left her cabin. Stepping out of the sanctity of the space she was making her own, she looked around, expecting to feel the phantom eyes stalking her. Tonight she felt nothing. She relaxed, her shoulders dropping, at the unwarranted fear she had developed. There was no one looking for her.

She headed in the direction of her thoughts—toward Sam. He must have seen her coming because his door opened before she reached it.

"What are you doing here?" Sam looked over her shoulder as if he expected someone to be behind her.

"I couldn't sleep." He pulled her into the room and quickly closed the door.

"I was having a glass of wine. Why don't you join me?" Rachel followed him into the living room. "Sit down. I'll be right back."

Soft music filled the room, playing from a stereo system concealed inside a smoked-glass cabinet. Only a single light, on a table next to the sofa where a wineglass sat next to an open book called *The Criminal Mind*, was illuminated. The overstuffed sofa showed no sign of depression where Sam had been sitting, but Rachel could feel his impression as she looked at it. She wanted to sit in that place, but decided to take the other end.

Sam returned and handed her a glass. "This is ginger ale," she said after sipping it.

"You've had medication today. No alcohol." He resumed his seat.

She'd forgotten the medicine and the pain that had taken her to the doctor earlier in the week. It felt as if it were an eon ago.

"Is the pain keeping you awake?"

She shook her head. "I don't know what it is. Probably the fact that I need a bed. I thought of buying an air mattress, but I haven't done it yet."

"Why don't you stay here? There's a comfortable bed upstairs that no one is using."

Rachel's heart nearly jumped out of her chest at his offer. She could be close to him. See him every day. Share meals and talk about whatever, the way she used to do under the stars. But Rachel knew better.

"Thank you, but no," she said.

"Don't want to accept any favors from anyone?" Sam sipped his wine.

"That's not it. The house is coming along. It won't be long before my bedroom is finished and I can order furniture."

"Is that going to be the loft?"

"I like the feel of the loft. With no wall over the downstairs, it's open and freeing. The view from up there is spectacular. I can look over the trees and see the lake and the mountains. But I'm going to use my old bedroom on the first floor. I'm redoing it, making it larger. I think I'll make the loft a reading room, a place to curl up and relax and watch the sun set."

Rachel yawned then. She took a drink, trying to hide it, but she was unsuccessful.

"You're sleepy."

"I am," she agreed. "I was wide awake when I got here, but the soft music and"—she looked at her glass—"ginger ale has lulled me into relaxing."

She stood up and prepared to leave. Sam stood too. "Sleep here," he said. "It's only one night. You can go back tomorrow. And with the medicine, it'll make me feel better."

Rachel stared at him. The idea of a soft bed was luxurious. Her body wasn't completely back on par and a good night's sleep would help her. Sam took the decision out of her hands. He put out the light and took her arm, leading her to the stairs.

At the door to the room where she'd slept before, he turned to her. "Good night," he whispered. "You know where the towels are. I'll get you something to sleep in."

Neither of them moved after Sam finished. She looked up at him in the darkened hall. It was impossible to tell what he was thinking. There wasn't enough light for her to see his eyes clearly, but Rachel could feel the heat increasing around them. She didn't know who moved first. Suddenly they were in each other's arms and Sam's mouth was on hers. This kiss wasn't like the one at her cabin. It wasn't slow and deliberate. This was the beach kiss, hungry, desperate, devouring. His mouth was hot and demanding and she gave as much as she got.

Their arms fought for position as Rachel and Sam tried to get closer to each other. He turned her into the doorjamb, her back pressed against the wood as his body aligned with hers. He was solid and hard against her softer curves. The contrast sent shivers up her spine and arched her closer to him.

His hands moved down her back, caressing her and outlining the contours of her frame. Fire burned through the fabric of her clothes where he touched her. She trembled and arched against him when his hands cupped her bottom and slammed her into his arousal. Rachel moaned as a delight previously unknown to her skated through her blood, singing a wild and insanely chaotic song.

"Stop me now, Rachel." Sam raised his head. His voice was a frog's croak of his usual authoritarian sound. His breath was hot against her already burning skin. Thoughts of stopping him were the furthest thing from her mind. She answered him by positioning her legs wider apart, giving him room to settle between them. The sound that came from Sam was primal, animalistic, and wonderful. Rachel understood Sam's groan at her action. Similar sensations went through them both. For a moment they were suspended, each staring at the other, but neither moving. Rachel felt him looking into her mind, yet she knew he couldn't see her clearly in the dim light.

When his mouth touched hers it was tender, reverent almost. She felt as if in that small space of time he'd asked her for a precious gift and in her goddesslike ability to grant wishes she had given it to him. The hands on her body were less binding, but more endearing.

After a moment, Sam pushed her backward into the room. He guided her to the bed and gently began the slow process of removing her clothes. He was patient, slipping her shirt over her head and bending to put his mouth on the sunbaked flesh of her shoulders. Her eyes closed as ecstasy flooded her like a wave of emotion cresting inside her.

Rachel pulled his shirt free of his khakis and ran her hands over flesh that was solid, yet quivered under her sensitized fingers. His skin was warm, but getting hotter with each touch. The heat around them kicked up several degrees in its quest to reach the point when they would spontaneously combust. Sam's fingers hooked into Rachel's shorts and pushed them over her hips, keeping his hands open wide as they traveled over exposed flesh, sending erogenous rapture straight to her core.

Breathing was hard as his hands and tongue made love to every section of her revealed by melting clothes. She was filled to overflowing with sensual rapture. Pushing Sam's shirt over his head,

Rachel took in the smell of him, and their day on the beach came back to her in vivid colors. She'd never be able to take in that unique scent again without thinking of him.

In seconds her hands went to his zipper and like a madwoman she tore at the offending device, trying to open it. Frenzy gripped them both as Sam helped her dispose of his clothing. Naked, they held each other, enfolded in each other's arms, foreheads kissing, ragged breath entwined as their hearts and bodies yearned together, one needing the other for completion.

Taking her mouth again, Sam pushed her down on the bed, keeping her fastened to him as if the two had been sculpted as a duet and not two single and distinct beings. He kept contact with her mouth, his tongue dancing inside as the sweet wine transferred and joined with the ginger ale, blending, mingling, fusing together.

Rachel never wanted him to let her go. He rested his weight on his elbows on either side of her as they lay on the soft coverlet. He looked down into her eyes. She saw his teeth flash in a smile. "I can't tell you how often I've thought of having you here." He kissed her then, softly at first, then deepening the kiss until the two seemed to gather strength from being together.

Sam's body pressed into hers. Rachel felt his erection in the cradle of her thighs. Her eyes closed in pure ecstasy. She let it wash over her like soft summer rain. He felt good as he moved up and down against her skin. Nothing in her memory had ever made her feel as good as this. Rachel wanted to lie here for the rest of her life.

Her hands caressed him, drawing up his back, her fingernails lightly outlining the long curve of his spine. She wanted to touch every part of him. She wanted to run her hands over the smooth contours of his body in a slow drive from toes to hairline. She wanted to listen to the soft sighs that came from his throat as her fingers worked a witch's magic over his skin.

Sam's mouth slid from hers and started a leisurely trek down the column of her neck. He lifted himself up, breaking contact with her to quickly slip on a condom. Air rushed in between them. Her skin cooled where his body freed hers. She had no time to reflect on air currents. Rachel was under the spell of a master wizard. Sam's sorcerous mouth, employing all the secret charms of a benevolent illusionist, invaded her mouth. He slipped his tongue inside and danced with the ages, engaging the most intimate feelings between man and woman as time ceased to move. Rachel moaned at the sensations rocketing through her. Her teeth clamped down on a scream when his lips covered her nipple, but she could do nothing to stifle the cry of ecstasy that escaped when their bodies joined. Sam absorbed her scream by again covering her mouth with his.

He moved inside her and she'd never felt anything to compare with the way he made her feel. Her hands curled around his biceps and her fingers dug into his skin as the two of them discovered the wonders of life on earth. Sam seemed to have more hands than she thought possible. He touched her everywhere, caressing her skin, causing mini-explosions along her breasts and stomach. His fingers worked through her hair and around earlobes that tingled and screamed for him to continue the pleasure-pain he was inflicting.

Suddenly Rachel was gripped by an impossibly hard wave, tsunami in strength and gaining as it roiled inside her. Sam must have felt it too. The frenzied pace between them increased to combustible ferociousness. Neither of them could stop what was happening. They rolled with it, with the fire chasing them, with the earthquake cutting a groove into the path where they stepped, with the flow of life that inevitably twisted into the crowning helix of climax.

They collapsed together, their bodies slick with sweat. They panted hard, drank in air as if it were liquid, filling lungs expunged of oxygen until they expanded to their full measure. Sam's hands slipped under her head and he lifted it into the curve of his neck. She heard him breathing against her wet hair. His fingers rolled her neck back and forth as he pressed reverent kisses onto her face and hair.

Pushing her back, he stared down into her face. He looked as if he was on the verge of saying something, but held it back. Rachel understood. She wanted to say something, but there were no words. It wasn't that she couldn't find them, they did not exist. For the experience they had just shared, for the strength of feeling, the depths of their lovemaking, there was nothing in any language she knew to express what she felt.

When Sam tucked her bottom into his stomach and pulled the covers over them, the room had the electrical snap of sex-induced ozone. The fires were receding and her heartbeat was returning to its normal pace, but the alteration to her world was irretrievable. The woman who got out of this bed, who slipped from the arms of the man holding her, was in no way the same as the one who'd earlier entered this house.

And she didn't want to go back to being that woman ever again.

Sex made her hungry. It was the only explanation Rachel could give herself for being in a grocery store with a cart of food. She had no stove, only a toaster oven, a hot plate, and a microwave.

And she couldn't cook.

She picked up a cookbook off the shelf. Richard Simmons, Patty LaBelle, Betty Crocker, Rosie, Oprah Winfrey's personal cook. So many choices. She had no idea what she wanted to eat or how it should be made. She threw three books in the cart. She could decide later.

Walking up and down the aisles, she wondered at the variety of goods. She often bought bread, lunch meat, cheese, cereal, and milk. She could make a decent spaghetti with store-bought sauce, but beyond that she was lost. Picking up a bag of rice, Rachel stared at it. She'd never made rice in her life. While her father had seen to her skills with hammer and nails, neither parent had attended to her education with a spatula or wooden spoon. Rachel dropped the bag in her cart. No time like the present to learn, she thought.

"Rachel, is that you?"

The question came from behind her, but the woman pushing a shopping cart in front of her stopped and stared. Rachel didn't know her, yet her gaze on Rachel was so strong she wondered if she knew her. Rachel searched her brain for something to make her recognize the woman, but nothing came. She was certain the two had never met. The woman was shorter than Rachel's five-foot-seven-inch frame by only an inch or two. She had short hair, strawberry blond, and her sleeveless blouse sported strong arms. They weren't very tanned, so she must stay inside a lot. Her eyes were the most beautiful shade of blue Rachel had ever seen, yet they were slightly cold as they openly stared at her. Rachel couldn't help feeling defensive.

"Aren't you a long way from home?" Bill came up behind her. She turned to him, breaking the tension created by the unknown woman who pushed her cart past them never saying a word. Bill pulled her into his arms, giving her a bear hug, before stepping back.

"I came over to order some furniture," she explained. "I thought I'd stop and buy some food on the way back."

He looked in her basket. An eclectic array of cans, frozen foods, meats, and staples lay haphazardly about the hard red plastic basket. Rachel had no idea how it had gotten there. Her mind had been on Sam and she'd picked up things without thinking about them.

"I'm just out for some diapers. We never seem to have enough."

The woman turned back and looked at her from the end of the aisle.

"Do you know who she is?" Rachel asked.

Bill looked in the direction she indicated. "Carly," he called. The woman looked at Bill as if it were the first time she'd seen him. He went toward her, pulling Rachel along. "What's going on? You're the third Lake resident I've seen in the last few minutes."

The woman smiled and Rachel looked around.

"Have you met Rachel?" he asked.

"Alex talks of no one else . . . when she talks at all," she said. "It's very nice to meet you."

Rachel didn't think she meant it, but she decided to be cordial. "Carly? Charlotte Lytelle, I'm glad to meet you too. I wanted to come by and introduce myself. Alex spends a lot of time at my house. I thought it would be good to talk to you about it."

Carly visibly relaxed.

"Gotta go, guys," Bill said. "I want to find Jess and have him remind Sam of something."

"Who's Jess?" Rachel asked.

"One of Sam's officers. It was a surprise to see him, but as it turns out he can do me a favor. See ya."

Bill pecked both women on the cheek and jogged off. He was still very much the seventeen-year-old boy she'd known a lifetime ago. Not at all like his brother, Sam. There was nothing boyish about Sam. He was all man.

"I was totally prepared to dislike you." Carly Lytelle's voice snapped her out of her thoughts of Sam.

"Why?"

"I'm sure Alex has told you we are having . . . growing pains."

"She never said that, but I could tell by her attitude. She misses her other life."

Rachel pushed her cart to the side to let another shopper pass.

"I know, but my job is here and I'm the only support she has. I'm trying the best I can."

Rachel could tell Carly was trying her best, but her daughter was seventeen and resented everything a parent did. "I know you are. She needs time."

"She told me you were working at the Community Center."

"Not exactly working. I went there once."

"Would you do me a favor and go back?"

Rachel frowned. Her presence couldn't have made that much of a difference.

"Alex barely speaks to me, but she likes you. I admit I'm a little jealous, but she's coming out of the shell she built around herself when her father died and you're the only new factor in her life."

"I have been thinking about the center," Rachel admitted. Sam had asked her to come back. And she'd enjoyed meeting the kids. Now one of the parents. Carly Lytelle didn't appear to be judging her or even thinking about the newspaper story that chronicled Rachel's arrival. She was interested in her daughter. "I'll try it again."

Carly smiled and reached over and squeezed her hand. "Thank you."

Both women moved again to let someone pass. "I suppose we'd better get out of everyone's way," Carly said. "And thanks for helping my daughter. Maybe one night we can have dinner together."

"I'd like that," Rachel said.

Carly walked away then, pushing her half-full cart around an end cap and out of sight down an aisle. Rachel went the other way. Her heart felt lighter. She thought she and Carly could be friends. Alex's mother would be her first friend since her return to The Lake. Carly didn't know anything about Rachel as a child or a teenager. Other than the slanted newspaper account of her disappearance and return, the two would start from an equal place. Again the place felt right to her.

Rachel looked in her cart. She had enough stuff. In fact, she had too much. She should either return some of it or leave the store. As she headed for the checkout counter, she saw Bill and Jess outside in the parking lot. She recognized Jess. She'd seen him that night at the center, but didn't know his name. She'd also seen him in the furniture store and now here.

Rachel started placing her stuff on the counter. She shrugged off her suspicions. There was a perfectly natural reason for him to be in the same places she was. It had nothing to do with witness security. She was being paranoid.

She looked through the huge glass windows again. Bill waved good-bye and headed for his car, a large parcel of diapers tucked under his arm. Jess turned his gaze toward the store and by the shiver that ran down her spine, Rachel would swear he looked directly into her eyes.

Chapter Ten

There was a contingent of people waiting on Rachel's porch when she pulled into the driveway. Alex was one and about six others lounged about. Some of them had books open and were reading. Some were writing and a few were talking to each other. Rachel wondered what was going on.

"Hello," she said as she got out of the Jeep.

"Hi, Rachel." Alex jumped down from the porch, not stepping on any of the four steps that led to the ground. "These guys wanted to come by and help, if that's all right."

"Help? With what?"

"Alex told us you were remodeling and how much she was learning." A young man with patrician good looks, long arms, and long hands spoke. "We thought after the center we could help you with some of the heavy work." He glanced at the four other young men behind him.

All of them stood. "We've done our homework and I worked on your roof," another said. He looked as if he should be at football practice, thick neck and shoulders as wide as a mountain.

If Alex couldn't see the real reason these guys were here, Rachel could. They looked at Rachel, but the four of them often glanced at Alex. Their gazes had the look of interest, boy-girl interest, budding-love interest.

"Homework?"

"They're all in summer school with me," Alex answered. "It will be over next week."

"I can't wait," one of them said. Rachel saw the relief on several faces at the prospect of ending school and having the rest of the summer to themselves.

"Is it all right?" Alex asked. "I didn't promise them anything for sure."

Rachel smiled. "Of course it's all right."

They went inside and Alex immediately began explaining what had been done and what needed to be completed. She checked with Rachel before setting two people to painting the newly finished Sheetrock walls of Rachel's downstairs office. Two others went to work cleaning up the debris that had been strewn about as they did the construction. All the walls were now built and finishing was necessary.

"Alex said you had some lighting problems." Rachel believed the girl addressing her was named Amy.

"I do. It's too dark for me. I like plenty of light."

"My dad's a board-certified electrician. He said he'd come by and help out." Just then there was a knock on the door. "Dad," Amy called.

He stepped inside. Rachel went to meet him. "Dad, this is Ms. Rachel Wells. My father, Mr. Winters."

"Josh," he said and Rachel took his hand and shook it. He was dressed in worn khaki pants with a leather tool belt around his waist. "I'm here to work."

"Here's the drawing." Alex came up with the plans that Rachel had shown her when she'd initially come and watched Rachel work.

Josh took the papers and looked at them, then at the walls and ceilings. "Do you have the lights?"

Rachel nodded. She led him to the kitchen where she'd stored the lights. They were still in the boxes they'd come in with neatly written labels as to which room and which wall or ceiling they were to be mounted on.

"I've pulled the wires through for the sockets and the sconces in the bathroom."

Josh walked through the house, amid the painting and clearing and one student working a refinishing machine on the kitchen floor. He nodded his approval as he checked her work.

"Campbell teach you to do this?"

Rachel nodded. "Did you know my father?"

"And your mother," he said nodding. "Your dad taught me to swim. I was sorry to hear that he'd passed on."

"Thank you."

"Now, let me tackle these lights."

Rachel found herself with almost nothing to do. Moments after Josh arrived, the football player's father showed up. He worked in home security and installed her new system. With all those people working, it was like a movie running at two times the normal speed. Three hours after they arrived practically everything was done. All she needed was furniture and a long bath.

By the time Sam pulled up, the whole contingent was sitting on the kitchen floor eating pizza and drinking cola.

"What's going on here?" he asked.

"We finished," Alex said proudly. "Well, except for the porch swing and the window."

"What window?" Rich, the football player's father, asked. He'd just installed a security system that included every window in the place.

"The big moon window."

"It hasn't arrived yet," Rachel said. "The wall leading down to the water will be a huge moon window."

"Here's a picture." Alex got up and handed the brochure with the window to Rich.

"Beautiful," he said, passing it on to Sam.

"Wow!" he said. "It's almost a glass house."

"No," Rachel countered. "Only one wall."

The wall would be completely removed and the half-moon window, with sections of different kinds of glass, would replace it. In the middle of the glass was a door that opened onto the patio leading to the beach.

"Call me when it's installed. I'll come back and wire it to the system."

Rachel agreed. Shortly afterward they began leaving. Rachel thanked them for their help and promised to put in a good word with the police chief regarding their community service. She said it with a smile as she looked up at Sam.

"I appreciate you coming to help. I can't believe how generous everyone is."

"A lot of us remember you and your parents," Josh told her. "It was our pleasure."

The moment the door closed, Sam turned her

into his arms and kissed her long and hard. Rachel melted into him, unable to stop the warm flow of heat that covered her like a birthing waterfall.

"Thoughts of you in my arms are the only thing that got me through the day," Sam said when he raised his head for air. He held her close, taking deep life-affirming breaths.

Rachel felt the emotion welling up inside her. What kind of magic had Sam woven over her? She was completely snared in his web. "What were all those people doing here?"

"I think I've been adopted." Rachel used the question to move away from him. She couldn't trust herself in his arms and the images of them making love last night flowed through her mind like an erotic movie. Her breasts tingled and her nipples pointed through the soft cotton T-shirt she wore as if they dared his hands to caress them. She began clearing away empty pizza boxes, pouring the residue of partially drunk colas into the sink, and dumping the wax-lined paper cups into the trash.

"What do you mean adopted?" Sam's long legs folded as he sat on a crate and lifted a slice of cold pizza from a box where Rachel had been consolidating the leftovers.

"Do you want me to heat that?" She stood reaching for the paper plate. Sam shook his head and continued eating. Rachel told him about meeting Alex's mother earlier in the day and then about the contingent waiting for her when she returned home. "They want me to come back to the center."

"They asked you?" Sam's eyebrows went up.

"Alex's mother did. Alex never said it, but her

actions make it clear. The other kids wouldn't have come if they didn't really want something."

"You make a difference. I think you should come."

"I'm no psychologist. Suppose I tell them something that ruins their lives?"

"There is only one true psychologist at the center. You can always consult with her. You won't be asked to do evaluations, just counsel some of the teenagers. Most psychology is based on common sense anyway and you have plenty of that; plus you've had psychology courses in college."

Rachel didn't remember telling him that. She dropped several handfuls of used napkins in the trash and shrugged inwardly. Maybe she had told him. In the aftermath of their lovemaking she could have said anything.

"Courses don't make up for practical experience."

"They also don't make up for the trust afforded you by those young people. And trust makes up for all the psychology courses in the world." Sam came up behind her. He put his hands on her shoulders and whispered in her ear, "You'd be good, Rachel. They need you."

"I'll come back next Tuesday and see what happens."

She finished cleaning up and the two of them walked through the house. She showed him the work that had been completed.

"All that needs to be done now is to finish the floors," Rachel said proudly. The scaffolding had been dismantled and stored in the small shed outside. Without the metal monster obstructing her walkway, she could move freely from the kitchen to the great room without being forced to weave around and through it.

"And furniture," Sam said.

"I ordered bedroom furniture today. After sleeping in your bed last night . . ." She stopped, realizing what she'd said and what images it summoned. "It's time," she finished weakly.

"You can sleep there again," Sam said seductively. "In fact, I'd like it if you slept there often." He reached for her, but Rachel sidestepped him.

"I saw Bill today."

"Oh, where was he?"

Rachel wondered about the note in his voice. "Grossman's Market out on Route 3. He was picking up diapers and talking to Jess."

"You saw Jess, too?"

"He was in the same market. Bill thought it was strange that three of us were all there at the same time."

"What three?"

Rachel noticed a change in Sam. Tension seemed to coil inside him. She hoped Jess hadn't told him he would be somewhere else. He wasn't in uniform, so she thought he was on his own time.

"Jess, me, and Carly."

He nodded, apparently remembering she'd already told him about her meeting with Carly.

He changed the subject. "When will your furniture be delivered?"

"In a week. I can hardly wait." Rachel sat down on the floor in front of the window. She'd be glad when the new window was in. Then she'd be able to see the mountains in the distance from anywhere in the room. "It's been so long since I've had a place that was really home." Sam pulled her closer, resting her head on his shoulder. "And I have to figure out that security system before I go to bed tonight."

She'd been there all this time without one, but now that it was installed she'd feel better activating it before going to sleep. Rachel suddenly smiled.

"What's so funny?" he asked.

"It's not funny, really. I was just thinking about this afternoon, all the kids and their fathers who came to help me. You want to know what I liked most about it?"

"That you found out you don't have to do everything all by yourself?"

"That too." She smiled and punched his arm softly. "But not a single person asked me how it felt to return from the dead."

In no way could this body ever be considered dead, Sam thought. He had convinced Rachel to learn her security system in the morning and spend the night with him. He made a mental note to have the system connected to the police department's monitoring facility before they left her house. If anything happened she'd have an instant response. So far everything at The Lake seemed to be normal, but he had a feeling it was false. Someone was there. He just couldn't see who yet.

But now everything was fine. Now he held Rachel to him, completely sated after making love to her. He should say she made love to him. He thought he'd lose his mind, the way she took control and brought him to the brink of ecstasy before taking them to their own private Valhalla.

She slept quietly beside him. Sam listened to her night sounds, her breathing. He watched the soft rise and fall of her breasts as she took air in and expelled it out. He'd never done this before, never thought watching a woman sleep could be erotic, yet with Rachel he wanted to pull her into his arms, feel the boneless weight of her as he placed reverent kisses over her face and neck. He wanted to coax her into wakefulness and ease her into lovemaking as if she were a flower opening to the sun's first kiss on a new day.

As he pressed his mouth against her shoulder, she stirred, but didn't awaken. He moved his arm and let her fall on her back. God, she took his breath away. She wore nothing under the covers. His body felt her heat as he watched her dark hair splay out against the pillow. He combed it through his fingers, remembering the silky feel of it. She smelled of love and a faint lemony fragrance from bath salts he'd seen in her bathroom.

Sam kissed her brow, as softly as he would that of a newborn baby. Unable to stop himself, he continued kissing her face. He gathered her to him, feeling her softness. He pressed her to him, her breasts to his chest, and his erection took on life as her legs moved over his.

"How long have you been awake?" she asked, her voice laced with the sexy depths of sleep.

"Since you returned to The Lake," he said, kissing her ear.

Her tinkle of laughter sent shivers through him. She moved her head back and looked at him. Sam kissed her mouth. Long, slow, drugging kisses followed, one heaped upon the next.

"Don't you have to work today?" she asked between kisses.

"No one would dare commit a crime today," he told her.

She smiled. He liked the way her face transformed. Her eyes shone and the hint of dimples in her cheeks depressed to the point that he wanted to put his tongue in them. For a long moment they looked at each other, basking in the openness of doing so. Rachel's light brown eyes fascinated him as did every inch of her.

She put her hand around his neck and pulled his mouth to hers. His body went taut and he reached for another condom before covering her with his body. Control was lost almost the moment he swung his legs over her. He kissed her mouth, but his body needed joining. He needed to be inside her. Sam wondered as the rhythm between them surged if he would ever be completely satisfied by Rachel. She drew something out of him, but she also filled a well inside his being, yet it was a phantasmal well. It filled but was never full.

He heard her moans, her lovemaking sounds. Her mouth was against his ear and Sam would never forget them. Each place he touched produced an erotic response. He drove her to fever pitch, but the act also pushed him closer and closer to a breaking point.

Finally he entered her, capturing her pleasure-scream like the braided links of a dream catcher that could hold all the sounds and pleasures of their lovemaking. Tidal waves of sensation coursed through him as Rachel's hands smoothed over his skin, while her legs held him prisoner. Their bodies had come together, creating fire, burning for each other, conquering walls and wars and showing them a place where possibilities were endless.

Sam's scream came on the wings of completion, on a high level of need that found its source and sank into it until he could only accept the power it lorded over him. Sam fell against Rachel, trying unsuccessfully to keep his weight from crushing the breath out of her.

She didn't appear to mind his weight. Her hands affectionately touched his back, skimming over his skin and painting circles in his flesh. He'd never felt so complete in his life.

After a minute, he felt her labored breathing and rolled away from her. She came with him, her hands still rubbing his skin. When she reached his scar, the hand stopped.

"What's that?" she asked, but didn't raise her head to look at it.

"A scar."

"From?"

"A bullet."

Rachel sat up and looked at the place where her hand was. Sam didn't move. Vainly he often covered it, making sure he didn't buy shorts or trunks that rode his hips lower than the point of the bullet's impact.

"This is the one you nearly died from." It was a statement. He wondered how she knew. "Bill didn't tell me the story. He only said you'd nearly died and that afterward you'd returned to The Lake for good."

Sam lay back against the sheets. He pulled the covers over the two of them, but didn't try to hide the scar.

"It was the same night," he began. "The night I shot P.J. When I realized it was her and not one of the guys from the house, I started down the alley. My mind was on her. Like a rookie, I forgot all the rules and regulations of police work. I was intent on saving my partner. Suddenly, as I neared that broken window, an arm came out and a single shot was fired. It hit me before I knew what happened. I was still running. I'd passed the window before I fell."

He stopped, feeling the scar and Rachel's hand, which hadn't moved. "I woke up in intensive care. I'd been there for five days. After I recovered I returned to DPD, but it wasn't the same. The fight had gone out of me and I decided to come back and try crime from the other side of the law table."

"Only you never did."

He looked at her. Her head was tilted back and she was looking at him. "I never did."

Rachel guessed she could say she had her first job. In her twenty-six years she'd never had a scheduled place to be. Her life was abnormal at best. Having a set day and time to report was unusual for her. The center was the first job she'd actually had and she loved it. In college she'd studied business administration thinking she would work in an office when she graduated, but when one of her courses dealt with the stock market she became very interested in how it worked.

She'd dabbled in it with the money she'd made working at the campus library and found she had a knack for buying and selling at all the right times. Her father had worked in investments and it had landed them in Witsec. She supposed she'd inherited some of his aptitude for the profession. Telling no one about the account she'd opened on the Internet or the amount of money she'd amassed, she knew she'd never have to work unless she chose to do so.

Pulling to a stop in front of the center on Tuesday night, she got out of the Jeep. Alex stood waiting for her.

"Hi," she said, standing next to Brian, the football jock who'd helped out at Rachel's house.

"Hello." Rachel pulled her purse strap onto her shoulder and glanced back. The feeling was there. It was always there and it was making her crazy. Why did she feel as if someone's eyes were always on her? Well, not always. When she was with Sam she could think of nothing else. That in itself scared her, but it was a wonderful kind of fear. She smiled to herself.

"Ms. Wells," Brian said instead of hello. She'd told them they could call her Rachel, but Brian said Officer Sam wouldn't allow it. Respect for older people had to be learned as well as how to place roof tiles. Alex was the only one allowed to call her by her first name.

Brian shifted from foot to foot, but Rachel could tell he was besotted by Alex and she appeared to return the sentiment.

"What are you two doing here? I thought you had finished your community service."

"We thought we'd come by and help out," Alex said.

"It is your first week," Brian explained as if he thought she needed support.

Rachel looked over her shoulder again. "Alex,

how are you and your mom doing?" They started moving toward the entrance. Alex shrugged and frowned, telegraphing to her that things were not the best they could be.

At the door she looked back again. "Are you looking for someone?" Brian asked.

"No," she said too quickly. "It's just a feeling."

"What kind of feeling?" Alex was all concern.

Rachel put her hand on her young friend's arm. "Like someone's watching me." She looked around again and forced a smile. "It's nothing to be concerned about. I'm just being paranoid. It's probably a by-product of resurrection. When you rise from the dead you have to expect people to be curious." They all laughed, but Rachel felt better when the center door closed behind them.

The night was very different from her previous venture. It was as if it were designed to test her decision to take this on. Rachel was assigned a permanent group. Alex wasn't in it. The counselor for her group had returned. Rachel's new group bickered and argued with one another for the first twenty minutes.

"That's enough," she said, standing up. "You're supposed to be young adults. You're going to start acting like it tonight."

They stared at her as if she'd suddenly materialized before their eyes. Sam gave her a look from across the room. He didn't come over, allowing her to handle the group in her own way. He'd said it was common sense and this made sense to her.

"Now." She smiled. "The first thing you need to do is realize you're all different, no better than each other, just different, and being different is a good thing. It's what made this country survive."

"How would you know? "You old, but you ain't that old." The group snickered.

"You're Glenda, right?" She didn't answer Rachel, only gave her a wide-eyed stare. "All right, Miss Glenda with a'tude. I'm not here to be your friend, although I would like to be. This is my second time here. I suppose it's your first." She looked at all the faces staring at her and the interplay going on between her and the young girl wearing too much makeup and clothes a size too small. Rachel was sure the clothes were her choice. They accentuated her bust and hips, giving off both the rebellious look to parental authority and the sexual awareness of her own young body. Rachel wanted to ask her about her mode of dress, but in this forum she would only get more and more defensive.

"Look, I gotta be here for two hours. Nobody said I had to talk."

Rachel nodded. "You just be quiet then and close your ears to anything that anyone else might say."

Her next trial began by asking the name of a kid hanging in the back. He looked timid and had a bad case of acne, but he blew up like a sudden hurricane at her question. The rest of the group took the same posture and she gave it her best. When it was time to let them go she was exhausted.

The other groups were breaking up. She heard the scraping of chairs and her own group took the signal to get ready too.

"Just a moment." She raised her voice above the noise. They stopped, but looked skeptical. "This hasn't been the best start, but I'd like you to know that I'll be back next Tuesday and the Tuesday after that until you get out of this program and another group comes in." She paused. "I know you act like it's a burden to have to go through this. It's a burden being a teenager, having no one *older* understand you." She smiled, indicating herself, and was rewarded when a couple of them smiled back. "If you want to talk without the group around, I'm sure you all know where I live." That caused a few giggles. "Good night."

Alex came over, Brian in tow, as the group dispersed. "How'd it go?" she asked.

"I think they hate me." Rachel spread her hands in defeat.

"Don't let it get to you," Brian said. This was the first time he'd said more than a greeting. "We were the same way at first."

"Well, I promised them, or rather I warned them, I would be back next week."

"Good," Alex said. Rachel could see a change in her. She appeared happier. It bothered Rachel that Alex and Carly weren't getting along well, but she could rack that up to hormonal changes in the seventeen-year-old. If Carly could be patient, Alex would straighten herself out.

"How'd it go for you two?"

"We were in Officer Sam's group. He's really stern with the kids, but they know he cares. Otherwise he'd have sent us to juvie hall instead of here."

Sam picked that moment to join them. Rachel wanted to move toward him, to slip her arm around his waist and lean into his strong body. But she remained still.

"See ya later," Alex said. "There's a game going on upstairs and they're waiting for us. Bye, Officer Sam."

Both Sam and Rachel turned to watch the teenagers leave. "She looks like a different person," Rachel said.

"What's this she tells me about someone following you?"

Rachel tried to laugh it off. "It's nothing. No one is following me. I have this weird feeling sometimes." Rachel looked around for her purse. She didn't want Sam to make anything of it. "I'm so used to having to look over my shoulder that I can't stop doing it."

Sam took her shoulders and turned her to face him. "Are you sure?"

"Sam, stop being a cop." She shrugged out of his grasp. "The is Lake Como, not Detroit. There is no one following me." As she said it she tried not to shiver. It *was* just a feeling. "If it makes you happy," she said seductively, "I feel perfectly safe when I'm with you."

Rachel expected a sexual response from Sam, at least a smile, but his face was straight and unreadable.

"Sam, is anything wrong? Do you know something I don't?"

"Of course not." He wrapped his arms around her. Rachel hugged him, fitting her body into his and forgetting everything except the comfort of his arms. "I'll see you home."

"Mine or yours?"

"Mine," he whispered and with his arm around her, led her toward the exit.

This was the third furniture store Rachel had been to and she'd found nothing she liked well enough to buy. She, Carly, and Alex were a hundred miles from The Lake and the most they had to show for their day was a good lunch and matching hats to keep the sun out of their eyes.

Carly excused herself from the table where the three had just finished eating to go to the ladies' room.

"Are things getting better?" Rachel asked.

"A little," Alex said, screwing her face up. Rachel knew that didn't mean a bad thing. It was a teenage thing. "We talk a little more when she's home. I'm surprised she isn't at work now. She works seven days a week." Alex glanced at the seat where her mother had been sitting.

"If my father—"

"Stop," Rachel interrupted. "You can't bring him back. You have to accept the world as it is. And go on. You can do that. It's not her fault that he died. And it's not her fault that she has to work to support you."

Alex's face dropped and she scooped a spoonful of ice cream into her mouth. Rachel knew she was talking to herself and to Alex. She'd given herself the same lecture after her parents left her alone in the world. She was older than Alex and she should be more mature, but her own life had been a series of controlled incidents. What she wouldn't give to be able to fight with her mother again.

The waiter showed two men to the table next to them. As their movement was close, Rachel glanced in their direction, then back at Alex. She was waiting for the girl to say something, but the voice she heard came from the next table.

"Did you see who that was?" one of them said. Rachel heard the comment and couldn't help following the direction the man was pointing out. It surprised her to find them staring at the disappearing back of Carly Lytelle.

"What's *she* doing here and looking like a real woman, not a boss?" the other asked. "Someone must have died to get her out of that plant and off some poor guy's back."

Alex tensed and Rachel covered her hand on the table to stop her from saying anything.

"Since she came here everything has changed," the men continued. "She's so fired up about efficiencies and production schedules that a man can't get in a good break. And this take-it-apart-and-do-it-right is getting on my nerves."

"Well, she won't be here much longer. We gave McLemore an earful when he came to inspect the operation."

"McLemore is the company president," Alex whispered to Rachel.

The guys laughed. "Won't she be surprised when they toss her out on that cute little tush of hers?"

"Then they can give the job back to a man who deserves it and we can go back to business as usual."

Rachel saw Carly come around the corner from the ladies' room and start for the table. She smiled at them as she wove her way through the busy restaurant. When she saw the men at the next table her smile faltered. She looked away for a second, checking her course to the table. When her head came up her smile was back in place.

Carly stopped at the men's table for a moment and exchanged a sociable word. Her back was to Rachel and Alex and they couldn't distinguish any words of her soft, musical voice.

"Mom—" Alex said when she sat down.

"Ready," Rachel said, cutting her off. "I'll get the check and we'll head out." She signaled their waiter.

"Do they always treat you bad at work, Mom?"

Carly didn't get a chance to answer. Despite Alex lowering her voice, the men at the other table heard her question.

"We don't treat you badly, do we, Ms. Lytelle?"

Rachel butted in. "Sorry to break this up, but if we're going to get to the next store we'd better move," She rose from her seat and Carly followed suit. Carly took Alex's hand and the three of them left the restaurant.

Rachel saw Carly take a deep breath when they were outside. She'd appeared happy and carefree for most of the morning, but now she looked as if someone had dropped boulders on her.

"Mom?" Alex was persistent.

Outside the restaurant were tables scattered about that people used to wait for seats inside. Carly walked over to one and sat down. Alex and Rachel also took seats.

"Alex, I don't want to bother you with this."

"Tell me."

"Tell her, Carly," Rachel agreed. "She should know what's going on in your life too."

Carly pondered this for only a moment before she looked at her daughter and started talking. "First, Alex, I want you to know that I am dealing with it and that it isn't everyone in the plant. Only a small faction of men who think this job belongs to a man."

"What do they do?" Alex asked, her voice lowered.

"They undermine me, claim they didn't get

order notices when they did, send out the wrong shipments or send them to the wrong clients. It's why I'm there day and night seeing that things are done right."

"Why don't you fire them and hire better people who will do what you want?" It was a simple solution from Alex's point of view.

"It's not that easy, Alex. It might come to that, but I'm hoping to get them on my side. The community around Lake Como is small and close and firing them might create more problems than solutions."

"Mom, I'm so sorry." Alex hugged Carly. Rachel saw the two of them grow closer in that moment. "I thought you were just trying to get ahead. I didn't know you had to fight to just do the job."

As Rachel wasn't really in the mood to shop anymore they decided to return to The Lake. Carly kept up a running conversation with Alex on things that had nothing to do with the plant or her problems there. Alex shared how she felt about her newfound popularity. Rachel and Carly found out Alex and Brian were no longer an item. But they *were* friends, Alex insisted.

Rachel listened, but stayed out of the mother-daughter conversation, leaving the two to talk as much as possible. Rachel drove along the highway, the Jeep eating up the miles. There wasn't much traffic today and the trees along the roadside provided a beautiful and peaceful scene for driving.

Rachel checked the rearview mirror. A black van was behind her. She was sure she'd seen it before. This highway was well traveled and the van could just be going in the same direction she was, but she had the feeling it was following her. She changed lanes. It changed lanes. She sped up. It sped up. She slowed down. It slowed down.

"What are you doing?" Carly asked.

Rachel noticed Alex and Carly were no longer talking.

"I'm not sure," she said. "But I believe we're being followed."

Carly and Alex both jerked around and looked out the back window. Rachel was unsure what she should do. She was too far from home to call Sam. And she wasn't even sure if they were actually being followed.

"It's the guys from the restaurant," Carly said.

"Are you sure?" Rachel asked.

"I know one of them has a black van. Who else could it be?"

"I don't know. What do you think they want?"

"To scare us."

"But on a road and with cars? We could have an accident and someone could really get hurt."

Rachel kept checking the mirror. They were getting closer, playing a deadly game of cat and mouse. She couldn't see through the windows; even the front ones had been illegally tinted.

"Alex, get my purse and find my cell phone," Rachel told the young girl.

"I got it."

"Call Sam. I have the police department under P."

"Sam's too far," Carly said.

"I know. Tell him I think we're being followed by a black van." She glanced in the mirror again. "I can't see a license tag number."

Carly turned around. "I can't see it either."

"Alex, tell him we're on Highway 3 in Dalton and that we need the local police."

Rachel heard the young girl asking to speak to Sam and then her controlled speech as she calmly related what was going on.

"He says stay on the highway. He'll have someone here in a moment. And drive carefully." She listened and continued saying things every few seconds.

"Make sure your seat belts are tight," Rachel said. She sped up as the van behind her got closer. "He's going to ram us."

"Where's a cop when you need one?" Carly muttered and braced her arms against the dashboard.

Impact snapped them forward and back against the seats. Alex screamed. Rachel kept control of the Jeep. She moved left, but the van moved with her. Depressing the accelerator, she inched the speed up several miles an hour. She was already pushing eighty.

"Mom, I'm scared," Alex said. Carly turned around in her seat to grab her daughter's hand.

"We were rammed," Alex said, still talking to Sam. Her voice had lost its calm and hysteria was replacing it.

"Alex, lie down on the seat and make sure you're strapped in," Rachel called. "Use the blanket in the back and put it against the door above your head, keep your feet on the floor."

She didn't know what the van would do, but Alex was the closest person to the impact.

"Yes, we're still here," Alex said. The van rammed them a second time. Alex dropped the phone and Carly reached for her. Rachel thought she heard Sam shouting into the phone.

The van was trying to get alongside her. She

knew letting it get to the side would mean whoever was driving could force her off the road. She bit her lip as she wove back and forth over the line keeping the van behind her and fighting to keep control of the Jeep. Thankful that the car hugged the road well and that she could switch to four-wheel drive on the fly, boosted her confidence but did nothing for the tension that increased inside her.

Her foot was on the floor now and the car would go no faster. If the police didn't find them soon she didn't know how much longer she could fight the van off. It rammed them again. Rachel felt as if someone had punched her in the back. The shoulder harness dug into her arm, and although it kept her from banging her head on the steering wheel, it didn't prevent her head from snapping forward and back. Or the split second when she had jerked the steering wheel and drove off the road.

Carly drew in a strangled breath. Rachel pulled back onto the road, the sound of loose gravel spitting against the metal hull. Yet she kept the van behind her. Farther back she saw the flashing lights of a police car.

"The police are coming," she said.

Carly looked over her shoulder. Rachel hit a pothole in the road. She saw it, but couldn't avoid it in time. It threw the Jeep sideways. She fought the steering wheel, but knew she was going to hit the guardrail. "Brace yourself," she screamed. The sound of metal crunching metal had her gritting her teeth. For the space of a lifetime the Jeep rode the rail. The van took advantage and pulled alongside her. It banged into the passenger side. They were crunched between the rail and the van. And it was trying to force them over.

Rachel looked ahead of her. The railing ended about fifty yards in front of her. If she didn't get out of this crunch in time, they'd be pushed down a gully. At this speed the Jeep would roll over. The police car was closer, but not close enough. Rachel hit the brake. She heard the squeal of tires, smelled the rubber burning as layers of it peeled off her tires.

Like a carnival ride, the van went forward, they went backward. The bumper was ripped off the van and they rolled over it. Like the pothole, it changed the direction of the Jeep. It spun around in a full circle, fishtailing backward like some improbable dance routine. Rachel tried to stop it, but the laws of physics were steadfast and unchangeable. Momentum whipped the Jeep like loose string. It wove across the highway, a slingshot released from a Y-frame, and catapulted into the side of the mountain. Rachel heard an explosion as the air bags deployed. Then nothing.

The constant beep of electronic machinery pierced her ears. Rachel's eyes felt heavy and her head ached. All of her ached. She tried to swallow and that hurt too. The accident, she thought. Was she dying? She opened her eyes. Sam was standing over her. She was in a room, a hospital. Sam's face was dark with concern. He hadn't shaved and looked as if he hadn't slept in days.

"You look terrible," Rachel said. He burst into

laughter, as if her words had broken a tension inside him. It was the beach laugh. She heard his sound. It was here, greeting her, familiar and welcome.

"How do you feel?" he finally asked.

"Like I've been flattened by a steamroller. What about Alex and Carly?"

"They're fine," he told her as she became agitated. "Carly has a fractured bone in her arm. She'll wear a cast for a few weeks. Alex is a bit shaken, but hasn't got a scratch. They've both been released."

"Am I hurt bad?"

He shook his head.

"You have a concussion, some cuts and bruises, other than that, you'll be fine."

"Can I have some water?"

Sam poured water into a Styrofoam cup, added a plastic straw, and held her up while she sipped it.

"I have a headache," she said when he lowered her back to the pillow.

"The doctor said it's to be expected. It will go away soon." He took her hand and held it.

"When can I go home?"

"Tomorrow. They want to observe you because of the concussion." Sam brushed her hair back. Rachel wondered what she looked like, but was afraid to ask. "Alex and Carly want you to come to them when you're released. I agree. You shouldn't be in that house with no furniture and no help."

"All right." He might have expected her to fight him, but on this point she had no energy. Rachel felt totally beaten. Each part of her was as heavy as lead and she was too tired to defend herself. She wondered what time it was. How long had she been in the hospital? But she couldn't ask the question. Her eyes closed and the only thing she felt beyond the pain was the pressure of Sam's hand.

When she opened her eyes again the room was much darker than it had been. Carly was holding her hand and Alex was asleep in the chair next to the bed.

"Hi," Rachel said, twisting her hand and alerting Carly that she was awake. She felt a little better. Her headache was gone and her eyelids didn't feel as if they had weights on them. "How long have you been here?"

"I took over for Sam. I wasn't sure I could get him to leave, but there are things a police chief has to do." Carly's left arm was bandaged and in a sling.

"Did they catch the van?" Rachel asked.

Carly looked away, shaking her head. "It wasn't the guys from the plant."

"Who was it?"

"We don't know. The police car stopped when it saw the Jeep hit the mountain. The guys in the restaurant didn't leave until after we'd already had the accident. The only explanation the police could come up with is random violence."

Rachel couldn't believe it. Why would someone just decide to run a car off the road? This wasn't road rage. It was deliberate. But it made no sense. Yet she knew there were people in the world who did those kinds of things. She just didn't think she'd encounter them at Lake Como.

"How's your arm?" She changed the subject, wanting to move her thoughts away from the path they were heading, places that involved the U.S.

Marshal's Service, high crimes, and even higher liars. Thankfully that part of her life was over.

"I'll be fine." Carly smiled. "It's my left arm so I'll be able to return to work."

Rachel looked over at Alex. "Do you think you could take a couple of days off and spend them with Alex? She's had a trauma and could use a mother right now."

Carly looked at her daughter. Alex hadn't stirred. She was curled up in the chair, her knees cramped against the armrest. Someone, Carly perhaps, had put a hospital blanket over her.

"Of course I will," Carly said. "I'm ashamed I didn't think of it myself. She's growing so fast. In another year she'll be gone off to college and only home for breaks and holidays." Rachel smiled and squeezed Carly's hand.

"Mothers and daughters don't lose the bond between them. They stretch it sometimes, even to the breaking point, before discovering how much they need each other. She'll always be there when you need her."

Carly nodded. "I can't tell you the horrible things that went through my mind when that van was ramming us." She paused, throwing another look at her daughter in the chair before saying, "I'm afraid your Jeep is a total loss. It's a good thing we only bought those hats." Carly used her right hand to plop hers on her head. "Alex insisted on bringing them."

"Who knows? Maybe they were our good luck charms."

"I don't know," Carly said. "I think a lot of it had to do with your ability to drive like you did. Who taught you to do that? And telling Alex to lie down probably saved her life."

"My father taught me a lot of survival techniques."

"I'm glad you were driving and not me. I could never have gotten away from that van. And even though we had an accident, we all survived."

When Sam came to get Carly and Alex and drive them back to The Lake, Rachel didn't immediately fall asleep. The medication had kicked in and she was temporarily pain-free. She lay in the twilight thinking, wondering who had wanted them dead and why. The thought of Graziano and his family came to mind. She didn't quickly discard it. Maybe there was someone after her. Maybe it wasn't over. Maybe Aaron McKnight had lied to her again.

She stopped, turning over and staring at the machines that beeped in rhythmic insistence. She could drive herself crazy with maybes. Sam could investigate it, but there was nothing to go on. They had no description of who was driving. They couldn't see a license tag. Even when the van was ramming them, there was no visible tag. And it got away.

Rachel had so many questions and no answers. Nothing she thought of made any sense. Not even that the van could have targeted Carly or Alex. It didn't have to be her. Carly was having trouble at the plant, but was it worth killing her over? Rachel didn't think the men in the restaurant knew she was going to be there. They were surprised to see her. And how could anyone know they would be that far from home? Going shopping that far had been a spur-of-the-moment decision.

The nurse came in. "How are you feeling?" she asked.

"All right," Rachel said without committing.

The white-clad women with starched white hats were a thing of old movies. Wearing rumpled blue pants and a pink and blue patterned nurse's top, she looked young and comfortable. She placed a cuff on Rachel's arm and slipped the earpieces of the stethoscope in her ears. She took Rachel's blood pressure and smiled. "It's fine," she said, "126 over 82." Her fingers were soft and strong as they took her pulse. "Good," she pronounced, then pumped something into Rachel's IV drip. "This should take effect in a few minutes. Do you want me to turn off the lights?"

Only the light above her head was on. The room lights had been turned off by a previous nurse before her shift changed. Rachel didn't immediately answer and the nurse mistook her silence for anxiety. "I'm sure you don't have anything to worry about. Your young man posted a guard outside your door. You just rest easy." She patted the bed and with a smile left the room, leaving the light burning.

In minutes Rachel closed her eyes. She was getting drowsy. The questions started to blur together. She found it hard to concentrate. The only thing she knew for certain, that she was positively sure of, was that the encounter with the van didn't end in this hospital room amid an assemblage of beeping machines.

It wasn't over.

Chapter Eleven

"What happened?" Sam stood in his kitchen nearly shouting into the phone. A long-neck beer dangled from one hand as he pressed the phone against his ear with the other. "How could you let her out of your sight? She could have been killed, along with two other innocent people. What the hell is going on over there?"

"Calm down, Hairston," the man at the other end said. "It was a mishap. One we couldn't have foreseen."

"I thought you were prepared for every eventuality. Weren't those the words you used when you explained this operation to me? Nothing could go wrong."

"It was a flat tire. A simple flat tire. And she was driving like she regularly played the NASCAR circuit."

"Another comment like that and I'll reach through this phone line and pull your throat out through your mouth."

The quiet on the other end of the phone was long and pregnant. Sam rolled the cold bottle over his face and neck, trying to calm himself down. He didn't need McKnight to tell him he'd lost his objectivity.

"All right," Sam said in a calmer voice. "I know I was out of line, but these are people I know, friends. I just want to keep them safe."

"I understand," McKnight said.

Sam knew he meant he understood that Sam was emotionally involved with Rachel Wells. What he didn't know was Sam was past emotionally involved. He was in love with her and he was doing his damnedest to keep her alive in an operation where he was rapidly coming to realize her other protectors viewed her as expendable.

"Have you found out anything about the van?"

"Nothing we can use."

Sam winced. It wasn't the answer he wanted to hear. They were U.S. Marshals, an arm of the FBI. Why couldn't they find a single black van?

"We found the van about ten miles from the crash site. It was burned to a crisp. No bodies were found with it. We assumed they fled on foot. We are combing the woods looking for them."

"What about the tags? Have you run them?"

"Yes, the van belongs to a couple from Caulder who have been away on a European cruise for the past week. According to their daughter, the van was parked at the airport."

"Dead end." Sam said it out loud although he didn't realize it until McKnight replied.

"I'm afraid so. We'll keep trying. Maybe we can find the driver."

"Thanks."

Sam was about to hang up when McKnight spoke again. "There's something you can do."

"What?"

"Find out if Ms. Wells suspects anything."

Sam hung up without responding. He wanted to strangle McKnight. Rachel had nearly lost her life and he wanted to know if his operation had been compromised. Sam knew now why he'd wanted to get out of law enforcement. The shooting in Detroit had been a catalyst. He had a law degree he'd never used. And McKnight had capped the decision. He knew law enforcement wasn't where he wanted his life to go.

He liked working with the kids. When this was over, he was resigning, turning in his metaphorical tin star, and working with them full time. He might even go into the classroom. But the law and all its machinations would no longer be part of the definition that made up Samuel Ahrend Hairston.

But for the moment he had a job to do. Sam went to the desk in the corner and pulled out the file he'd hidden behind the computer. He sat down and opened it. An eight-by-ten color glossy of Rachel fell onto his legs and he picked it up and scrutinized it. For a long moment all he did was look at her face, staring deep into her eyes as if he could make the single-planed image change into the living, breathing woman.

He read over the file again. It was the fifteenth or twentieth time he had gone over the details of her disappearance, of her father's part in the Graziano trial and their success at adjusting. The details were sketchy, only what McKnight thought he needed to know.

Rachel had filled in some of the details, but there was much more to her story than what was written on these few sheets of paper. The phone rang then. Sam shuffled everything back into the folder and dropped it behind the computer before picking up the receiver.

As he spoke he stared at the back of the computer's screen. The folder poked out a bit. Rachel's eyes looked at him sideways, as she did sometimes in bed when she rolled onto her side. He savored the feelings of her in that position and drowned in those amber-gold eyes.

"Hi." Leanne came into the room with a wide smile on her face. Rachel looked up in surprise. "How are you feeling?"

"I'm fine," Rachel told her. "It was only a slight concussion."

"I was amazed when Sam called me and of course this morning it's the lead story in the newspaper."

Rachel groaned.

"Yep, Lori Stiles strikes again."

"She wasn't even here. At least I never saw her."

"You'll learn that Lori doesn't need to actually interview the parties to write a story."

Rachel was aware of that from her first encounter with the woman and the subsequent release of the story on her return.

"Thanks for coming to see me, but I'm being released this morning."

"I know. I'm your chauffeur. Sam couldn't make it. He enlisted me to come and get you."

Rachel loved Leanne, but she was a little disappointed that Sam wouldn't be with her.

"Although, when I saw Cindy, I was surprised he asked me."

"Saw who?"

"Cindy Wornersmith. You know. One of Sam's officers. I saw her in the lobby. If she was already here, she could have driven you back. But I'd have jumped at the chance anyway. We'll have at least an hour to talk."

Leanne walked next to the orderly who wheeled Rachel to the exit. Leanne quickly got into her vehicle, a black customized SUV with the mural of a western sunset on the side. Leanne's husband, in addition to being an engineer, was both an artist and a nature lover.

For a short moment Rachel remembered the black van that had run her off the road and memories of her near-death had her heart beating fast. Gritting her teeth, she closed her eyes and waited for the moment to pass. Then lifting herself stiffly out of the wheelchair, she climbed into the passenger seat.

The orderly handed her her purse and the hat that had started the previous day in such delight. He snapped her seat belt across her and Leanne leaned over and thanked him. Rachel put the hat on her head.

Leanne pulled away from the entrance slowly and entered the quiet street where the hospital sat. No words were exchanged between them until they reached the entrance to the highway.

"What happened, Rachel? Sam didn't say much, only that you'd been in an accident. The paper this morning said a black van had forced you off the road."

"That's what happened. I was out looking for furniture. The construction is finally finished in the house and Carly and Alex were helping me find things for the rooms." Rachel recounted the events of yesterday afternoon. "Sam thinks it's random violence. I have to agree with him."

Leanne glanced at her. "Do you think it has anything to do with you being in the witness program?"

Rachel shook her head, but in the back of her mind she had thought of it. "I was never the target of that program. Everyone involved is dead. I'm sure one has nothing to do with the other. It's more likely, as Sam said, random violence."

"Things have changed around here in the last ten years. We never had much crime and still don't compared to cities like New York and Rochester, but it's more than we've ever had."

"I just don't understand it," Rachel said.

"I know, honey." Leanne's voice was full of sympathy. "Try not to think about it. I'll be careful and drive slowly. I'll get us home."

"I'm not afraid of the road," Rachel said. "I'm not even afraid of getting behind the wheel again. I did everything I knew to avoid the van and keep us alive."

Leanne took the SUV up from the minimum speed to the limit posted for the road. An hour later when she bypassed the turn onto Rachel's street, Rachel spoke up. "Where are we going?"

"Sam left me explicit instructions to bring you to his house."

"But I want to go home. I need a shower and clean clothes."

"I know you've been doing a lot of work in your house and that it's all done, but you have no furniture, not even a bed. After getting banged up in an accident you need someone to take care of you and Sam seems willing."

Rachel wasn't sure she liked how Leanne said *Sam seems willing*. It implied an intimacy that, even though the two of them had made love, she was still unsure of. Sam was definitely the most unusual man she'd met in her entire life. He was persuasive, confident, intelligent, and she thought he knew his limitations. Most men, even her father, felt they had no limits. If they wanted something, it was attainable. Those men had the hardest time adapting to new surroundings, new situations, and new controls. Rachel's family had been lucky in that her mother complemented her father in every way and together the two of them adapted.

"What about Carly? Didn't Sam say something about me staying with them?"

"He did, but he knew you wouldn't stay put there."

Rachel didn't agree with Leanne, but she was right. Rachel wanted her own surroundings. She felt more comfortable knowing where everything was and . . . She stopped. How to escape, had been her thought. The fact that she didn't need to know that anymore hadn't sunk in. As much as she tried, told herself she was safe, she still thought she would need to run someday and her house was the best place for her to be if the need came.

"Sam isn't home," Rachel remembered. "He's at

work. I'll be just as alone at his house as I will be in my own home, so I may as well care for myself there."

"You won't be alone. I'm staying until Sam comes."

"Leanne, I don't need a nurse."

"Well, you've got one." She spoke more sharply than Rachel had ever heard her speak. "Bask in the glory, girl." Leanne's voice was softer. "The man is obviously concerned about you. He's not in the habit of bringing accident victims to his home, so I can only infer that a little more has transpired between you two than has been printed in the local papers."

Rachel blushed, averting her face to keep Leanne from seeing the color staining her cheeks.

"What's it gonna hurt if you find out Sam Hairston has a heart? And it's bleeding for you?"

"Maybe it's not Sam, Leanne. Maybe it's me."

Rachel had worked herself into fighting mode when Sam called to say he was on his way. Leanne answered the phone and hung up without giving Rachel time to talk to him. "Sam will be here in fifteen minutes," she said. She came back to the kitchen table where Rachel was sitting and picked up the cup of tea she'd been drinking. Rinsing it and putting it in the dishwasher, she restored the kitchen to the condition she'd found it in. "I believe that's my cue to leave. I'm going to run and get my dinner started before hubby gets home." A twinkle in her eye and a wide smile accompanied Leanne's comment.

Rachel smiled and hugged her, but the moment her SUV was out of sight, Rachel left for her own cabin. She would not be held prisoner by Sam or anyone else. He should understand that. She had been closer to him than anyone else. She'd told him more about her life in Witsec than she'd shared with any of her former or her new friends. Yet knowing all this, he had her picked up and literally kidnapped until he could get away.

Rachel's footsteps beat a path through the sandy beach, up through the trees toward her house. She could hear her blood rushing in her ears, along with the pounding of her heels.

Getting to the house, she was winded and tired. Sweat beaded on her forehead and upper lip. Now that she was home, she thought better of her headlong rush through the trees. She unlocked the door and went into the great room. The room was empty and for the first time she wished there was a sofa or a bed she could lie on. She was tired and thirsty. Sitting down on the floor against the wall, she pulled her knees up and rested her head on them. Her heart pounded in her temples. Consciously she took breath into her body and let it out, trying to calm her rapidly beating heart and regain her breath.

A few minutes later she raised her head and looked around at the newly painted room. She shouldn't have been in such a mood when they went shopping. If she'd bought furniture it would probably be available for delivery in a few days. But her thoughts had been in a different place. They weren't on Carly and Alex, although outwardly she kept up a conversation. What she was really thinking of was leaving The Lake.

She understood her reasons. Sam was getting too close. Her usual action at this time in a relationship was to cool it. Stop seeing the guy. Make up an excuse why she shouldn't continue dating him. She couldn't call what she and Sam did dating. He'd taken her to a diner exactly once. They'd never watched a movie together, danced at a local club, or even visited the one and only relic of a bowling alley halfway between Lake Como and Caulder. Yet his kisses drove her nuts and making love with him offered her the promise of a life that she never imagined could be hers.

Frankly, it terrified her. She was sure that her life was not meant for any of the things that Sam's touch led her to believe. Yet she craved it, wanted it, dreamed of how things could be. Then the need to run seeped into her mind and the dilemma of staying at The Lake or finding a new place where no one knew her tore her to pieces.

Finally succumbing to thirst, Rachel got to her feet, heading for the kitchen and a bottle of water.

Sam burst through the door without knocking.

"I knew you wouldn't follow directions," he said by way of a greeting.

Rachel was startled, but recovered quickly. "I'm not your prisoner or responsibility. Stop trying to control me."

"I'm not trying to control you," he said, coming closer to her. "I'm trying to keep you safe."

"Safe from what?" she asked. "Or should I say from whom?" She'd meant her voice to be censorious, but it came out sultry and suggestive.

"You'll never be safe from me."

Rachel didn't have a comeback. Her stomach

dropped as if she'd fallen from a high mountain. She was trying to think of something to say, but every cell in her body was being used to combat the feelings rushing through her at the sight of him.

It was a losing battle, made more so the moment Sam slipped his arm through hers and dragged her body to connect with his.

"How do you feel?" he asked, his voice husky and strained. His mouth bent close to hers. She could see his half-closed eyes and feel his breath on her mouth. The combination rendered her unable to speak. She said nothing and he closed the tiny distance between them and kissed her.

Rachel went limp in his arms. As pliable as putty, as weak as Jell-O, terms Rachel would never use to describe herself, yet when Sam entered the picture she was little more than the eighty percent water that made up the human body. He could pour her into any form he wished and she'd gladly go.

She flung her arms around his neck and gave herself, full body, into the kiss he bestowed upon her.

Her arms snaked up his chest, her fingers scraping over the golden badge on his chest. Caressing the skin of his neck, she drove her hands into his hair, as her mouth attached to his. Her body turned into him, aligning itself with his strong legs and the bulky belt at his waist. Rachel forgot her anger. She let her hands rove over him. She'd missed this feeling, this out-of-body experience that turned her into someone else, someone who craved this man, who wanted to eat every inch of him and then begin her feast all over again. She'd missed the smell of him, that combination of the outdoors and the musk of his own skin. She'd missed being pressed against him, having his arms wrap around her with both strength and tenderness. She'd missed the feel of his mouth, the invading nature of his tongue as he tasted her nectar. She'd missed the fire they created, the tightness in her loins as they made themselves ready for his eventual trespass.

His mouth slid from hers. She felt his hard breathing as he kissed her throat. "I think I'm losing my mind," he moaned against her ear.

"You're taking mine with you," she answered.

His hot mouth placed wet kisses on skin that sizzled when he touched it. She could feel the steam searing off her as his lips traveled over her neck and throat. His hands opened her blouse to gain more access to naked skin. She could hear her own moans of pleasure, but she couldn't stop them. She wanted him to go on, to never stop this exquisite torture he was putting her through. She knew that torture led to a greater event.

His mouth closed over her bra and the nipple that ached for him to touch it without the separation of the cloth. It puckered and hardened at his touch. Deftly his hand released the hook at her back and her breasts, finding themselves unconfined, grew fuller in his hands.

Rachel caught her lower lip in her teeth at the pleasure that shot through her when his mouth found and circled her bare skin. She could hardly remain standing. Weakness turned her knees to jelly and she clung to him.

Fire flared around her with the suddenness of a

dam breaking. She knew if he didn't satisfy her soon she would burst into flame. Her hands went first to the belt at his waist. It was large and heavy, holding everything from his gun and cuff links to tear spray and tape. Like a madwoman she undressed him, pulling at both his clothes and hers at the same time.

Thinking only of her own satisfaction. Pulling his pants free, Sam reached into a pocket and pulled on a condom. Then she pushed him to the floor, their clothes a pallet under him. Then she took his body into her own. Penetration was heaven. Her eyes rolled back in her head as her mouth opened and let out the sound of ecstasy. Sam grasped her waist and thrust into her. Rachel cried out at the delight that fissured through her core. Sam's hands roved over her skin, creating tiny fires wherever they touched.

He took her breasts in his hands and rubbed his thumbs over the sensitized nipples. They seemed to stand at attention for him and her body moved to a rhythm created and sanctioned by some inner force that asked for no instruction and took no orders from any other part of her. Sam thrust into her as she came down to meet him. Their joining was hot, wet, and fast. She felt the familiar note of climax coming. She reached for it, stepping up the beat, hearing the ancient drums of communication in her whole body, answering them with each downward movement.

Colors formed before her eyes. Bright reds and brilliant yellows. Sam had his hands back on her waist. He pumped her up and down over him. His eyes were closed and his face contorted in rapture.

She recognized his climax, knew it was coming, and worked to make it as pleasurable for him as it was for her. Hearing his cry of completion, she threw her hair over her shoulder and with one final thrust collapsed onto him.

Rachel breathed hard, her throat as dry as the Sahara, her body spent, and her heart pumping like a bilge keeping the *Queen Elizabeth* afloat. Neither she nor Sam said anything for a long while. Rachel couldn't speak after the experience and she wasn't sure if he could either. They lay together, her on top of him, until the air around them began to cool their bodies. Sam's hands rubbed her skin, keeping her warm.

"I didn't come here for this," he said, pushing her onto the mound of clothes next to him. "I thought you'd be tired, need to sleep." He punctuated each phrase with a kiss to exposed nipples. Then he stopped. "Your bruises?" He inspected them, making Rachel self-conscious.

"They're all right. They will fade in time." Rachel pulled her blouse from the floor next to her and started to put it on.

"You're beautiful, Rachel. Even with bruises, you're the most beautiful woman I've ever seen." Sam's voice nearly cracked when he said it. She turned to look at him. His eyes were full of some emotion she couldn't read. They had just made love and she wasn't completely back to normal yet, if she ever would be. She didn't trust herself to read what was in his eyes and not what she wanted to be there.

A week later Rachel had convinced herself it was the medication that made her believe someone was out to get her while she was in the hospital. There was no van after her. Sam had been right. It was a case of random violence, nothing more.

Rachel hadn't ventured out of The Lake since Leanne brought her back. She had no vehicle and no need to leave. As far from home as she'd gone was to the Tuesday night meeting at the center. After the kids heard of her accident they were surprised to see her and maybe a little compassionate. They didn't give her the same reception as the previous week.

She felt safe in the tiny community. That feeling of being watched still came and went, but here she was on home turf. Her old friendships were being renewed and she was making new ones. Like family they insulated her from all she did not wish to endure.

Rachel had thought of leaving, but of all the places she had lived this was the only one that was really home, that felt like home.

And Sam was here.

Rachel was about to go off into one of her musings over Sam, but at that moment the doorbell rang. It was her bedroom furniture. Finally, she had her own bedroom. The deliverymen set it in place even through three changes of her mind. When they left she tore open the new sheets and started getting everything in order.

She'd just thrown the comforter open and begun straightening it when the phone rang.

"What are you doing?" Sam's voice was low and seductive.

"Making the bed," she told him.

"You have a bed?"

"It was delivered an hour ago."

"We'll have to try it out."

She heard him laugh on the other end of the line. Rachel smiled herself and heat rushed into her face.

"I called about dinner tonight."

"If you cook, I'll eat," she said lightly.

He laughed again. The sound did something to her.

"I'm not asking you to cook. I thought you'd like to have dinner at my place."

"Candlelight and chocolate?"

"Required menu items."

"What time?"

"Seven o'clock."

"Should I dress?"

"It's optional."

Rachel laughed. "I mean, should I dress up?"

"I stand by my former answer."

"I'll see you at seven." She hung up with a smile and a warm feeling. The bedroom looked great when she had everything in place. The comforter was a soft rose color with satin ribbons running through it. The walls were white, but with a deep maroon border at chair rail height from the floor. The rug was the same color maroon.

She turned completely around, feeling a part of the cabin. This was where she was meant to be, she told herself.

Tonight she would sleep here. But first she was having dinner with Sam. She wished she had something pretty to wear. Most of her wardrobe was made up of jeans and T-shirts. She had a couple of dresses, but nothing that could show herself off the way she'd like Sam to see her.

Rachel caught a glimpse of herself in the mirror. She looked out of place in her feminine room.

But she had a plan.

* * *

Everything was ready. The food was warming in the oven and Sam had run upstairs and showered and dressed. Straightening his tie, he skipped down the stairs anticipating Rachel's arrival. He'd thought of nothing else all day. Since he'd called her she'd been on his mind. He planned the menu in his head, made a mental note to pick up the perfect wine to complement it, and called Doris out at the Castle to order a chocolate dessert no woman could resist.

He had lit the candles a moment ago and now turned around to get the salad from the refrigerator. Rachel walked through the archway from the dining room and he nearly lost it. He'd never seen her look so beautiful. She wore an elegant white dress made of some soft fabric that combined nothing with its message of sex. It begged to be smoothed and caressed. He wanted to take her in his arms and run his hands over her breasts and hips, down her long, long legs, and over her polished toes.

The dress hung from one shoulder to the floor, taking its time by defining every curve on her well-stacked frame like a road map twisting down a mountain road. Her hair was swung to one side and cascaded over a bare shoulder. The effect left her face unframed and open. He could see the beauty in her high cheekbones and the regal look of amber-gold eyes. Her feet were scantily held in shoes made of rhinestone straps that disappeared under the hem of the dress.

"Wow!" was all Sam could say. He set the salad on the kitchen table to keep from dropping it. "That dress has *got* to be illegal. Should I arrest you?"

She waited a moment before speaking. "This old thing?" She looked down at herself, then slowly her eyes came back to him. They made a slow trek up his body from feet to face. Sam knew seduction when he saw it and Rachel had all the equipment to get what she wanted. But she didn't need anything to get him.

He took her into his arms and kissed her. It was a back-bending kiss. A change-your-life kiss. An I-love-you kiss.

Chapter Twelve

Campbell Wells had treated his daughter like a princess. Rachel knew what that was like. Sam treated her like a queen. He took her hand and led her across the threshold to the dining room. They sat down at the table, which was laid out with the finest linens. The plates were a china pattern that had silver threads running around the wide rims. They sat on a silver charger, and a shrimp cocktail cup with jumbo shrimp arched over the sides sat in the middle like an exotic flower.

Sam had thought of every detail, from the proper lighting to best display the table to the choices and preparation of the food. Even Hollywood couldn't do better.

Food had never been sexy to Rachel. It was sustenance, a body fuel necessary for the functions of survival. But in the capable hands of the police chief of Lake Como a feast worthy of a queen had been prepared.

"This looks wonderful," Rachel said, as Sam held

her chair. She lifted an ice-cold shrimp and slipped it between her teeth when she was seated. The taste was heavenly. "I can't believe you went to all this trouble. You must have worked at it all day."

"Not the whole day. I had to rope and tie a few bad guys before I could don my white hat and ride my horse over here."

Rachel laughed. "Did I ever tell you I never learned to cook?"

"What, you were too busy building scaffolding and mastering the fine art of drywall to take time out to boil water?"

"I can boil water," she told him. "I can also start a fire using wet wood, although dry is better. I can survive on things I forage for in the woods." She picked up another shrimp to punctuate her point. "And I can drive anything from a sports car to a tractor-trailer."

"I bow to your superiority." He lifted the wineglass that was already filled with white wine and clinked his glass with hers. "Have you ever driven a sports car?" he asked.

"A white Lotus, a Maserati, even a DeLorean."

"Where'd you do that?" The frown that marred his forehead was both interest and jealousy.

"Someone I used to know owned them."

"*All* of them?"

"He had quite a bit of money."

"He?"

"What, you thought I was hatched from an egg this morning?" She looked surprised on purpose.

Sam cleared his throat. "Of course not. It's just that you never mentioned anything about anyone except your family."

"I was seventeen when I left. I'm not anymore."

His look of appraisal told her he agreed with her. "Tell me about this race car collector."

"You don't want to hear that." Rachel was sorry she'd brought it up. His comment on her cooking had stung a little and she'd retaliated as she only did with Sam. With any other man, including Rayford Pitt-Lawrence, the race car collector as Sam had called him, she could hold her tongue, remain in control of her senses and her logic. With Sam all her well-laid plans lost their way in the glow of his presence.

Sam got up and took her charger plate and all the contents on it, including the shrimp cup that was now empty of the mouthwatering seafood. Even though his hands didn't even shake the fine-cut class container, his eyes never left her. "Oh, but I do," he finally said in a voice that could melt teeth.

He went into the kitchen and returned moments later with their dinner. He set the beautifully adorned plate before her. Rachel wasn't sure what it was, but the presentation was like her host, unexpected and startling. The fish didn't lie flat on its china surface. Instead three thick pieces were angled over a bed of brown rice. From the center rose carrot and broccoli stalks that had been cut with slit pockets. Dangling from these were small shrimp hooked like earrings on a tree.

"It's striped bass stuffed with swordfish and shrimp," Sam told her.

Rachel cut a small section from the bottom and tasted it. Like the appetizer the entrée had her eyes closing in sheer bliss. The fish had been prepared the Moroccan way. She could taste the cumin and a hint of tumeric. Rachel thanked who-ever taught him culinary arts. He'd been a good student.

"Tell me," Sam said, filling her wineglass from a bottle that impressed her. Trimbach Pinot Gris Reserve Personnelle 1997 was a bright, dry, smoky pinot gris. It felt lush and rich on the palate, but was quite dry and nicely acidic.

"Tell you what?" Rachel asked, hoping he didn't mean to resume their previous conversation.

"Tell me how you came to drive sports cars." He reseated himself and sipped from his own glass.

Rachel pressed her lips together remembering Ray and her treatment of him. "We went to college together. I was a day student and he . . ." She stopped, trying to think of a way to describe him. "He was taking some classes on the same campus. We met one day near the library. I was coming out. He was going in."

Sam smiled as if he could see the collision that resulted from them both zigging when one of them should have zagged. At least that was how Ray had put it.

"We did that three days in a row and were left with no choice but to introduce ourselves." Rachel lifted her fork and ate part of her meal. "Eventually, we began dating and during one holiday we went to his mother's house in Virginia."

Rachel would never forget how her stomach dropped when he turned into the driveway of the estate that was his mother's home. She'd expected a beach house in Virginia Beach, a two-story, maybe near the water. What she found was a center hall she could put an efficiency apartment in and still have room for a full-size basketball court. Ringing this palatial homestead were fifteen bedrooms all with their own bathrooms and personal maids.

"His mother loved speed and she was the real collector of cars. Other than sporty models, she had several classic cars. We took them out one day."

Rachel looked down at her meal. She took time to eat several bites in silence.

"What happened, Rachel?"

"Why do you think something happened?"

"Because you always drop your head when you don't want to answer a question."

"I'll have to remember that so I don't give myself away."

"We'll talk about why you think giving yourself away is a bad thing at a later time. Don't get distracted now. What's the rest of Ray's story? By the way, what's Ray's last name?"

"Pitt-Lawrence. Rayford Pitt-Lawrence."

Sam stared at her. "Former Attorney General Rayford Lawrence's son?"

She nodded. Ray's full name came from a combination of the Pitts and the Lawrences, two old southern families who'd survived the Civil War and settled on small plots of land butting up to each other. As time went by, when a lot of black people were selling their land and escaping to the North, the Pitts and the Lawrences acquired land rather than sell it until both their estates and fortunes were in the millions. They were the original African-American old-money families. Marriage joined the lands and Rayford was the heir apparent.

"Ray knew many of the little-used roads around

the area where he lived. A few miles from the house he asked if I wanted to drive. I was afraid and thrilled. Behind the wheel my hands were sweating, but the rush I got from driving fast enough to create a tail of dust behind the car was priceless. In an open field he taught me to turn on a dime."

Rachel felt the heat in her face at the memory of spinning the car around.

"If his mother had seen us she'd have died on the spot." She laughed. "Several times the car rose up on two wheels, and I admit, often I thought we might roll over. But all the cars held the road, or the ground I should say, in many cases. We walked away from them with no mishaps and a lot of good memories."

"You speak about him fondly. Normally, when someone takes you home to meet their parents, wedding bells are imminent. What happened to you two?"

Rachel forced herself not to drop her head. She did take the time to eat another bite of food and drink the delicious wine before continuing her story.

"I broke it off," she said quickly.

"Broke it off? Why?"

"You don't know what it's like to be in hiding. I had to be so careful. I had to think before I spoke, evaluate how someone might read what I say before I said it. I could have continued a relationship with Ray if he was just plain Ray from Virginia Beach, but he wasn't. His parents would have had me investigated, started digging into my past, my parents' past. I couldn't risk it. They might find something, or even worse if they only found out we began life when I was seventeen years old they would want explanations. They'd ask questions I couldn't answer. I thought it best to let it go."

"Didn't you have a complete cover?"

"I thought I did, but with the police you never really know anything. Only what they want you to know and I'd learned not to trust that. I had no choice."

Rachel remembered sitting in her room, letting the phone ring and ring. She didn't open his e-mails, finally changing her address so he didn't have it. When she ran into him one night coming out of a grocery store he told her he loved her and wanted to marry her. Rachel lied to him. She turned him away, telling him she didn't love him and never would. She never saw him again after that night.

"A few years ago I saw a story in a newspaper that he'd been a professor at Harvard, but had been tapped by the present administration and appointed to a minor post in the Middle East."

She was quiet for a moment, eating the delicious-tasting food. She didn't regret her decision. Although she enjoyed Ray's company, she would never have fit in with the Pitts or the Lawrences.

Sam interrupted her thoughts. "Well, at least he taught you something very useful. Something that probably saved your life."

"What was that?"

"Driving skills. From Carly's account of your technique you could be a stunt driver for the movies."

"Interesting. I once really wanted to do that kind of thing."

Sam threw his head back and laughed, a deep belly laugh. "You surprise me. I thought you were a quiet, reserved person. And all the while, under that facade beats the heart of Mario Andretti. What changed your mind?"

"My mother got sick and needed me at home. I started playing with stocks on the computer and made my living that way. Eventually, I gave up the idea."

They had finished the meal. Sam got up and took their plates, carrying them into the kitchen.

"Let's have dessert on the beach."

"In this dress?"

He looked at her. "Take off your shoes," was all he said. He helped her up and holding her hand led her to the sliding glass door. They went down the patio steps and followed the path to the beach.

Rachel gasped when she saw the blanket spread on the sand and a covered dessert tray already set as if it had been waiting for them. A champagne bucket held a bottle of dessert wine.

"When did you do this?" she asked.

"Earlier tonight, just before you came."

She went up on her bare toes and kissed him on the cheek. "Know that I'm suitably impressed."

"Then it was worth it."

They sat down on the blanket and Sam removed the clear plastic bubble-cover that protected the cheese and fruit. Rachel lifted the wine bottle.

"This must be a good wine," she commented.

"Santa Julia Tardío 2000," he answered. "It's made using torrontés, a minor Galician grape, more popular in Argentina than in Spain. This is a medium-sweet dessert wine comparatively light in body, with an aroma of honey and lemon and a nice fruit and slightly sugary finish."

"The clerk in the store told you that, right?"

"Right." He took it from her and pulled out the cork, which had already been freed. He filled flutes that had accompanied the fruit. "What shall we drink to?" He lifted his glass.

Rachel looked about at the perfect night. A full moon, a slight fragrant breeze, a gorgeous man. Romance came to her mind, but she kept her voice from saying it.

"To the future," she said, lifting her glass.

"To the future," he repeated, clinking his to hers.

She drank, keeping her eyes on him. She was falling in love with him. The news didn't surprise her. It had been coming for a while. All the signs were there: her inability to rebuff him when she knew his job reminded her of terrible things that had happened in her past, the ease with which they talked, the super way he kissed her, and the out-of-this-world flight he took her on when they made love.

Sam lay back on the blanket. He set the champagne flute on his chest and looked up at the sky. "Have you thought about what you're going to do now?"

Rachel joined him, lying down. The stars were brighter than she remembered them being. "Now, tonight? Or now, the rest of my life?"

He picked up the glass and turned to her, resting his head on his hand. "Now, tonight, sounds like an interesting topic. But I meant now, the rest of your life."

"I have been thinking about that. I thought I'd check into returning to school. Maybe take some more psychology classes. Although I have been asked to teach some building and woodworking techniques."

"Really?" His eyebrows went up. "Who asked you that?"

"Some of the kids. They wanted to know how I learned it and if I would show them sometime." She turned her head and smiled at him. "You know, this is just like my last summer here, lying out under the stars and talking. The only thing we don't have is a raft and the bobbing water under us."

"And this." Sam leaned over and slipped his hand around her neck. He kissed her, softly kneading her lips. Rachel's eyes swept down as the familiar feelings of desire spread through her. Sam no longer wore his dinner jacket. Her hands slipped over the stiff cotton of his starched shirt. She rolled into the space between them, her body spanning the length of his. He pressed her back as his mouth deepened the kiss. His tongue forayed inside her mouth, tangling with hers and feeding as if they hadn't had dinner moments ago. Rachel couldn't believe how he made her feel, precious, loved, cradled in a world so safe she need never think of mistrust. Was it all right to feel like this? Was this what her parents had shared, this intangible need for another human being? It was as if there were a huge empty well inside her and he filled it.

It was good Rachel was lying down. Her bones had long ago turned to liquid and dissolved inside her. She couldn't believe the things that went through her mind, when her mind was working, as Sam kissed her. He filled her thoughts as much as his body filled that empty place. He held her as if she would break and made her feel as if she were more important to him than anything else on earth. His mouth made love to hers, his lips soft, but his resolve determined. Why hadn't she seen him in this light ten years ago?

The breeze stirred around them. Sam moved from her mouth and began a searing trip down her neck. Rachel was surprised she could move, but suddenly she could no longer remain still. Her leg skimmed over his, the roughness of his pants fabric contrasting against her bare legs. She kicked something and felt something wet and cold on her foot.

Jerking up, she broke the kiss.

"What's wrong?"

She laughed. At first it was a small hide-behind-the-hand laugh, but quickly turned into a full-blown-relief laugh. "I kicked over the wine."

"There's more in the kitchen." Sam leaned in and nuzzled her neck. Sensation swizzled through her.

"Maybe I'd better get it." Rachel wasn't thinking of the wine. Sam's ministrations were causing explosions on the nerves of her brain. Her thoughts were too jumbled for her mind to form anything logical.

"Why?" he asked. "Is there something going on out here you don't like?" His lips were on the skin right above the rise of fabric near her breasts. Her breath was coming fast.

"I'm burning up," Rachel breathed out as her head fell on his.

"Wine isn't going to help that." Sam continued his torture of her. Rachel forgot about the wine. She pushed him back, taking his face in her palms and returning her mouth to his. She kissed him with everything she had inside her. Pushing him down on the blanket, her body half covering his, she ravished his mouth with hers as if her life depended on them connecting.

Her feet dug in the wet sand. She was sure the heat between them could dry the spilled wine.

"Maybe you better go get that wine," Sam said when they came up for air. "If you don't I'll take you right here, right now."

"You're not going to get an argument out of me."

They looked at each other for a long moment, then burst into laughter.

"But maybe I'd better go check on the wine staining my borrowed clothes."

"Borrowed?"

Rachel traced his eyebrows with the nail of her finger. "Your invitation gave me no time to buy a dress. I'm strictly the tomboy type."

"The word *boy* and you are mutually exclusive terms."

She kissed the side of his mouth. "It pays to have friends," she answered. "Carly loaned me the dress."

"I've never seen her fill it out the way you do."

"I'd better go get that wine before you say something else like that."

She got up and pulled the hem of her dress up. It was heavy at the bottom due to the wetness.

"The wine's in the refrigerator."

Her heart was light and beating with a song of love when she went up the stairs and into the kitchen. Checking the dress in the bathroom, she lifted the hem and cleaned the wine out with soap and water. Then she repaired the lipstick Sam had kissed off and went into the kitchen. She passed his cluttered desk next to the refrigerator. She smiled thinking how much his desk looked like hers. In that, the two of them would be compatible. With her hand on the handle of the refrigerator, the thought stopped her. She was thinking of things they had in common. She was thinking of a future, one with Sam, one in which the two of them walked as a couple.

The sensation that went through her made her knees weak. She leaned against his desk chair and took in deep breaths. Suddenly she was unsure of the two of them. Did he feel like she did? Were his feelings as deeply entwined in his core as hers appeared to be? Had he ever stood in a room and realized that the time they'd spent together wasn't just as two separate people, but two people merging into one? That he wasn't being the police chief and protecting one of his citizens, he was pulling that citizen out of a deep hole in the earth where she'd dug herself in and shown her what life in the sun could be like?

Rachel's knees weakened and she sat down at the desk. She closed her eyes and propped her elbows up, holding her head for several moments. Her feelings had changed. She was in love with Sam and she was going to be different when she went back to him. She didn't know how to hide these new feelings or even if she should. She needed to know that the revelations in his kitchen were the same for him.

As she started to get up something caught her eye. It was a photograph sticking out from the back of the computer. She recognized herself and automatically pulled it out. Why did Sam have a photo of her and when did he take it? Moments later her heart dropped to the floor. Her mouth went dry and her heart jump-started and began to beat with a fury. The heat emanating from her could morph sand into glass. She was looking at her life. Photos of her parents, a long description of her time in the program submitted and signed by Aaron McKnight, United States Marshal's Service.

Sam knew.

All the months since she'd returned, he'd known everything about her. What cities she'd lived in, how she supported herself, who her friends had been.

And then there was the progress report on the Grazianos and their part in her life.

"Oh my God," she said as she read Aaron McKnight's report on the progress of the sting in progress. She was a target! It wasn't over. They'd lied to her.

"What's taking so long in here?"

Rachel whirled around at the sound of Sam's voice. She was still holding the report in her hand. The photos spilled out onto the floor. She felt as if she'd been caught doing something wrong, but the feeling quickly changed to rage.

"Rachel, I can explain."

Rachel felt a sudden calm come over her as if she'd just stepped outside her body and the woman standing before Sam was someone else.

"No explanation necessary. I've been here before," she said, and lifting her shoes and purse, walked from the kitchen.

Sam could have kicked himself for not making sure that file was completely concealed. His heart felt heavy. He hadn't known how much Rachel meant to him until she walked through the door.

He thought you fell in love gradually, that there were stages that went deeper and deeper as the years passed. Sam had no doubt he was in love with her, but he felt as if all the stages had suddenly merged together and he'd die if he lost her.

She was gone and he knew she wouldn't come back. All the things she hated in policemen, the lying, the concealing of a conspiracy, he'd passed the tests with flying colors. And deserved her hatred.

He picked up the two-way radio and called the officer on duty. While Sam had her at his house he was the duty officer, but someone was stationed at her house in case anything surprising happened.

"She's on her way," he said. "Let me know if anything happens."

"Will do, out."

Her dress slapped against her legs as Rachel walked toward the trees. Sam didn't even call her name as she walked away from him. Her eyes were dry, too dry to cry. When she reached the tree line she broke into a run, holding the gown up. She didn't stop, but burst through the secure door and went inside her cabin. She closed it and tried to remember the security code to deactivate the alarm. She got it on the third try, then hung against the wall in the silence.

She expected the tears to come, but nothing happened. Her heart beat like a drum, pounding through her head. Her body was numb, a feeling so strange she had no way of describing it. Rachel didn't know how long she stood there. She hadn't turned the lights on and was slightly disoriented after her run through the trees.

Her decision had been made tonight. She would leave The Lake in the morning. She slid down the wall. She'd miss Carly and Alex, the kids at the center, the new friends she'd begun to make, but it didn't matter. She couldn't stay here any longer with Sam only a few yards away. Not after he'd betrayed her, lied to her, even by omission. McKnight was at the root of it, but Sam knew. He was part of the plan. She, the target, was the only one who wasn't consulted.

Suddenly things started to make sense. They fell into place like all the pieces of a kaleidoscope, painting a colorful picture. All the occurrences she'd shrugged off and her own paranoid behavior were real. The accident, the van, they were designed to kill her. The Grazianos weren't all dead. Someone out there wanted her to pay. And to draw them out, McKnight and Sam had conspired to use her as an unwitting target.

Feeling was returning. She was scared. Being back in Lake Como had lulled her, called to her emotions as the perfect place to be. But she had to go. Now that she knew she was still a target, she had to leave. She had no car. The Jeep had been totaled and she hadn't done anything about replacing it. Tomorrow, first thing, she'd buy a car and head out. She was one to travel light. All she'd take was her laptop computer so she could have access to her accounts.

Pushing herself away from the door, Rachel went to her new office. Turning on the light, she looked about the room. She'd been proud of it, with the space and light and the fact that it looked out on the trees and the water. It didn't matter, she told herself. She had to leave it. And this time it would be for good. She wouldn't be back during the summer to stay in a motel and walk the trails through the woods. This time there was no looking back.

She thought of Sam and reinforced her vow that the split was for good. Unplugging the silver-colored, sleekly designed machine, Rachel stuck it in her backpack. The car plug, however, had been left in the Jeep. She shrugged. She'd have to buy a new one.

Rachel held the backpack and looked about the room as if it were her last time. She switched the light off at the same time something hot seared across her shoulder. Instinctively she dropped to the floor. Putting her hand on her shoulder, she brought it away wet and sticky.

She'd been shot.

"Hairston, get over here. I heard a gunshot. I'm going in."

Sam burst through his door at a dead run. Jess hadn't finished speaking and he already had his gun out and was running through the trees.

Changing channels on the two-way, he called McKnight. "You there, McKnight?"

"Yeah, I'm on it."

Still wearing his suit pants and shirt, he flipped the radio onto his belt and stopped near a tree where he had a view of the cabin. Holding his gun up with both hands, he was ready for the unexpected. Sweat poured off him as if he'd been in the water. Glancing at the house, Sam wondered why there were no lights on. Everything looked normal except that he was too used to seeing her lights burning, even into the night. For a while he thought she slept with them on.

Sam made his way to the house. His progress was slow. Images of Rachel lying hurt inside flooded his mind and he had to force himself to work by the book. Look in every direction, then look again and a third time. Make sure he didn't back himself into a corner. Every step he made he kept looking around, wondering where the shooter was **and** if he had hit Rachel. He wanted to call to her, tell her he was outside and that he was coming to her rescue, but he knew better than to alert anyone that he was there.

Pulling the radio out, he contacted Jess. "Where are you?" he asked.

"Porch, left side." Jess wasn't one to use any unnecessary words.

"Have you seen Rachel?"

"Not since she went in."

"I'm at the back door. Ready?"

"Ready."

Sam counted to three and they burst through the two doors simultaneously. Methodically working their way through the house, they found it empty.

"Where do you think she is?" Jess asked when they'd relaxed and turned on the lights.

"I don't know." He walked across the newly laid carpeting and looked down at the bloodstain.

His heart stopped.

Rachel held her breath, willing the pain in her shoulder away. Her mind told her to run. Get out of the house. Get away from here. Her feet moved and she ran to the loft. Grabbing the security blanket, filled with the pullover blouse, jeans, socks, running shoes, and hooded sweatshirt, she went through the skylight. She wasn't sure if using the doors would be safe. Someone could be waiting out there for her. She was taking no chances of that happening. Whoever was there wouldn't think she'd planned for an escape. Why would she need to? From everything she'd been told, she was safe.

Taking the time to carefully close the window, she opened the concealed ladder she'd installed after the roof was done and lowered it over the side of the house. Quickly she climbed down and hit the hidden switch midway between the electrical meter and the ground. The stairs retracted and would reseal themselves inside their housing on the roof. No one would know she wasn't still in the house. She set off for the woods.

She ran, ignoring the pain in her shoulder. It wasn't as bad as it had been at first. The bullet only grazed her, but blood covered the fabric of Carly's dress. Rachel ran until she couldn't run anymore, until the sandals she was wearing were broken and useless and she had no more breath than a swimmer trying to cross the Atlantic Ocean.

The woods were dark and she was sure no one had followed her. She ripped Carly's dress off. When she settled in whatever new place she decided to stay she'd see that another one was sent to her. Using the dress to press against the bloody shoulder, she cleaned the wound and fished in the blanket pack for some medication. Applying it burned a little, but in the long run it would help.

Dressing in the dark clothes, she pushed everything else inside the zipper blanket and stuffed it in the backpack. She had to get out of the woods and find a car. But she needed to get to her money first, her hidden cache, her rainy-day, just-in-case money.

A twig crackled close by. Rachel froze. She clamped her teeth down on the gasp of air that would give away her position. Moving an inch would make the backpack rub against her clothes and a smart tracker would be able to hear it. Rachel had no doubt the man looking for her would be the smartest they could find.

"Don't move," a voice said. A cold chill went down her spine, paralyzing Rachel into immobility. It was the voice of death. Her death. He was here for her. This was the final stand.

"I knew you'd come one day. You or someone like you."

"Then this is no surprise. You should be prepared for me. You seem so prepared for everything else."

Rachel didn't know what he meant.

"I've been keeping tabs on you since you got here."

"Watching me, following me around, the van."

He nodded. It was dark, but she could see his outline, if not his face, clearly. "You're a damn good driver. Too bad we can't have a runoff and find out who is the better of the two."

"I believe that's already been proven. I'm still alive."

"Bravado." He laughed, a ruthless sound. "I like that, but it will have no effect on me."

He took a step forward. Rachel wanted to move back, but she remained still. The woods were very dark and even in the sliver of light she could barely make out his features. He was six feet tall and solid.

"I don't know you. You're not one of the Grazianos."

"That's where you're wrong. Carmine Edgecomb, I'm the last of the Grazianos. No one would associate me with them unless they knew that we were cousins. I grew up with Tony. But I didn't join the business. I worked legitimately until your father wiped out my entire family."

"But I didn't do anything. And my father is dead."

"Yeah." He grinned. "Like me you're the last of the Wellses."

"What do you want?"

She saw the flash of his teeth. "That's easy. I want you dead."

Sam had been all around the house and couldn't figure how Rachel had gotten out, but she was definitely not there.

"The only logical place she would be is in the woods." Sam spoke into his two-way. McKnight and Jess were both listening. "We've got to go in and find her. Whoever shot through her window is probably in there too, so keep your eyes peeled. And remember she's wounded."

"Even so," McKnight said, "I know her to be very resourceful. Does she have a weapon?"

"Not that I know of."

"I know she can shoot the head off of a pin at fifty paces, so let's go under the assumption that she does," McKnight said. "It's dark out here, so stay out of her line of fire. She won't know it's us."

"Understood," Sam said. Thoughts of Pearl, his former partner, went through his mind. He pushed it aside. "I'm at the house, so I'll take the middle. Jess, you follow up on the lakeside and, McKnight, take the right flank. If you see anything out of the ordinary, alert us."

"We pair off," McKnight came back. "My men are about." He called them on his radio and told them whom to pair up with. "Hairston, I'm with you."

"What about in town?" Jess asked. "Just in case she didn't take the most likely route."

"I have Finley and Gallant searching," Sam said, naming two of his officers. "And I've called Sheriff Wise over in Caulder and alerted him."

"We've got men on the other side of the woods," McKnight said. "And a few down by the water. If she's here, we'll find her."

"Got it," Jess said. "Moving out."

"McKnight out," McKnight repeated.

Sam glanced once more at the house, then headed toward the woods. Where was she and how badly was she hurt? He hoped Mcknight was right and they would find her.

They combed the woods. Sam let McKnight take point. He knew his objectivity was compromised and McKnight was the professional in this case. Sam realized how much he didn't know about Rachel. Where were her favorite places? How did she get out of the house? What was her favorite color? Did she like hats? She'd said she was a T-shirt and jeans person. He had to find her.

How far could she have gotten? Sam wondered.
It seemed as if they had been searching for hours.
She'd left his house wearing that white gown. She
hadn't had enough time to change before Jess
called to say he'd heard a shot. So Sam looked for
anything that might glint in the darkness.

Then he heard it.

Another shot.

Rachel didn't wait after he started to raise the
gun. She kicked him in the groin. The gun flew
out of his hand as he grunted and doubled over.
She took off. She knew the woods, knew the trails.
Finding her bearings, she headed back toward the
lake. Logically he'd think she'd head deeper into
the darkness, hide where he couldn't find her. But
Rachel thought getting back to the lake and finding a way out of town was a better idea.

She doubled around, keeping to the far side,
away from the water. She'd borrow Carly's car and
leave it in Caulder. There she could catch a bus or
a train and disappear again. Only this time she
couldn't call McKnight. She wouldn't be set up
with a new identity. This time she was on her
own.

Rachel heard something and stopped. Someone
was in front of her. How could he have anticipated
her so correctly? The thought scared her more,
knowing he'd guessed her motives. Rachel held
her breath and didn't move. She pressed herself
into a tree, trying to blend into the night. The
sound came again. Rachel let her breath out slowly,
making as little noise as possible and still sustain-
ing her life.

After a lifetime the sound moved away from her. Forcing down her heart, which was lodged in her throat, she started again. Cautiously she moved from tree to tree. Checking over her shoulder, she moved forward, but kept her eye on the fact that Carmine Edgecomb could shoot her at any time.

He wanted her dead, he'd said. She was the last of her family, no cousins, no aunts or uncles, the last of the Wellses. Rachel saw the stretch of land leading back into the residential section of town. She checked all directions around her. For twenty or thirty seconds she'd be exposed, in clear view of anyone aiming at her. But she had to try it. She wanted to make the moment right. Discarding the backpack would make her flight faster, but she needed the laptop. She also knew it afforded her some protection against a bullet in the back.

Three steps into the clearing, Rachel was stopped by the voice again.

"That's far enough," he said.

Sam whirled around at the voice, his gun ready, crouching. He didn't recognize the voice, but the tone was clear. And deadly. He looked around, wondering where the other agents were. McKnight was close by. They exchanged looks that said to remain silent. Sam knew who the voice was talking to—Rachel. A fear he'd never known fissured through him. It was quickly replaced by rage. If he, whoever *he* was, harmed her his fate would be worse than anything Sam could describe.

Quickly, he reined his anger in. Emotional, he was no good to Rachel. He needed to remain rational or he could get her killed.

McKnight took a step away from the tree he was pressed against. He signaled Sam to move. Three yards apart, they both crept in the direction of the voice.

"How did you find out I was here?" Sam heard Rachel asking. "I'm sure Loretta Stiles's column doesn't have that wide a coverage."

"Loretta who?"

She had him talking. That was good, Sam thought. The longer he talked the greater the odds were they would get to her before anything happened. But Sam had no doubt the man had death on his mind.

"Your friends. They led me right to you."

"My friends?"

"The FBI."

Sam glanced at McKnight. Both of them took ballet steps forward, wide and quiet. He swept the area around them from left to right, making sure the gunman was indeed alone. Finally he could see them. Rachel had her back to him. She was dressed in dark clothes and wore a backpack. The man stood a couple of yards in front of her. Sam didn't have a clear view of his face. He could see an outline only.

Suddenly the man turned and fired a shot. The bullet hit the ground an inch in front of McKnight's foot. Startled, Sam clamped his teeth together and adjusted his sweaty palms on the gun in his hand. A triangle of dirt popped up from the earth and splattered his pant legs.

"Welcome to the party, Marshal McKnight," the man said, his voice edged with the venom of a past unfriendly association. "You know the drill. Do it or it's her." Sam saw McKnight throw his gun on the ground and step forward. "That's good. Now the other one."

McKnight had a second revolver. It was standard for a U.S. Marshal. McKnight reached to his back.

"Easy," the man said. "One hand. Your left."

His struggle was awkward, but McKnight pulled the small handgun out and let it join the one of which he'd already lost possession.

"You won't get away with this," Rachel said. Her voice was strong and confident, although Sam was sure her heart was drumming as fast and hard as his.

"You don't need to worry about what happens to me. Now be quiet before I forget I want to draw this out and pop you right now."

Sam held still, but wanted to rush to her defense.

"I know you weren't out here taking in the night air." He addressed McKnight, but said it loud enough for Sam or anyone else within range to hear. "Whoever you are out there, throw out your gun. I know you got one."

Sam didn't move. His heart hammered in his chest, but he knew if he was caught by this man none of them would survive the night.

"You've got five seconds," the voice came strong and sure. "After that she gets it." He started counting.

"He means it," McKnight said.

Without a choice of anything else to do, Sam threw his gun on the ground. It hit the dirt with a thud close to Rachel's foot.

"Come on out."

Sam stepped out from behind the tree where he'd concealed himself. He stepped up to stand on one side of Rachel. McKnight stood on the other. "Hello, chief, I don't think we've met."

Sam was surprised the man knew who he was. He'd never seen him before.

"I've been keeping tabs on you." He looked at Rachel. "You and the young lady here spend a lot of time together."

"How I spend my time is none of your business," Rachel said. She looked straight ahead, but Sam couldn't help but look at her.

"Don't you just love her?" The man swung his gaze and his gun back and forth between Sam and McKnight. "I got a gun pointed at her heart and she thinks she's in command."

"The gun makes you a big man, right? You come looking for me after nine years. I was a child. How old were you? And what do you think happens now?"

Sam noticed McKnight was moving an inch at a time away from Rachel and toward the gunman. He was putting distance between the three of them so they'd be too far apart for the gunman to get off clean shorts and they could take him down. He was sure McKnight had a third weapon. Sam had another gun. He'd grabbed it on his way out of the house and stuffed it in his sock. It felt useless against his leg. He couldn't reach for it. At least not yet. He moved sideways an inch. Eventually he and McKnight would form an arc, putting the gunman at a disadvantage.

"Move another breath and I'll put a hole in you."

Sam stopped, standing as still as a statue. He'd been caught. Out of the corner of his eye he saw a flash of movement. Rachel dove to the ground.

She went in the opposite direction of both Sam and the exposed gun lying on the ground. The man shifted toward her, sweeping his gun around. He took a shot. McKnight dove in front of Rachel. Sam lunged for the gun on the ground. The man swung back and hit the gun cleanly, bouncing it out of reach as if it were a billiard ball sunk into the corner pocket.

Rachel rolled over on the ground and came up on her knees. "Look out, Rachel," Sam shouted. The man was rounding on her again. Scrambling to his feet, Sam headed for him. McKnight lay still.

"Down," Rachel shouted. Sam hit the dirt. A shot rang out. The man screamed in pain. Sam's head snapped toward Rachel. She was holding a gun. He didn't know where it had come from. She'd hit the man in the shoulder. He dropped his gun and McKnight, getting up slowly, ambled over to kick it away while Rachel held the small gun on the man. Sam came over and cuffed him.

"Call the others," McKnight said. "Tell them to check for anyone else who might be hiding out."

Sam did so. Then he saw McKnight fall over, blood staining his shoulder. He called Jess and had him send the ambulance. It had been standing by and quickly arrived. McKnight was being treated when Sam went to Rachel. She was crouched on the ground with her face in her knees.

"Are you all right?" he asked.

"Fine," she said without lifting her head.

Sam touched her. She was shaking, trembling. She'd wrapped her hands around her legs as if she needed to hold herself together.

"It's over, Rachel."

"Is it?" She looked up at him. Her eyes were

glassy as if she was holding back tears. "Will it ever be over? I thought I was safe here. I thought there was no one left. No one that I needed to look for, check to see over my shoulder. I thought, I was *told*, there was no one left. No one! And all the while I was just being set up."

She scrambled to her feet. The gun she'd used was still in her hand. She looked at it, put the safety back on, and walked away from them.

"Rachel." The man called her name. "You're right. You'll never be safe." He began to laugh. Rachel walked away from them. Sam knew she wasn't just going back to her cabin. She was leaving him. He'd lost her.

Chapter Thirteen

Rachel thought they would never leave. Why did police take so long to report everything? Jess had stopped her hasty exit and insisted she get medical attention for her shoulder. It was only a scratch. The damage to her heart was much worse than any bullet to her shoulder.

She'd told her story five or six different times. Sam had been there all along. He was still dressed in the suit he'd worn to dinner, although he'd abandoned the tie long ago.

FBI agents combed the woods. Curiosity onlookers gawked outside the yellow police tape. Once or twice Lori Stiles tried to barge her way into the room. McKnight escorted her out the second time. Rachel couldn't hear the words he said, but she was sure "riot act" was among them.

At last she closed the door on everyone. She went to her finished bedroom and climbed into her new bed. It held no pleasure for her. Rachel knew that with the rising sun she would begin her plans to leave. She had no destination in mind, but she would work that out. She'd rent a car and relocate. In the past when she knew she had to begin anew, she was upset, but resigned to her fate.

Today she was devastated. Leaving The Lake and Sam would be more difficult than anything she'd ever done. Leaving before hadn't been her choice and she had missed Bill, but her feelings for Bill were nothing like what she felt for Sam.

Rachel had worn out her welcome. She knew it was time to leave, time to pick up the pieces of her life and try fitting them together in some semblance of order. She knew what the pieces would do. She had changed in her time here. She cared about Carly and Alex and the kids at the center. But mostly she cared about Sam.

He was here and she'd fallen in love with him. But he was part of the group who manipulated her, who cared no more for her than they did for a common criminal. She'd never know when another Carmine would come for her. She'd never be sure that she wasn't an unwilling pawn in someone else's plan.

She had no choice anymore.

She'd run.

Rachel breathed in the smell of the rich, full-bodied coffee that Doris poured into her cup.

"Heard there was quite a ruckus out at your place the other night," she said.

"It's over now." Rachel wanted it behind her, as far back as she could get it.

"Looks like you're packed for good." Doris looked at the Jeep outside the window. Rachel had rented it yesterday, packed it this morning, and stopped here for breakfast on her way out of Lake Como. Her usual table was occupied and she had to sit at one near a window.

"Where you heading?"

"I don't know. I just thought I'd point the car in a direction and drive until I find some place I feel like stopping."

Doris set the pot on the table and took the seat opposite. "Are you sure that's what you wanna do?"

A lump appeared in Rachel's throat and she swallowed hard.

"You and Sam looked like you were going somewhere."

"Well, we aren't."

"What happened?"

"Doris, I really don't want to talk about it. Let's just say we're incompatible."

"Not from where I was sitting," Doris contradicted. "You probably haven't talked to Sam. Why don't you do that before you just run away?"

"I don't want to see him again."

"He came to your defense the moment he knew you were in trouble."

"Doris, he's a cop. It's his job."

"Do you really believe that?" She paused and stared directly into Rachel's eyes. "From what I hear he didn't even take time to put on his uniform."

"You make it sound as if he wasn't dressed."

"He was wearing a suit. Like he'd just had dinner with someone special."

"How did you know that?"

"Never mind how I know. The point is he rushed to your rescue and you're not even talking to him before you leave town."

"I came for coffee and food, not advice."

Doris raised her eyebrows and hunched her shoulders. She got up and started walking away.

"Doris," Rachel called. "I apologize. This is something I have to do."

"All right," she said. "Breakfast, same as usual?"

Rachel was about to nod when she suddenly changed her mind. "No, an egg and bacon sandwich on wheat bread. And make it to go."

Five minutes later she hugged Doris for the last time and took her bag with the sandwich and a cup of coffee.

"I'll miss you," Doris said. "I'm usually a good judge of character, working here and all. I thought for sure you were here to stay. Well, when you get settled drop me a line."

"I will," Rachel promised, but she had no intention of keeping in contact with anyone in Lake Como. It was better to make a clean break than to torture herself with news of a lost love. And Doris would be sure to keep her informed of Sam's actions.

Placing her cup in the plastic holder in the Jeep, she got inside and turned the key. The engine purred to life. On the seat was a set of maps. Rachel didn't care to get lost in the concrete jungle of New York City, so she pointed the Jeep west and started to drive.

Five miles down the road she came around a curve and saw the flashing blue lights of police cars blocking the road ahead. Her stomach dropped as if she'd fallen from a high place. She knew it was Sam. He'd picked his location well. He was on a bridge. She couldn't go around him even with an off-road vehicle like the Jeep. Anger reared its head at his manipulation. She stopped, refusing to allow him to control her life.

She'd turn around and find another direction. If she didn't break the law, he had no right to stop her. Glancing in the rearview mirror, she noticed the road behind her had also been blocked. McKnight got out of one of the cars and stood at the apex where the two cars met. His right arm was in a sling. She felt a little guilty about him. He'd taken a bullet meant for her.

"Damn." She slammed her hand down on the steering wheel and gunned the engine. The Jeep leaped forward, tires squealing. She sped forward, forgetting her promise to keep within the law. Sam stood his ground. Twenty yards from him she spun the wheel. The Jeep turned, but continued its forward motion and rocked to a stop a few feet from him. Road dust and the acrid smell of burning rubber filled the cab.

She jumped down from her seat. "What is wrong with you? Get that car out of the way and let me pass."

"No," was all he said and he didn't raise his voice. The singular word and his apparent calm angered Rachel even more than she was already.

"Why?"

"I'm in love with you."

"Too bad. I never want to see you again."

"Liar."

"You have got some nerve." Rachel went toward him. "You lie to me. Put my life in danger. Nearly get me killed. And you think saying you love me wipes all that out?"

"I didn't nearly get you killed." He took a step toward her. Rachel took a step back and Sam stopped.

"I wanted to tell you about it, but I couldn't. It was the law and I had to cooperate."

"Or what?"

"Or you probably would have been killed." There was anger in his voice. "Anyway, it's over now so there is no reason for you to leave The Lake."

"Liars, manipulators. How do you think I can trust someone who doesn't tell me the truth?"

"On faith," he said. "Rachel, I know how this looks. I know for nine years you've been at the mercy of people who only told you part of the story. I know that I am guilty of the same thing. But I do love you and I promise you that if you give me a chance, I'll never again do anything to test your trust."

Rachel's heart started to melt. Sam looked as if whatever she said would break his heart.

"Aren't you in love with me?" he asked.

"I never said anything like that," she hedged.

"That wasn't my question."

"How did you know I was on this road?"

"Doris called me and told me you were in the restaurant. When you left she said which direction you headed. Now answer my question." He came to her and took her arms, forcing her to look at him. "Answer my question." His voice was soft, drugging. "I'll cherish you forever. I'll love you and keep you for all the days of our lives. Just tell me you love me."

He was so close she could feel the heat of his skin, smell his unique male smell. "I love you," she said, unable to stop herself.

Sam kissed her. Rachel went into his arms with

the relief of a reprieved prisoner. His mouth devoured hers. They matched each other kiss for kiss, bobbing their heads from side to side as they connected and separated, each turn deepening the kiss to a feverous pitch.

"I love you," Rachel whispered. "I thought I was going to die when I left this morning."

"I thought I was going to die too. Promise me you'll stay forever. Promise me you'll marry me and have my children. I promise you I'll always love you. I'll never put you in danger and I'll never manipulate you."

Rachel stared at him. He'd said all the words she wanted to hear. His heart was in those words. In his eyes was a love so clear and shining that she was surprised she'd never seen it before.

"I promise," she said.

They went on kissing until McKnight cleared his throat from somewhere behind Rachel.

"I assume congratulations are in order."

They both turned and looked at the marshal. Rachel left Sam's arms and ran to him. She hugged him tight, only releasing him when she felt him winch.

"Thank you for saving my life," she said, indicating his arm.

"It's a life worth saving," he said.

Sam came up behind her and put his hands on Rachel's shoulders. "She's just agreed to be my wife."

McKnight smiled. Rachel had never seen him do that. "I'm sorry I was such a horrible protectee," she told him.

"You weren't bad. I understood a lot of your frustration, but this time you are well and truly free. We got word this morning that the Graziano family never condoned Edgecomb's actions. He was working alone and the family doesn't like anyone stepping outside. I have no doubt they'll deal with him in time."

"What are you going to do now?" Sam asked. "Do they assign you someone else."

McKnight shook his head. "I resigned this morning. I'm going to go back to some land I own in Montana and never think about the marshal's service again." He looked at Rachel then. "But I had to wait until I knew you were safe." He bent down and kissed her on the cheek. "Invite me to the wedding," he said and turned to walk away.

Rachel smiled for the first time since she'd fled from Sam's cabin last night. That had to be a lifetime ago. She was finally through with shedding lives. She was Rachel Wells, soon to be Rachel Wells-Hairston. She had friends, who knew everything about her. And she would forever live in Lake Como.

Dear Reader,

I hope you enjoyed reading *You Made Me Love You*. I was thrilled when the Dafina line of books added romance novels. This is my first Dafina romance and I was pleased to write it.

I first saw the Finger Lakes Region of New York State when I was a high school student. I loved it and wanted to go back and visit it again. It was the most romantic place I had ever been, a beautiful lake surrounded by mountains and a full moon large enough to lasso. I longed to set a book there and finally *You Made Me Love You* is that book. Exactly as the title implies, the area captured my heart and made me love it.

I receive many letters from the women and men who read my books. Thank you for your generous comments and words of encouragement. And thanks to those of you who think the books would make great movies. Some of you even cast them. I love reading your letters as much as I enjoy writing the books.

If you'd like to hear more about *You Made Me Love You*, and other books I've written or upcoming releases, please send a business-size, self-addressed, stamped envelope to me at the following address: Shirley Hailstock, P.O. Box 513, Plainsboro, NJ 08536. Or you can visit my Web page at http://www.geocities.com/shailstock.

Sincerely yours,

Shirley Hailstock

Check Out These Other
Dafina Novels

Look For These Other
Dafina Novels

Grab These Other
Dafina Novels
(mass market editions)

Grab These Other
Dafina Novels
(trade paperback editions)

Every Bitter Thing Sweet
1-57566-851-3

by Roslyn Carrington
$14.00US/$19.00CAN

When Twilight Comes
0-7582-0009-9

by Gwynne Forster
$15.00US/$21.00CAN

Some Sunday
0-7582-0003-X

by Margaret Johnson-Hodge
$15.00US/$21.00CAN

Testimony
0-7582-0063-3

by Felicia Mason
$15.00US/$21.00CAN

Forever
1-57566-759-2

by Timmothy B. McCann
$15.00US/$21.00CAN

God Don't Like Ugly
1-57566-607-3

by Mary Monroe
$15.00US/$20.00CAN

Gonna Lay Down My Burdens
0-7582-0001-3

by Mary Monroe
$15.00US/$21.00CAN

The Upper Room
0-7582-0023-4

by Mary Monroe
$15.00US/$21.00CAN

Soulmates Dissipate
0-7582-0006-4

by Mary B. Morrison
$15.00US/$21.00CAN

Got a Man
0-7582-0240-7

by Daaimah S. Poole
$15.00US/$21.00CAN

Casting the First Stone
1-57566-633-2

by Kimberla Lawson Roby
$14.00US/$18.00CAN

It's a Thin Line
1-57566-744-4

by Kimberla Lawson Roby
$15.00US/$21.00CAN

Available Wherever Books Are Sold!

Visit our website at **www.kensingtonbooks.com**

Grab These Other
Thought Provoking Books

Adam by Adam
0-7582-0195-8

by Adam Clayton Powell, Jr.
$15.00US/$21.00CAN

African American Firsts
0-7582-0243-1

by Joan Potter
$15.00US/$21.00CAN

African-American Pride
0-8065-2498-7

by Lakisha Martin
$15.95US/$21.95CAN

The African-American Soldier
0-8065-2049-3

by Michael Lee Lanning
$16.95US/$24.95CAN

African Proverbs and Wisdom
0-7582-0298-9

by Julia Stewart
$12.00US/$17.00CAN

Al on America
0-7582-0351-9

by Rev. Al Sharpton
with Karen Hunter
$16.00US/$23.00CAN

Available Wherever Books Are Sold!

Visit our website at **www.kensingtonbooks.com**